BLOOM

ALSO BY KENNETH OPPEL

THE OVERTHROW BOOK 1

BLOOM

KENNETH OPPEL

A Yearling Book

Text copyright © 2020 by Firewing Productions, Inc.
Cover art copyright © 2020 by M. S. Corley
Interior art used under license from Shutterstock.com

All rights reserved. Published in the United States by Yearling, an imprint of Random House Children's Books, a division of Penguin Random House LLC, New York. Originally published in hardcover in the United States by Alfred A. Knopf, an imprint of Random House Children's Books, a division of Penguin Random House LLC, New York, in 2020.

Yearling and the jumping horse design are registered trademarks of Penguin Random House LLC.

Visit us on the Web! rhcbooks.com

Educators and librarians, for a variety of teaching tools, visit us at RHTeachersLibrarians.com

Library of Congress Cataloging-in-Publication Data is available upon request.
ISBN 978-1-5247-7300-7 (trade) — ISBN 978-1-5247-7301-4 (lib. bdg.) —
ISBN 978-1-5247-7302-1 (ebook) — ISBN 978-1-5247-7303-8 (paperback)

Printed in the United States of America
10 9 8 7 6 5
First Yearling Edition 2021

FOR SOPHIA, WHOSE DREAM STARTED IT ALL

Air tumbled into the helicopter as the soldier shoved the door open. Anaya looked down at the island's rocky slope. She spotted a scrawny goat standing on a boulder, and then they were over forest, the helicopter's shadow flashing across treetops.

Impatiently, she searched for a break in the tree line. A marshland, a lake—that's where they'd find Dad.

Her insides gave a twist when she remembered how he'd looked on the video call. His wild, dirt-streaked face. The things he'd said.

Can't get off . . .

They're everywhere . . .

Above the pounding of the helicopter's rotors, the soldier shouted, "I'm not seeing any lake!"

Neither was Anaya. Her eyes skittered anxiously across the forest.

"Thought you said you knew where this place was." The soldier sounded testy.

"I do. It's sort of bean-shaped. I've seen pictures."

"You said you'd been there."

"It was a while ago." Years ago, actually, when she was just five. "It's on the northeast end of the island," she said.

"Should've seen it by now," the soldier told her. "This place isn't that big."

"It can't have just disappeared!" Anaya said firmly.

"One more circle," the soldier told the pilots over his headset.

Anaya shook her head in frustration. "It should be right here!"

"All I see are trees," said the soldier.

Anaya stared down, then stared harder. Cold electricity prickled across her skin. "Those aren't trees," she said.

And then the helicopter dropped suddenly, like something was yanking it from below.

TWO WEEKS EARLIER

CHAPTER ONE

ANAYA

ANAYA WOKE UP, BLIND.

With a sigh, she touched her fingertips to her eyelids. Glued shut. She sat up in bed and sneezed seven times in a row. The inside of her nose was granular with dried snot. She stood and expertly felt her way to the bathroom. She found the stack of washcloths by the sink, and turned on the hot water. The first few times she'd woken up like this, she'd freaked out. By now she was used to it, especially at the height of spring allergy season. Patiently she held the moist, warm cloth against each eyelid in turn, melting away the gunk. She slowly pried her eyes open and stared blearily into the mirror.

"Where have *you* been all my life, you thing of beauty?" she said to her reflection.

Her face was puffy around her eyes. Normally, she thought her eyes were one of her best features, but right now they looked piggy. The end of her nose was chafed and flaky from blowing it all the time. To jazz things up just a little more, a new bouquet of pimples had blossomed across her skin.

The fading echo of a headache pulsed in her skull, and reminded her of last night's dream. It was one she'd had many times. She'd been running really fast, and it was exhilarating, even if it did always seem to leave her with a headache.

She opened the crammed medicine cabinet. Special cleansers and ointments for her acne, extra puffers for asthma, plastic vials of monster pills for her allergies. She slugged back two. This was definitely a two-pill day.

Anaya started to wash her face, then stopped. What was she doing? She wanted to look as rough as possible. She should've left at least one eye glued shut.

She dragged herself down to the kitchen, trying to shamble like a hunchback. With her nose plugged up, it was pretty hard to smell anything—but she could definitely smell the toast. She imagined a piece of thin, crisp bread with just a swipe of butter, and some marmalade soaking into the glistening surface. She loved toast—before she became allergic to practically half the food on Earth.

Mom was already in her uniform, loading her breakfast things into the dishwasher.

"I can't go to school," Anaya said.

Her mom turned. "Sweetie . . ."

"Can you please just call the school?"

"We let you skip two days last week. Technically, you're not even sick."

Anaya pointed at her face. "If I walked into a hospital, they'd have me in the ICU in two seconds."

Mom laughed softly, then came close and brushed Anaya's long, wavy hair away from her face. "You're lovely."

"My skin's volcanic!"

"They don't see your acne, they see *you*."

"Only if they have X-ray vision!"

Mom had no idea. She'd always been beautiful, and she was still the most glamorous mom Anaya had ever seen. Just look at her, tall, slim, raven hair spilling over the crisp collar of her white shirt with the epaulets: four stripes, the only female captain flying for Island Air. Lilah Dara—even her name was pretty. When she put on her sunglasses and bomber jacket, she made a pilot's uniform look like Paris fashion.

Meanwhile, Anaya was shorter; she definitely had Dad's sturdier body type. She didn't mind that—what she minded was her acne, and not being able to make it through class without having an asthma attack, and feeling generally feeble.

"Are you using the acne cream?" Mom asked.

"At night."

"You're supposed to do it during the day, too."

"It smells so bad!"

"The doctor said it was important."

"So I can be hideous *and* gross-smelling!"

"You are *neither*," her mom said, and gave her a hug.

"If I stay home, I can work more on my history project."

"Your marks couldn't get any higher, Anaya."

Anaya gave a pitiful cough and wheeze. "There's gym today," she said, giving it one last kick at the can.

"For gym, I will write you a note," Mom agreed.

Anaya sighed in defeat. Mom was not letting her off school today. Dad, on the other hand, might.

"I've got to go. There's moong dal cheela, warm in the oven," Mom said. "Tell Dad not to forget the chutney."

"Thanks."

Anaya knew that Mom herself preferred scrambled eggs and toast for breakfast, but for Anaya she often made the lentil pancakes, folded over with paneer inside. Lentils were safe. And even though she was lactose-intolerant, for some unknown reason paneer was one of the few cheeses she could handle. Also, the pancakes were delicious.

Mom adjusted the knot of her black tie. "I'll be back for dinner."

"Anywhere good today?"

Mom flew floatplanes, usually de Havilland Beavers, and most of the runs were between Victoria and Vancouver, but there were also plenty of charters between the Gulf Islands, and even farther north.

"I'm bringing back a group that was sport-fishing off Sonora. I'll probably come home smelling like salmon."

She hastily wrote a note on the pad by the phone and handed

it to Anaya. "It gets better," she said, kissing her on the forehead. "See you, sweetie."

She wanted to believe her mother. She wanted to believe that, one day, she'd *bloom*. She imagined a dull flower suddenly opening its petals, and they were dazzling, and everyone would look up from their phones and whip out their earbuds and gasp and say, *Where did that come from!* and *I've never seen anything so beautiful!*

She smiled at the fantasy, and grabbed an apple from the fruit bowl. Cutting it in half, she popped it into the microwave for forty-five seconds. If she ate it raw, she got bumps all over her lips, and a really itchy tongue.

Basically, she was allergic to everything. Gluten, eggs, milk. She was allergic to smoke and dust. There were entire months she was allergic to. April was tree pollen, and May, too. June was grass. July was still grass but also mold spores; and then August and September were ragweed.

It hadn't always been like this, just the last couple of years. Now her picture was plastered all over the staff room like a WANTED poster, alerting teachers to her food allergies, and telling them where her EpiPens were. Anaya carried one with her everywhere.

She spooned some honey into her mouth. Someone had told her that local raw honey was a good way of curing allergies because it exposed you slowly to all the pollens in your area. She put the kettle on for her green tea—because someone *else* had told her it was the healthiest thing in the world for you. When you lived on Salt Spring Island, people were always telling you the best things to eat and drink. Things to make you wise and healthy and live forever.

Dad came into the kitchen, bringing with him the smell of soil. No matter how often he showered, he still smelled like leaf mold and pine needles, and had a line of dirt under his fingernails. He wore the same green merino wool sweater pretty much every day, even though it had frayed at the elbows. He mostly kept his beard tidy, but sometimes it started creeping out of control, like the unruly plants he studied.

Dad was a botanist with the Ministry of Agriculture, and worked at the island's experimental farm. When she was younger, Anaya thought an experimental farm was a lot weirder and cooler than it turned out to be. She'd imagined giant cows, and chickens the size of velociraptors—but in reality it was a bunch of greenhouses and scraggly plots with boring-looking plants. His specialty was grasses—which her friends thought was hilarious. "Hey, Anaya, can your dad score us some grass? I hear he grows the *best* weed." Really, his specialty was figuring out ways to *stop* things growing—like invasive species that shouldn't have been here, but *were,* and were making life miserable for other plants.

"How're you?" Dad asked.

"I was thinking maybe I should live in a bubble," Anaya said.

"A bubble," Dad said, opening the oven and peering in at the pancakes. "Are these all for me?"

"No, I'd like two! You know, like a giant hamster ball. They're called Blorbs or something. Except mine would filter out allergens."

Dad set the plate of moong dal cheela in the middle of the breakfast table and sat down. "So, you'd just roll around in it?"

"Pretty much," Anaya said, helping herself to the lentil pancakes. "I could roll to school."

"That hill might be tricky," said Dad.

"I'd have to get up some speed. Anyway, they could clear a space at the back of the classroom, and I'd just kind of wobble around."

"They could pass you Anaya-friendly snacks through the air lock."

Anaya couldn't help grinning. "And maybe one day I'd meet a boy just like me and we'd get a bigger bubble and raise a family of bubble babies."

Dad nodded thoughtfully. "I think this is a very good idea."

"Can you please call the school and tell them I'm sick?"

"No," Dad said sympathetically. "But I'll give you a lift."

FOR THE PAST two weeks, Anaya had been eating lunch with Tereza in the small room off the library where they worked on the yearbook. It was due at the printer's in ten days and they were rushing to finish layouts.

At the start of the year, a ton of people had volunteered for yearbook, and then all dropped away until it was just her and Tereza. Anaya didn't mind. She got Tereza to herself. Tereza was a few years older and smoked and wore her boyfriend's shirts, and there was nothing she hadn't read. Her parents were European, and she spoke with a weary drawl, so no matter what she said, it seemed profound. Basically, Anaya just wanted to be her.

Anaya also loved the yearbook room. It was a refuge from the crowded hallways, the splayed legs, the noise, the bathroom lineups, the bathroom toilet paper (or lack thereof), the bathroom paper towels (nonexistent), the bathroom toilet seats (too disgusting to contemplate). Really, the school bathroom alone was a good reason to hate school.

Anaya sneezed for the thousandth time today.

"You sound rough," Tereza said.

Anaya shrugged. She didn't like talking about her allergies: it made her feel boring. And she already felt like a dull little moth around Tereza's bright butterfly.

"My aunt, she has wicked allergies," Tereza said, "and you know what she said helped?"

"Does it involve hanging an onion from my ear?"

Tereza smiled slyly and tapped a cigarette from her pack. She lit it with her Zippo (it had a picture of a jeweled skull on the side), then opened the window, leaned out, and released a plume of smoke from between her lips. Turning back, she offered the cigarette to Anaya.

"You're kidding."

"I know, it sounds crazy," Tereza said. "But my aunt said it soothed her throat—maybe relaxed it or something."

"It makes no sense."

"Nope."

Anaya had never smoked. Everyone said it was one of the worst things you could do to your body; she also hated the smell. But when Tereza raised her eyebrow in that way she had, Anaya took the cigarette.

She leaned far out the window, sneezed three times in a row, and looked around to make sure no one was watching. The sky was low with dark clouds. Definitely rain coming. Quickly she lifted the cigarette to her lips and took a long, hard suck . . .

And almost immediately was spluttering and hacking. Tereza took the cigarette from her hand and stubbed it out against the brick. Anaya sat back down, eyes streaming.

"Okay, I'm sorry, that was a stupid idea," Tereza said.

Anaya dabbed at her eyes with a tissue. She took a deep breath through her mouth, exhaled.

The rain came suddenly, battering the glass, drumming against the school roof.

"Geez," Tereza said, shutting the window.

Anaya was glad. The rain tamped down all the pollen and made her life easier. On the computer, she scrolled through the class photos to make sure they'd got everyone.

"I am so done with all *this*," Tereza said.

This was a big word for Tereza. It didn't just mean yearbook. It meant the entire school. It meant the whole island. Next fall she was headed to university in Toronto. Anaya wondered if Tereza would miss her as much as she was going to miss Tereza. She'd be making new friends and meeting interesting people from all over the world.

Tereza's eyes flitted wearily over the class photos. "These boys, these *boys*. No. Just *no*."

"What about Fleetwood?" Tereza was her only friend to have a boyfriend.

Tereza gave a small, dismissive wave of her hand. "Oh. Fleetwood."

"He seems pretty nice," Anaya said, even though he came across as a bit dopey and was named after a band from the 1970s. "I mean, what's it like to have someone just . . . *look* at you that way?"

Tereza sighed. "I know, I know, it's terrible, so much *neediness*."

There was a quick knock on the door before it opened and Fleetwood himself bounded in. With his shaggy hair and big hands and feet, he always reminded Anaya of an oversized puppy.

"You've *got* to see this," he said.

"Fleetwood, no," Tereza said. "Remember, we talked about this. This is yearbook time."

"Can it be Fleetwood time for just a second?" He leaned between them with his phone so they could watch the video. "Kangaroo-fighting!"

"Oh, Fleetwood," Tereza said sadly.

Anaya had to admit the kangaroos were impressive. Standing upright, they looked uncannily human. The slope of their shoulders, the muscles of their upper arms, their chests. It was actually a bit creepy. Then she noticed their feet. It looked like they only had three toes, and the middle one was much longer, with a wickedly pointed claw.

"Look at these guys!" said Fleetwood. "They're totally pumped! Look at their *biceps*! Okay, wait for it . . . check it *out*!"

The bigger kangaroo jumped straight up, and seemed to balance in midair—was he actually balanced on the tip of his tail?—then *kicked* out with both feet and slammed the other kangaroo in the stomach. Anaya winced. At least, he hadn't drawn blood.

"Can you believe that?" Fleetwood exclaimed.

"That was very nice," said Tereza. "But Anaya and I have work to do. Go play now, Fleetwood. Go find that boy with the baseball cap you like."

"See you!" Fleetwood said, and kissed her on the mouth.

After he left, Anaya turned back to the monitor. In one of the class-photo layouts was a blank rectangle.

Tereza tapped the screen. "We need a picture of that new boy. He missed photo day."

Seth Robertson. He'd arrived just a couple of months ago. No one knew much about him, except he was very quiet and kind of odd-looking and always wore long-sleeved shirts and a hoodie, even in gym class. He was being fostered by Mr. and Mrs. Antos, who had an organic vegetable farm.

Tereza looked at Anaya. "Can you go and get a picture, please, of this *boy.*"

It was Anaya's turn to sigh. She hated wading out into the hallways, especially when she looked like an extra from a horror movie.

"Please don't make me go out there," she said.

"I'm going to tell you something," Tereza said. She looked right and left, as if she were going to impart a big secret. In a hushed voice, she said, "You are way cooler than you think."

"No," Anaya said, but she desperately wanted to believe it anyway. "Really?"

"Yes. Now get out there! You take better pictures than me."

Anaya laughed, still glowing from Tereza's praise. She stood and grabbed the camera.

Outside the library, shoulders hunched as if fighting a gale-force wind, Anaya charted a course through the crowded hallway. Todd Salter and some buddy of his were goofing around at the water fountain, splashing each other. She gave them a wide berth, but heard a small cry behind her. When she looked back, Petra Sumner was brushing some water droplets from her neck.

"Oh my *gawwwwd*!" said Rachel, Petra's surgically attached

friend. "Are you okay, Petra? Does anyone have a tissue? Petra needs a tissue!"

Already a little crowd of super-concerned kids was forming around Petra, offering tissues.

"Way to go, *Todd*!" said Rachel, who could make any name sound like the worst-smelling thing in the world. "You know she's *allergic*, right?"

"Oh man," Todd said. "Did I get her?"

Todd looked like a dog that had just been caught taking a poo on the coffee table.

"Guys, I'm fine," Petra said, doing that pouty thing with her lips that guys liked.

She was very pretty, and wore her blond hair in a pixie cut. Anaya had read that you had to have a beautiful face to carry it off, and Petra Sumner definitely did.

Anaya now saw two small, angry red splotches on her neck. Petra truly was allergic to water. It was incredibly rare. It had some Latin name, and there were maybe a hundred people on the planet who had it.

Petra's gaze drifted across the hallway and met Anaya's. Quickly Anaya turned away and kept walking, knowing she probably looked heartless. But she'd seen all this before, so many times. People loved making a fuss over Petra.

Anaya had been there when her allergy started. When they were little, she and Petra were best friends. The two of them spent half the summer at the community pool. Then, one day, after they got out of the water, Petra had broken out all over in a scary rash, and her voice got hoarse, and they'd rushed her to the hospital.

It wasn't long afterward that Anaya's own allergies started up, like some weird curse. The difference was that Petra was still beautiful, but Anaya wasn't, not when she was wheezy and snotty and had acne spread across her face. Petra had dumped her pretty fast.

Whenever Petra got a splotch, everyone was all over her, asking if she was okay. Anaya could probably swell up to the size of a giant cinnamon bun and people would just go *eww* and step around her.

Petra's allergy was adorable and heartbreaking; Anaya's was just gross.

ANAYA FOUND SETH Robertson sitting hunched at the bottom of the north stairs, nibbling a sandwich and drawing on a sketch pad.

It was funny to find him here, because she sometimes sat here herself, despite the crumpled yellow tissue that had been on the floor for almost two years. There it was, lurking in its shadowy corner. This was as deserted as the school got, right here. She liked it that Seth was someone who hid himself away, too. It made her feel less awkward, meeting him. Also, Tereza's words still chimed pleasantly in her head: *cooler than you think.*

Seth had an almost-handsome head, but his body seemed out of proportion. Maybe it was just the hoodie and flannel shirt that made his chest seem so barrel-shaped while everything else was skinny. Skinny stooped neck, long skinny legs in jeans. Bony hands jutting from too-short sleeves.

Anaya caught a glimpse of a small scar on the underside of each wrist. She wondered if he cut himself sometimes, but the round shiny patches looked more like cigarette burns. Had someone done that to him, or had he done it himself? Either way, it made her feel heavy and sad.

He still hadn't looked up from his sketchbook. Anaya couldn't see much of the page, but she got a glimpse of a wing, and the way he'd drawn it made it look like it had just caught the wind. There was a sense of incredible speed. How had he done that with so few lines?

"Wow, that's really good," she said.

Now he looked up, startled. He closed the book in his lap and leaned forward, as if protecting it. Swiftly he pulled his sleeves down over his wrists. It looked like a move he did a lot. Anaya found his gaze unsettling. It was the gaze of a startled animal waiting to see what you were going to do next.

"I'm Anaya Riggs," she said. "I think we're in the same—"

"Math class, yeah."

She was surprised, and pleased, that he'd noticed. She felt a sneeze coming on but managed to stop herself. "Do you draw a lot?"

He shrugged. "It's nothing much. Just sketches."

"Well, I'm working on the yearbook and we could use some good artwork."

He looked at her, unblinking. It made her nervous when people looked at her too intently; she always wondered what exactly they saw, and whether they thought she was hideous.

"It makes the layout a lot more interesting." She sneezed and had to pause to blow her nose. "I mean, we've got a lot of Melanie Drake's stuff, but there's only so many unicorns you can take, you know what I mean? But your stuff looks a little edgier."

"Yeah, maybe," he said, and Anaya knew that was a no.

"Anyway, like I said, I'm working on the yearbook and we need a photo of you."

He looked at the camera around her neck. "Do you have to?"

Anaya laughed in surprise; she'd never had that reply before. "No, we don't *have* to . . ."

"What happens if you don't?"

He tilted his head to one side, like this was a very serious question, and she couldn't help smiling at his oddness. She found him just the tiniest bit adorable.

"Well, nothing. You just get a blank box with your name underneath. And you look like a crazy loner."

That got a small smile out of him. "Okay, let's do the picture."

"Can you come out where there's a bit more light?"

He got up and shambled closer. She caught a whiff of him. Not unpleasant, exactly. Like warm celery.

"Do I have to smile?" he asked.

"Just do your thing," she said, looking through the viewfinder.

He looked at her straight on. He didn't smile. His eyes were slightly too close together, but it didn't make him look goofy. It made him look incredibly focused, like a bird of prey.

IT WAS STILL raining hard as Anaya walked home from school. She took a deep breath. The air smelled wonderful. When she inhaled, her whole chest felt like it was filling—which was rare. She'd hardly sneezed at all.

She turned up their driveway. Having a botanist father did not mean their front yard was a wonderland of sculpted bushes, exotic flowers, and ornamental trees. Quite the opposite. Dad never paid the yard one bit of attention. He was, after all, more of a weed man. Their yard was definitely one of the weediest going.

Scraggly cedar shrubs lined the driveway, except for the gap where nothing grew. The dead patch was a bit of a family legend. Every so often, Mom tried to plant something there and it would die within weeks. Another cedar, a fern, a hydrangea, native drought-resistant ground cover—it all croaked. Dad said they should just plonk down a garden gnome and call it quits.

As Anaya walked past the dead patch, she stopped.

Rain *drip-dripped* from the edges of her umbrella.

Her first thought was that someone had jammed a stake into the dead patch. She went closer. From the muddy earth, a black shoot jutted a full foot high.

It was sturdy, its sheath bristling with a spiral of tiny hairs. The very tip of the plant was pointy.

This thing hadn't been here this morning. She would've noticed it.

Which meant that it had grown a full foot in a matter of hours.

In the dead patch, where nothing grew.

CHAPTER TWO

PETRA

PETRA WALKED INTO TOWN, hoping this new doctor would be able to cure her.

From school it was only a five-minute walk to downtown—if you could even call it that. There was a supermarket, a couple of bakeries, a hardware store and banks, and a bunch of bookstores—people liked reading on the island. The town was built around the marina, where there was a boardwalk and a few restaurants. There weren't that many cool places to hang out. The Royal Cinema got movies weeks later than anywhere else. There was the pizza place, the gross donut place and the good donut place, and a bowling alley, which always smelled faintly of cat pee. When the weather was good, you could hang out on the playground at night.

The town was pretty, everyone said so. In summer the main street bloomed with hanging flower baskets. Every Saturday a market was held in the field near the marina, and day-trippers would pour off the ferries from Vancouver and Victoria to buy organic fruits and vegetables, and beeswax candles, and weird crafts made out of yarn, or driftwood, or beach glass.

Rain clattered against Petra's umbrella as she walked down the main street. Luckily, Petra had probably the best umbrella in the world. It was the biggest you could buy. She knew because she'd searched online. It was like a plastic torpedo that covered her entire body down to her waist. It kept her completely dry, so long as she had pants—and rain boots, which she did because she watched the forecast constantly. If you were going to live in a coastal rainfall zone with a water allergy, you needed an umbrella like this and a lot of Gore-Tex clothing.

Mom and Dad were always talking about moving someplace drier—apparently, Saskatoon got the least rain in Canada—and there were places in the US that were even drier, but they'd lived on the island their entire lives, and moving, especially to another country, was a big deal.

Next to the Scotiabank was a small office building. Inside the lobby, Petra carefully folded her umbrella so it didn't splash her, then walked down the corridor until she came to a door that said ALICIA DUMONT ND.

She reached for the doorknob and faltered.

Her parents didn't know that she'd secretly made herself an appointment with a doctor of naturopathic medicine. Dad especially would flip out. He was a nurse practitioner at the island hospital, and he didn't think naturopaths should even be called doctors: their medicine wasn't scientific and it didn't work, and it only distracted people from getting real treatment.

But it seemed to Petra like no one really knew what the real treatment for her was, not even her specialist in Vancouver. The disease was so rare. Aquagenic urticaria.

Petra had seen the way Anaya rolled her eyes today in the hall-way. Anaya thought she was such a martyr because she was *sniffly* and had zits, but at least Anaya's allergies weren't degenerative. Petra felt afraid every time she even *thought* that word. Degenera-tive: getting worse, and never stopping.

Maybe her skin would become a permanent red, itchy mess, and maybe one day she wouldn't even be able to *drink* water! She'd heard of a woman who could only drink soda. Tap water was lit-erally dissolving her esophagus. But there must be water in soda, too! So it didn't make sense, did it? You needed water or you died. What if it got so bad she couldn't drink *anything*? What if she needed an IV in her arm? What if she got allergic to her own saliva and couldn't even swallow? She would become a hideous monster and no one would love her and she would die.

Her heart started to race, and Petra took slow, deep breaths, the way her therapist had taught her. She knew she was supposed to look calmly back at all her catastrophic thoughts, and question them scientifically. So.

Her allergy might not be degenerative. So far, it hadn't gotten any worse. She could still drink water. Even if her skin did get worse, it didn't mean she would be hideous. And if she *did* get hideous . . . This one always stalled her.

This exercise was supposed to make her feel better. She wasn't sure it did this time. She took one last deep, slow breath and turned the doorknob.

She didn't know much about naturopaths, except they used different medicines that were supposed to help the body heal itself. That sounded pretty good to her. Being cured. She pushed the door open and went inside.

Petra had expected the naturopath's office to look like a medieval alchemist's shop, with shelves crammed with dried herbs and weird-smelling elixirs. But it was just a normal waiting room with ugly chairs and old magazines she didn't want to read, and a window with a male receptionist behind it, looking up at her with a smile.

He looked like an older version of the high school principal on that TV show about the kid who keeps skipping school because he's a supermodel, and the principal keeps trying to expel him but never can.

"Hi, Petra," the receptionist said cheerily.

Oh great, Petra thought, wincing at the sound of her name. This island was way too small. With only ten thousand people, practically everyone knew, or at least recognized, everyone else.

The receptionist's name tag said TOM THRESHER, and Petra figured he was probably the father of Marlene Thresher, who was in the grade above her. Petra glanced furtively at the two other people in the waiting room. She didn't want anyone telling her parents they'd seen her here.

She tilted her dripping umbrella against the wall.

"Still pouring out there, Petra?"

Petra wished he'd stop calling her by name. She went to the window and handed over her health card. "Yep."

"Your mom or dad here with you?"

"They couldn't make it."

Mr. Thresher's smile folded itself into a frown.

"Oh. Our office policy with minors is we can't give a consultation without a parent present."

Petra had prepared for this. "I have a note from my mom." She pulled it from her pocket and slid it over the counter.

She tried not to look concerned while Mr. Thresher read it. She'd written it in her best handwriting, used her best old-person vocabulary, and practiced her mother's signature before signing it.

Mr. Thresher said, "Maybe I'll just give her a call."

Petra's heart sank. "Really?"

"If I could just get her number—"

"She's at work," said Petra hurriedly. "You'd probably just get voice mail. Isn't the note enough?"

Mr. Thresher leaned forward and lowered his voice. "Petra, there are two spelling mistakes in this note. I went to school with your mother, and she was the best speller in our grade."

Cursing inwardly, Petra forced herself not to blink. Of *course* they went to school together. And of *course* her mother would be an excellent speller. Mom loved rules! The more the better!

"She wrote it in kind of a hurry," Petra persisted.

"They don't know you're here, do they?"

She decided she needed a new strategy: pity.

She made her eyes as big as possible. "I have a really, really serious allergy . . . ," she began.

Mr. Thresher's forehead creased sympathetically. "I know, Petra, I have heard about that, and—"

"And I'm sorry I forged the note—that was wrong—but my parents would never let me come." She was whispering now. "They think it's all fake, like witchcraft."

The receptionist sighed sadly.

"So, I walked all the way here. In the pouring rain. I could've died!"

This last bit was completely over the top, but Petra thought she needed to pull out all the stops.

"You poor thing," said Mr. Thresher. "But you still need your parents' permission. Maybe if they read this booklet—"

"That won't help," Petra said. She'd just given an Oscar-winning performance; what was wrong with this guy? "Can't I even *talk* to the doctor?"

Another sad shake of his head.

Petra's frustration flared into anger. "Come on, it's not like

I'm getting *brain surgery* or anything. Not that she could even *do* brain surgery. I mean, she's not even a real *doctor,* is she!"

"*Who's* not a real doctor?" said a woman in a white coat, walking into the room with a file folder.

Petra felt her cheeks burn with embarrassment. "Forget it." She spun around and marched straight out of the office. She'd lied, she'd been rude, and she'd totally failed in her mission. No hope for a cure today. She felt a hot tingle behind her eyes.

But she wouldn't cry. She'd taught herself not to, because she was allergic to her own stupid tears and would only end up with a splotchy, itchy face. So she used her trick. She pretended she was looking at everything through the wrong end of a telescope, so everything was far, far away—even her own feelings. Nothing mattered nearly as much. It got her through feeling sad, and feeling nervous, and feeling downright terrified. At least, for a little bit.

So it was just a necessary trick, but at school, some kids thought she was all aloof and tragic and brave, and they *liked* it, and wanted to hang around her. Like Rachel, who was an okay friend, but didn't really understand her, not like Anaya had. But Petra had lots of friends and it was nice to be popular and, yes, pretty. It wasn't a crime.

The last time she'd cried was after Anaya had betrayed her. And since then, not another tear.

In the lobby, she zipped her coat, pulled up her hood, and

realized she'd forgotten her umbrella back in the office. No way could she go back, after the scene she'd made. She couldn't face them.

She peered out at the rain. It wasn't so bad right now. She thought it was brightening in the west. If she went fast, she could make it home in under fifteen minutes. Anyway, she had her emergency umbrella. Being well-organized was one of her top ten strengths. Everything neat and tidy. And dry.

From her backpack, she pulled out the stubby compact umbrella. One good gust of wind would finish it off. She held it low, so it scraped the top of her head. She angled herself through the lobby door, plunged her free hand into her pocket, and headed down the street.

The weird thing was, Petra actually *wanted* to walk in the rain. Even after she'd become allergic to water, she still loved the sound of the rain, the smell of it drying on the road in the sun.

And she still had swimming dreams all the time, like the one last night. They were intense: the feeling of being immersed, water pushing against her face as she slid through it. She always woke up from those dreams excited but sad, because swimming was something lost to her—along with her plans to become a marine biologist. It sounded like a bad joke, but that really had been her dream job when she was younger.

The rain came down harder. Big fat, fast drops. She heard a car—no, something larger, a truck—coming up behind her and moved off to the side. As she angled her umbrella slightly, to deflect the spray, she stumbled on some stupid black plant poking up. The umbrella jerked back and a barrage of raindrops smacked her exposed face.

No . . .

She righted the umbrella and swiped at her face with her sleeve, but really just smeared more water around, and got her hand wet in the bargain. She sped up, waiting for the itching to start, and she hated Mr. Thresher for not letting her see the doctor—and she might as well hate the doctor, too. Petra was going to have hives because of this.

She saw the gas station coming up and thought she'd better get inside, where she could at least dry off her face. For all the good that would do. She imagined the water sinking into her pores, bubbling like a witches' brew.

And here it came, the familiar heat, the crazy-making itch. All over her cheeks, her forehead, around her mouth. It was going to be bad; this one was going to be a real mess.

Heart thumping, she hurried for the gas station. Behind her a car honked, and she turned to see a white car with the Royal Canadian Mounted Police crest on the door.

Petra growled, actually growled. She did not need this. The patrol car pulled over, sending a skiff of water against her boots. The passenger window rolled down and Sgt. Diane Sumner leaned over.

"What're you doing? Get in!"

"I'm okay," she said, and kept walking.

"Petra! Get in!"

She looked around to see if anyone was watching. Her mother had an uncanny habit of showing up in her cruiser, usually at the worst possible moment. Like that time she was skipping school with Rachel, or kissing Marco Gasparini (who looked *exactly* like the older teen brother in that movie about the kids who were actually robots) after a dance. *No* was pretty much her mother's favorite word. No to using her phone after eight at night—which made it *extremely* difficult to manage her social media brand—no to dating until she was sixteen, no to a body piercing.

The rain intensified. Petra shrugged off her backpack, opened the door, and dropped into the car. She jammed the umbrella and pack at her feet.

"You're wet!" Mom said.

Very good, Sherlock, she thought.

"There's tissues in the glove compartment."

Petra grabbed some and started dabbing her face. Was it already red and welty? It felt so itchy!

"You have your cream with you?" Mom asked.

"I forgot it at home."

"You said you were going to Rachel's after school."

Here we go, thought Petra. *May as well turn on the siren.*

"Things changed."

"You weren't at that piercing parlor, were you?"

"Maybe you should take me down to the station for questioning," Petra said.

Her mother pulled onto the road and glanced over without amusement.

"There better not be a ring in your belly button."

"There's not!"

Petra dragged out her phone so she could look at her face. Usually after five minutes of getting wet, her skin was a complete mess.

She stared in amazement. Her face was fine. It was still damp, but she couldn't see a thing. She kept staring, waiting for a rash to spread. When Mom pulled into the driveway, Petra had the door open before the car was even fully stopped. She ran for the front door.

Inside, she dumped her things in the hallway and rushed to the bathroom. She turned on all the lights and stared. Not a single red spot anywhere on her face. Instantly the raging heat and itchiness she'd felt outside evaporated. All imagined!

"There's nothing!" she cried, turning to her mother. "Look!"

"Well, it does look clear," Mom said. "Let's just wait a bit longer—"

"It's been way over ten minutes! I got splashed right in the face!" Giddy elation overtook her. "I'm cured!"

She ran to the kitchen and turned on the tap and put her hand under the water. Within seconds, a red patch spread over her skin, and she felt the itch coming. Her breath caught. It didn't make sense. Why the tap water and not the rainwater?

Beyond the sliding door, rain danced off the wooden deck. She rushed to the door.

"Petra!"

Before Mom could stop her, she shoved open the door and stepped out.

"Petra, come back inside!"

The rain pelted her. She stretched out her bare arms and turned her face to the sky. Rain pooled in her closed eyes, dribbled down her cheeks, traced the outlines of her lips. The red patch on her hand wasn't even itchy anymore. It was like the rain was cleansing her.

Rain drenched her hair, dripped onto her shoulders, ran in rivulets down her midriff.

"Mom, it's okay! Look! Nothing! This rain's different!"

It was her first shower in three years. Her personal hygiene was chemical wipes and special cleansing lotions. Never water from a tap. But this rain! She wanted more and more on her. She tipped her head back, opened her mouth as wide as it would go, and felt the drops hitting her lips and teeth and tongue. She felt like a desert wanderer who'd just discovered a clear lake.

"Petra! What if it's just delayed . . ."

She hurried past Mom, back into the kitchen, leaving wet footprints across the tiles. Rummaging through cupboards, she grabbed every big bowl she could find. Outside, she set them on the deck to collect the rain.

As if applauding her idea, the rain came even harder, clattering on the deck like a heartbeat gone crazy with joy.

CHAPTER THREE

SETH

SETH DIDN'T KNOW ANYTHING about farming, but he was pretty sure that the stuff growing in Mr. Antos's field was not broccoli.

It was tall and black and spiky, and seemed to have shot up overnight as the rain hammered on the roof. Even as he'd slept, he was aware of it—and of the aching in his arms and hands. A weird, impatient pain in his joints. He had a dim memory of pain like this when he was little. Growing pains, wasn't that what they called it? Just before dawn, the rain had stopped, and he'd drifted off until the smell of coffee and bacon woke him up.

He turned away from the window and pulled on some clothes. He'd lived in a lot of places, but never on a farm. As he went downstairs for breakfast, he couldn't remember the last time he'd actually *felt* like leaving his room. Even *having* his own room was pretty rare.

"It stands tall, almost like bamboo," Mr. Antos was saying, coffee in hand, gazing out the window at his field.

They got up early, Mr. and Mrs. Antos. They always told Seth he could sleep in on weekends, but Seth was an early riser, up with the birds. Anyway, he liked their Saturday breakfasts: bacon, fried eggs, blueberry pancakes with butter and maple syrup, and toast if you had any room left. In his last place, they'd just line up a few boxes of cereal on the counter.

"I'm going to ask Mike Riggs to come have a look," Mr. Antos said to his wife. "He might know about this stuff."

"Good idea," Mrs. Antos said. "Pancakes, Seth?"

A place was already set for him at the breakfast table, like they'd hoped he would join them. Sitting, he speared several pancakes with his fork. The Antoses' dog, an old, friendly Lab called Maddox, nosed around under the table, brushing Seth's legs, hoping he'd drop something.

"Mike's with the Ministry of Agriculture," Mr. Antos told Seth, joining them. "They've got an experimental farm here on the island. He's their weed expert. Maybe he can tell me how to tackle this."

"You probably know his daughter, Anaya," said Mrs. Antos. "She's in your grade, I think."

Seth nodded. Just yesterday she'd taken his picture for the yearbook. She wasn't pretty, like Petra Sumner in his English class, but she was friendly and he'd felt at ease with her. Which was weird, because it usually took him a long time to feel comfortable with people. With Anaya, though, it was like they'd already met.

"A nice girl," said Mrs. Antos. "Poor dear's allergic to every-thing under the sun. I can't even imagine."

Seth doubted the Antoses had ever been sick a day in their lives. They were both big people. They had big heads and the big-gest hands he'd ever seen. They could pick big things up and move them anywhere they wanted. They were always working. They made Seth feel weak and spindly—and tired, just watching them.

"We can't force you to help out," Mr. Antos told him when he'd first arrived. "But we think you'd really enjoy it. It's very satisfying. And knowing how to grow your own food is a pretty useful skill."

The first few weeks Seth hadn't helped out much. He kept to his room. He sketched, plugged into his headphones, with his mind as far away as he could fling it. He'd never been a talker. He hadn't been convinced there was much point in making an effort, or getting used to anything. He tended to get moved around. There were all sorts of words to explain why. A family might have a "change in priorities" or there was a "personality conflict" or "certain needs that weren't being addressed" or there were "insur-mountable challenges as a result of attachment disorder."

After his last family, his social worker, Shayla, had asked him what he thought about living on a farm. It was funny. People were always asking how he felt about things, but it seemed stu-pid because it wasn't like he had choices. He didn't have all these families lining up for him. He went where they sent him.

Shayla had said the Antoses were an older couple who wanted to welcome a young person onto their farm. Their own children were grown up now, and had left the island, but the Antoses were in good health and still farmed organic vegetables. Shayla told him this was a great place for him. Seth asked her why. The country, she'd said. The fresh air, the chance to be active and get in touch with the earth and its cycles. A new start.

"Seth," she'd said. "You've had your share of rough patches. You don't have too many years before you're of legal age. Then you're on your own. So right now you've got a chance to think about your future. What kind of things you might want to do. School. Job. Whatever. I think this could be a really good place for you. They're good people, Seth, and I told them you were a good person who would thrive in their home."

Seth didn't feel like he'd thrived anywhere yet. The Antoses were his seventh family since his mother gave him up. In the early days, he felt like he was waiting for something—maybe his mom, coming to take him back. But as the years went by, and she never came, he knew it wasn't her he was hoping for. It was something else that he still couldn't quite figure out.

Maybe this small new feeling he had with the Antoses—maybe this was it. He liked the island. It was the first time he'd lived near so much water. He liked the way you could see the weather coming, the way the light slanted low in the mornings and evenings. He felt like something better might be starting.

"I'm going to weed after breakfast," Mr. Antos said.

Seth hadn't taken much interest in farming. He didn't know anything about how you planted things or took care of them. But for the first time, he thought he might want to.

"Can I help?" he asked.

If Mr. Antos was surprised, he showed no signs of it. "You certainly can. I'm not planning on losing my crop to this stuff. Eat up."

As he got up from the table, he put his hand briefly on Seth's shoulder. It didn't feel like other hands that had been placed on him. He looked at his plate for a moment, just breathing, feeling the warm imprint of Mr. Antos's hand.

After helping clean up breakfast, Seth went out to the field with Mr. Antos. There were eight rows of the small green broccoli seedlings Mr. Antos had planted just two weeks ago. The black grass grew between the rows, sometimes right up close to the plants. Seth walked in for a better look.

The grass had no leaves, but spiky hairs spiraled up its stalks. He touched a smooth bit. It was hard, and completely black, not even a hint of color. It was like something that didn't belong. The blackness of it kept pulling his eyes back. Like it had a gravitational force, and was swallowing light itself.

Seth got his first lesson in using a hoe. Mr. Antos gestured a lot with his massive hands, and his instructions were calm and clear.

"Usually weeds just rip out fairly easily," he said, demonstrating. "These guys are stubborn."

With small, strong blows, he chopped away at the base of the black grass. It took three tries before the stalk fell over.

"Deep roots," Mr. Antos said, bending down and making a small cluck of disapproval. "You'll want to angle the blade to get them up."

Seth took his hoe and started on the next row. It was hard, but he liked it.

"Good work," Mr. Antos called out from the next row over.

After an hour or so, they took a break, and Seth was soaked with sweat, and his arms ached, but in a good way. They drank water from the outdoor tap and sat on lawn chairs.

"Good thing you had a second helping of pancakes, huh?" said Mr. Antos.

Seth gave a quick grin.

"I love the smell of the earth," said Mr. Antos. "It always makes me feel a bit younger. Ready for some more hoeing?"

Seth nodded.

After a while, he suddenly realized he hadn't been thinking about anything else. It was such a relief to feel so calm inside. He came to a thick stalk, and even after he hacked at its base five times, he couldn't chop it down. He grabbed it and yanked. His hand skidded along, and he winced as a line of pain cut across his palm. He looked down and saw the bright blood.

"You get cut?" Mr. Antos said, looking over. He put down his hoe and walked over. "Let's get that cleaned up."

"It's not so bad."

"We both need gloves with this stuff."

At the tap, Seth washed off the blood and Mr. Antos came back with a dishcloth, gloves, and a box of Band-Aids.

"Take a break if you want," said Mr. Antos.

"No, I'm good," said Seth, and took the pair of gloves Mr. Antos offered.

Close to noon a truck came up the driveway and parked. Seth watched as Anaya hopped out of the passenger side. His stomach knotted up a little. He hadn't expected her to come, too. She walked toward the field with Mr. Riggs, arms jostling, talking animatedly, and Seth thought, *That's how someone walks with their father.*

Mr. Antos went to greet them, and for a second Seth wavered. He was used to hanging back. Then he remembered how Shayla was always saying he should make an effort with people. He stood tall and stretched. He realized he genuinely wanted to talk to Anaya.

"Hey," she said when he walked over.

"Hi."

She sneezed and blew her nose, which was red at the end. A lot of her face was splotchy, because of the acne. He could tell she was self-conscious about it, because she kept resting her hand on her cheek, like she was trying to cover it up. He knew what it was like to feel different, to want to hide away some part of yourself. He liked how lively and intelligent her eyes were. He already knew she was smart. In math class, she answered more questions than almost anyone. He wondered why she'd come along today. Probably she just liked spending time with her dad.

Maddox ambled over to greet her, and she dropped to her knees to pat the dog enthusiastically.

"Hey, gorgeous," she said, burying her hands in his fur. Maddox literally lapped up her praise, licking her face. Anaya grinned at Seth. "I'd love a dog, but—"

As if on cue, she sneezed three times in a row.

"Allergies," he said.

"Yep." She stood and took a hit of her puffer, then looked out over the weed-infested fields. "Man, look at this stuff."

"You're not alone," Mr. Riggs was telling Mr. Antos. "I've had other calls. When did you first notice it?"

Mr. Antos shrugged. "All this happened overnight."

Anaya's father took a cloth measuring tape from his pocket and held it against one of the standing stalks of black grass. "Three foot four in, let's say, twelve hours." Mr. Riggs whistled softly.

"That's a lot, right?" Seth asked.

"Sure is," replied Mr. Riggs. "There are species of bamboo that grow three feet in twenty-four hours, but this is twice as fast."

"We have some in our yard that's even taller," Anaya said. "I saw it yesterday when I got home from school. This morning it was like we had a hedge."

"This isn't something you're familiar with?" Mr. Antos asked Mr. Riggs. "Something you've seen on your farm?"

Anaya's father shook his head. "I posted it on Plant ID this morning and I'm waiting to see if we get any matches."

Anaya grinned at Seth. "It's a site for plant nerds. They post pictures of weird stuff from all over the world and ask if anyone knows what it is."

"People are usually pretty quick," Mr. Riggs said. "Anyway, I'll know more Monday when I talk to the Ministry."

Mr. Antos blew air from his cheeks and looked out at his fields. "Lucky I've got an extra hand." He nodded at Seth.

"Looks like you guys have got a good start on it," Mr. Riggs commented. "You might want to spray."

"My customers expect herbicide-free," Mr. Antos said.

"I know it's a tough call," Mr. Riggs said, "but spraying could be your only chance. This stuff is aggressive. It might crowd out your entire crop."

Mr. Antos looked at Seth and said, "What do you think, Seth?"

Seth blinked, wondering if Mr. Antos was seriously asking his opinion.

"Well," he began, "if it's between something or nothing . . ."

"A true pragmatist," Mr. Antos said. "We'll see how it goes. Thanks for coming by, Mike."

"No worries," said Anaya's father. "If you don't mind, I'm going to take one of these guys back to the farm with me."

"Please, take it all," Mr. Antos laughed. "But use my gloves. Seth already got cut."

"Here, I'll do it," said Seth. He grabbed it with both hands and yanked. It took two tries before the stalk ripped free, trailing soil-clumped roots like jellyfish tentacles. He handed it over to Mr. Riggs.

"Thanks, Seth."

Mr. Riggs took hold of it carefully and gave it a shake. "Sheesh. Deep roots and a couple of rhizomes already coming off it."

"What are rhizomes?" Seth asked.

Anaya explained: "Underground shoots the plant sends out to start a brand-new plant."

Seth heard Mr. Antos give a sigh. "Which means tomorrow we could have a whole new crop."

"See you Monday," Anaya said to him with a backward wave as she returned to the truck.

"Bye."

After the Riggses left, Seth finished hoeing with Mr. Antos, then went upstairs to take a shower. Water steamed around him. It felt good hitting his skin. He soaped his face, his chest, his long, skinny arms. He counted the small pink scars, which started at his wrists and were spaced every inch or so, all the way up the side of his arms to his shoulders. Twenty on each arm.

Soon you'll forget you ever had them.

That's what the surgeon had said, after the operation. He'd smiled when he said it, trying to be kind. Seth remembered that smile, those words.

And the doctor was wrong.

Seth had never forgotten them.

DRIVING TO THE experimental farm with Dad, Anaya saw the black grass everywhere. Growing from ditches alongside the road, stabbing up from lawns. Some people were already out with their mowers and Weedwhackers.

"Sheesh," said Dad, "this stuff is speedy."

Dad said a lot of things like *sheesh,* and *wow,* and *hoo boy!* He was a pretty quiet guy, but when he talked about plants, he got very excited and talked like everyone in the world was just as enthusiastic. Sometimes he referred to plants as "guys" or "dudes" and used words like *sly* or *wondrous* when describing them.

Anaya kept glancing at the rearview mirror. In the bed of the pickup, the black grass slid around, its roots waving in the breeze like they were alive.

"This is what you'd call an invasive species, right?" Anaya asked.

"Oh yeah. I have a feeling this scoundrel's going to cause a lot of grief on the island."

Anaya couldn't help smiling. *Scoundrel.*

"Seth seems like a nice kid," Dad said.

"Yeah." On the way over to the Antos farm, she'd told her

father about how she'd met Seth yesterday at school, and seen those scars on his wrists. She'd come because she liked helping out Dad, but also because she wanted to see Seth again. She didn't have a crush on him or anything like that. For some reason, she just found him intriguing. "He seemed pretty happy, actually."

Maybe it was just seeing him outside with a hoe, instead of hunched up in a dark stairwell. And she got the feeling he was glad to see her, too, which was nice.

Dad nodded. "He's ended up in a good place. I like the Antoses."

The parking lot of the experimental farm was deserted when they pulled in. Dad grabbed the plant from the back of the truck, and they walked past the humble collection of buildings and greenhouses to the fields.

"Well, I certainly don't need to plant a trial plot," Dad said.

Everywhere Anaya looked, the black grass was already bristling up.

"The good news," Dad added with a chuckle, "is at least I found something that outcompetes that rotter over there."

He pointed. Anaya looked at a plot where small, boring green weeds were now impaled by the black grass.

"What was in there?" she asked.

"It was a bit like garlic mustard. Grows like crazy, and releases allomones."

"Allomones?" Sometimes Dad forgot that not everyone knew all the special plant words he did.

46

"Yeah, it's like chemical weapons. The garlic mustard wages warfare in the soil. It releases chemicals from its roots to keep anything else from growing. Basically, it poisons the soil for other plants."

"But not the black grass," Anaya said.

"No. Seemingly, the black stuff's immune. It just outbullied the bully. One tough customer. Want to help me spray?"

One of the things she liked best about hanging out with Dad was that he let her help. Even after she became allergic to everything, he didn't treat her any differently.

Still, whenever she worked outside with him, she always made sure she had her puffer and EpiPen handy, and that she wore sunglasses, and that she took her pills—a double dose of antihistamines today because the pollen count always spiked after a big rain. So far, she wasn't doing too badly.

She helped Dad stake out four separate plots of black grass. They sprayed the first plot with Roundup, the second with fluroxypyr, and the third with triclopyr, which Dad said killed pretty much everything. The last plot they left alone, so they could see how tall the grass would grow naturally.

Afterward they went inside the laboratory and cleared space on a table for the black grass they'd taken from the Antos farm.

"So, let's take a good look at our friend here," Dad said, adjusting a flex lamp.

"What d'you think it is?" Anaya asked.

"My guess is a species of phragmites."

Anaya heard it as *Frag-mighties*. "It sounds like some kind of superhero."

"Just about. There's a strain that's gotten into Ontario, wild grass, stuff grows ten feet high, almost impossible to get rid of. So what do you notice about this guy?"

She liked the way he asked for her opinions. "Really thick, lots of roots. Those spikes are wicked. And the black color. There's no other plant that color, is there?"

"There's stuff called black mondo grass—but it's more purply. No, this stuff is truly black. Which means it can photosynthesize any wavelength of light. Which is pretty cool, right? This guy's adaptable."

"So, if it's not black mondo, or phragmites, what is this?"

"No idea. It's probably always been around; we've just never noticed it. But I think I'll send this guy out for genetic testing." He got up and started to prepare a specimen bag. "Someone else on Plant ID might've seen this by now. You mind opening up my laptop? I'm still logged in."

"Sure."

Dad had shown her the site plenty of times, and every time she was amazed how many freaky plants there were out there. She flipped open the laptop, and swallowed.

"Dad?"

He was labeling the bag. "Uh-huh?"

"You've got over two hundred messages."

Before she could even start reading, three new messages

scrolled onto the screen. Dad dropped the bag and sat down in his chair. He rolled the messages back to the beginning and clicked the first one. A picture of the black grass popped up.

Seen it. Not Black Mondo grass. No idea what it is.

"That's from Vancouver," Anaya said, reading over Dad's shoulder.

Click after click: more pictures of the black grass, more bewildered comments.

"Portland, Oregon," Dad murmured. "Little Rock, Arkansas."

Already four feet tall in my barley. Anyone else?

Click.

"New Orleans," said Anaya, reading the locations. "Saint Lucia."

Click.

Photos of black grass jutting up among banana plants.

Click.

Black grass rising from people's gutters in Finland.

Click.

Black grass reaching skyward alongside the Great Wall of China.

CHAPTER FOUR

PETRA WOKE UP, EAGER to wash her face.

During the big rain, she'd collected enough water to fill three plastic bottles. One and a half liters total. She kept them in the medicine cabinet, carefully labeled so no one would throw them out by accident.

On her way to the bathroom, Petra glanced out the window at their front lawn, overgrown again with black grass. In the three days since it appeared, they'd mown it down a bunch of times, but it always came back. People couldn't keep up with it. It killed lawn-mower blades. You needed a chain saw if it got too tall.

Pretty much all anyone talked about now was the black grass. How it was crowding out the crops, how nothing killed it. You couldn't go on your phone or turn on the TV without people talking about how it was showing up everywhere, and what was this stuff, anyway? So far, lots of guesses and no answers.

In the bathroom, she stood in front of the mirror. Morning and night she'd been washing her face with the rainwater—just a little bit on a cotton ball. She didn't want to waste it.

It was stupid, but every time she put some on her skin, she felt like it was cleansing her, going into her pores and changing her for the better. Sometimes she even took a little sip. Just to let it sit in her mouth against her tongue, tasting it, and feeling the *wetness* of it, before swallowing. Like some magical elixir that would cure her.

She'd asked her father if he could get it analyzed at the hospital, and he'd promised to send it to a lab in Vancouver. Petra hadn't wanted to part with even the fifty milliliters in the specimen bottle. But whatever it was in that water, she wanted *more*.

If they could *make* it, maybe she could get a lifetime supply! And it would change her life—maybe even *save* it.

She opened the medicine cabinet and reached for one of her bottles. Her hand stopped halfway.

"What the . . ."

Squinting, she leaned closer.

"Did you guys do anything to my water?" she shouted into the hallway.

Mom showed up first, already in her RCMP uniform. "What is it?"

"Look!"

Petra pulled out one of the bottles and held it out to her. "There's all this crud floating around."

Suspended in the now-murky water were three shriveled black peas, each with a tiny sprout curling out of it.

"Huh," Mom said.

"Did you put anything inside?"

"Of course not! When's the last time you saw them?"

"Last night! When I washed my face! And there was nothing in them. Look at this one!"

Inside the second bottle was a skinny stem with two black leaves that looked like bat wings.

"What's going on?" Dad asked, appearing in the doorway in his bathrobe, hair still damp from the shower.

"Her rainwater," Mom said, showing him the two bottles.

Dad shrugged. "Some seeds must've blown in when you were collecting it, Petra. They just germinated in the bottles."

"Overnight?"

She saw Dad blink. "This happened in one night?"

"Yeah. Nothing normal grows that fast!"

Her thoughts started coming fast and blurry, like animals on a dark carousel. Her skin crawled. She'd been washing her face with this stuff—she'd even drunk a little of it! She grabbed the last bottle from the cabinet and looked closely. Inside bobbed two prickly black stalks, with wispy roots.

She swallowed and turned to her parents. "This stuff looks exactly like the black grass."

"SEE THAT, GROWING at the very top?" Mr. Antos said, pointing.

Seth looked up. The grass was about eleven feet high now, and from the top grew a slightly thinner stem. From its branchlets dangled small, spiky black buds.

"Those have got to be the flowers," Mr. Antos told him. "Once they open, the wind spreads the pollen everywhere. . . ." He shook his head. "A million seeds hit the soil, and that'll finish the growing season for us."

"Are you going to try herbicide?" Seth asked.

Mr. Antos shook his head. "No point. I was talking to the Drakes and Johannsens and they said none of the herbicides are working for them, not even the heavy-duty stuff." He turned his face in all directions. "Wind's nice and light today. I think I'll burn it all down."

Seth blinked. "Are you allowed?"

Mr. Antos raised an eyebrow and in a James Bond accent said, "I have a license to burn."

Seth laughed.

"No, seriously," Mr. Antos said. "I have a license for my property. After the burn, we'll overseed like crazy and see if we can crowd out the weeds that way. And then we might be able to get a late crop." He turned to Seth with a grin. "So. You want to burn this stuff down with me?"

"Yeah!"

It was Wednesday after school, and he'd had a good day, mainly because Anaya had talked to him. He hadn't known if she would, with other people around, but she'd actually sat with him on the stairs during morning break. He still wasn't much of a talker, but she made up for it. They talked about the black grass a bit, and she told him about a book she was reading. He wondered if he'd made his first friend. He turned his face to the sun and closed his eyes.

The day was still warm and Seth decided to take off his hoodie. It was the first time in a long time that he'd worn just a T-shirt in front of anyone. Mr. Antos's eyes flicked to the scars lining his long, pale arms, but he didn't look at Seth questioningly, just nodded at his overgrown field and said, "All right, let's get to it."

The black grass was everywhere on the island now—except a few places, including the school playing field. Down by the marina, the big plot where they held the weekend market was okay, and the playground, too. Mr. Antos had said there were a few farms and grazing pastures that were untouched, no rhyme or reason to it.

From the shed, Mr. Antos brought out two drip torches. They looked like small fire extinguishers, only they were filled with a mix of diesel and gasoline. He showed Seth how to hold and tilt one so fuel squirted out in a small, precise stream. Then he let Seth light the wick. Seth held the torch in his hand nervously.

"It's pretty straightforward," Mr. Antos said. "We'll start here and work in opposite directions around the whole perimeter. We'll meet up at the far side. Just keep moving, laying down a line at the base of the grass. Nice steady pace."

Seth nodded and started walking. He wasn't sure the black grass was catching at all. When he glanced back, he only saw little licks of flame, and some smoke, curling from the base of the stalks.

He rounded the first corner, dripping out his line of fire, and it still didn't seem like the flames were doing much. But about halfway along he heard a sound like a giant balloon being burst. Looking back, he saw stalks of black grass igniting, one after another, like rows of giant Roman candles. Flames shot skyward. The smoke was black and yellow. Was that normal? With great huffs and cracks, the fire hurried toward him in a blazing wall, and he picked up speed, the drip torch lighting a trail after him.

He thought he heard Mr. Antos shouting from across the field, but the dragon roar of flames was now too loud to make out words—and the grass was too high to see across. The sweat on his neck suddenly cooled as the wind hit it. He glanced up at the thick plume of smoke hanging over the field, and saw it flatten like an anvil, then pour down away from him, toward the opposite side of the field—and Mr. Antos.

Seth rounded the corner to the field's far side and didn't see Mr. Antos coming toward him. He should've been here by now.

"Mr. Antos!"

The smoke was wafting toward him now. He heard Maddox barking. Staggering around the corner came Mr. Antos, holding his sleeve across his face. He stumbled and fell. The smoke thickened and crashed down over him.

Seth ran blindly into the smoke. He'd never smelled anything like it. His eyes streamed. He squinted and kept going. The wind shifted direction again, and the smoke cleared for a moment. He almost tripped over Mr. Antos, sprawled on the ground and making a terrible sound.

"Mr. Antos!" he shouted, kneeling.

Mr. Antos's breath came in wet gasps. He tried to stand up, but teetered. Seth ducked under Mr. Antos's left arm, and tried to raise him. He felt like his spine might buckle. But his legs straightened and his back didn't snap, and he raised Mr. Antos up. Together they hobbled toward the house, until Seth couldn't manage it anymore and they both collapsed to the ground.

"Sorry, Mr. Antos."

Mr. Antos looked confused. His eyes were unnervingly blue, and Seth realized it was because his pupils had contracted to tiny needle points. Maddox appeared from the smoke and circled anxiously, barking. Seth looked back and saw the molten stack of smoke sliding toward them again. He had to get Mr. Antos farther away.

Teetering, he tried to heft him up again. Suddenly Mrs. Antos was taking her husband's other arm. Seth felt a huge weight lifted. Mrs. Antos could lift anything and her husband was no exception. They hurried him toward the house.

Another thin wash of smoke blew over them. Mrs. Antos was coughing now, too, her eyes streaming. Seth's eyes were teary, but didn't even sting. He felt okay. By the time they hauled Mr. Antos onto the porch, he heard sirens.

"All right, Gregor," Mrs. Antos was saying to her husband, her own voice hoarse, "you're all right. Try to stop coughing. Catch your breath. . . ."

Seth turned to look back at the field, boiling with smoke and flame. He wondered if it might jump across to the nearby fields or trees—or the house.

A female firefighter appeared on the porch, kneeling down in front of Mr. Antos and asking questions while checking his blood pressure and pulse. Mrs. Antos had to answer the questions because Mr. Antos was still coughing so much. The firefighter put an oxygen mask over his nose and mouth.

"What are you burning?" the firefighter asked.

"The grass," Seth said. "The black grass."

"That's it?"

"Yes."

The firefighter's face flinched at the smell of the smoke. "Masks and oxygen!" she shouted at the two firefighters hurrying toward the field. "Smells like an oil burn." To Seth and Mrs. Antos she said, "The ambulance is on the way. We're going to get you inside, okay?"

Seth looked down to see Mr. Antos's hand on his arm. It gave a weak squeeze, before falling away. And then they were being hurried into the house as the firefighters uncoiled their hoses, and the field burned and burned.

CHAPTER FIVE

"HERE'S WHAT WE KNOW," Anaya's father told the people crammed into the community center. "Its spread is worldwide. We've seen it growing in tundra, in rain forest. There's even reports of it in the desert. So far, it's totally herbicide-resistant. We've tried them all. It shares characteristics with a bunch of known plants, but right now the thinking is it's an entirely new species."

Anaya was relieved that Dad managed to use "it" when talking about the black grass today. She wasn't sure anyone wanted to hear it referred to as "dude" or "fascinating" right now, especially after what had happened at the Antos farm.

Every chair in the community center was filled, and people jostled along the sides and crunched together at the back. Even with all the windows open, the smell was pretty ripe. Salt Spring was *earthy*. There were lots of people who didn't believe in things like deodorant, or soap, or even socks. They believed in composting and damp wool. And meetings. Most of them seemed to *love* meetings.

From the sidelines, Anaya watched her father. He was right

up front with the island trustees and governing council, sitting behind a long table with flex microphones. Sergeant Sumner, Petra's mom, was up there, too, representing the RCMP. Scanning the crowd, Anaya caught sight of Seth near the back in his usual hoodie, standing beside Mrs. Antos, who looked pale and weary.

"Anaya, how are you?" someone asked, and she felt a soft touch on her arm. It was Mr. Sumner and Petra.

"Oh, hi," she said. She always felt awkward and sad when she ran into them. Mr. and Mrs. Sumner were always polite to her, and sometimes seemed a bit wistful, like they didn't understand why she and Petra weren't friends anymore. Like they didn't know their own daughter was a disloyal backstabber who'd chucked her aside when she got ugly.

She lifted her hand at Petra. "Hey."

Petra stretched her mouth into a grudging smile.

"How's Mr. Antos?" Anaya asked. She figured Mr. Sumner would know since he worked at the hospital.

"He's okay. He was very lucky, really. He inhaled a lot of smoke, and it really damaged his lungs. Seth probably saved his life."

Anaya glanced back at Seth. Everyone had heard how he'd dragged Mr. Antos clear.

"We have some stuff we wanted to show your father," Mr. Sumner said to her. "Some plants Petra found—it might be useful."

"I'll tell him," Anaya said, and felt relieved when they moved on through the crowd.

From the front of the hall, her father was saying, "Under no circumstances should you try to burn it—"

"How come no one told us it was toxic?"

Anaya looked around, trying to find the person who'd shouted out the question. It was Thom Gutman, who had a farm near Wicked Point. Normally, at meetings people lined up at the mic and patiently waited their turn.

"We should have known!" someone else shouted.

Anaya shifted awkwardly—they were almost making it sound like Dad was to blame for what had happened!

"We didn't know yet," he replied.

Sergeant Sumner leaned into her mic. "We're imposing a fire ban, effective immediately. We can't have any more of that stuff set alight."

"So, where d'we put it all?" someone else asked. "I'm running out of space!"

"And it starts rooting again, even after you cut it down!" another person called out. "We need it off our land!"

"We're finding a site where you can haul it," Sergeant Sumner said. "We'll have that location for you by the end of tomorrow."

"What're we supposed to do about our crops?"

That was Thom Gutman again.

"I know this is very hard," Dad said, "but for now tilling is your only option. . . ." And he started outlining possible ways to save crops.

Someone tapped her shoulder, and Anaya looked over to see Tereza and Fleetwood.

"I thought you didn't believe in town meetings," she whispered to her friend.

"Fleetwood wanted to come," Tereza said in her weary drawl. "He has *theories.*"

"Doesn't everyone?" Fleetwood said.

Tereza looked at Anaya closely, smiled, and whispered into her ear, "Your face!"

Anaya flushed with pleasure. The last couple of mornings, when she'd peeked warily at herself in the mirror, her acne looked a bit calmer. There were definitely fewer pimples, and they looked less angry. Also, the skin around her eyes wasn't nearly so puffy, so you could actually *see* her eyes.

Anaya couldn't help smiling, even though it seemed completely frivolous to be thinking about her complexion right now.

"We might lose our entire growing season," a woman in the hall said loudly. "Is the government going to compensate us?"

"Or feed my goats?" someone else called out. "There's no grazing for them. They can't eat that black grass, it's too spiky."

While one of the trustees stuttered out a reply, Anaya noticed Ralph Jenkins step out into the aisle and make his way toward the mic. He was one of the oldest residents of the island, and generally considered a weirdo. He'd built his very own druidic standing stones and rented out his land as a spiritual retreat.

He tapped the mic, sending a metallic shrill through the hall.

"My name is Ralph Jenkins," he said slowly and clearly.

"Here we go," murmured Anaya.

"We know who you are, Ralph!" someone called out, to a few chuckles.

"There is something you are not telling us," Ralph Jenkins said, his amplified voice cutting through the chatter. "There is something you're not telling us and we have a right to know."

"I *love* this guy," said Tereza, who looked interested for the first time.

Anaya noticed that Fleetwood was nodding intently.

"Our *government* is not telling us where this weed comes from."

"Very good point," said Fleetwood.

"Because it sure seems to me," said Ralph Jenkins, "that this weed could only be bioterrorism."

There were shouts of agreement, and scattered applause.

"We want the truth!" someone called out. "This stuff didn't just come from nowhere!"

Ralph Jenkins said, "I hear the news like everyone else. The US blames China, and China blames them right back. And then everyone blames North Korea, because they're so secretive. You've got the Middle East blaming people . . ."

"Nobody's blamed Canada yet," Tereza said wryly. "We're too nice."

"Please, Mr. Riggs," said Ralph Jenkins, "tell us what you

know. Is this something that escaped from your farm, or some other experimental facility?"

Anaya looked back to her father. He'd been an islander most of his life, and everyone knew and mostly liked him (the guy at the Esso station had a weird hatred of him for some reason). But Dad was also an employee of the Ministry of Agriculture, which was the federal government, and so that meant Dad knew things and kept secrets. Which was ridiculous.

"Ralph, I can honestly tell you, this plant did not escape from my farm—or any facility in our country. And I know there's been a lot of finger-pointing in the media, but every country on the planet has been equally hard-hit."

"That could just be part of their plan!" Fleetwood whispered.

"Oh, Fleetwood," said Tereza.

"No, seriously," he said, turning his intense gaze from Tereza to Anaya. "Don't you think?"

She smiled back awkwardly, feeling herself blush. Fleetwood hardly ever looked at her.

"Well, it seems to me," said Ralph Jenkins, "that unless we can get rid of this stuff, the planet's not going to be producing much food this year."

Anaya chewed on her upper lip. Ralph Jenkins wasn't sounding so crazy right now. According to Dad, and the news, all across the northern hemisphere farmers were having trouble planting their crops.

"We're working on it, Ralph. Not just Canada but every country in the world. We'll get this stuff under control."

"Seriously," Fleetwood was whispering, "if you wanted to take over the world, you'd make it *look* like you were infested with black grass, too. So no one suspected you. Right? But you'd actually *have* the antidote! And when everyone else ran out of food and started to starve, then you'd *sell* the antidote for a trillion dollars."

"That's a pretty good plan," Anaya admitted.

"For a James Bond movie," Tereza added, then, "Oh my gosh, he's *still* talking!"

"And I can't be the only person here," Ralph Jenkins rambled on, "who noticed that all this stuff started growing right after that big rain we had."

"Sorry, Mr. Jenkins," said Dad, "you're saying the rain—"

"Very next day, up it comes! Is that a coincidence? I think not. I did predict this, of course, in my podcast last year. . . ."

People started telling him to sit down. Eventually Ralph threw up his hands in disgust and stalked off.

"I think Mr. Jenkins might be right," said a voice near the front, and with astonishment Anaya realized it was Petra. There she was, walking up to the mic with perfect poise.

That took guts, Anaya thought grudgingly. Then again, Petra had always loved being the center of attention. When they were little, they were both bossy, but Petra usually managed to end up with the best crayons, the best action figure, the best part in the basement plays they'd put on. She loved being in front of people—but what on earth was she doing right now?

"I think the seeds were inside the rain," Petra said.

The crowd was very quiet suddenly.

"Whoa," Tereza mouthed to Anaya. "Hot gossip."

"What makes you say that, Petra?" Anaya heard Dad ask.

"I collected some of it, the rain, because, well, for some reason I'm not allergic to it."

Anaya rolled her eyes as a murmur of sympathy burbled up from the audience. Did the entire island know about Petra's tragic water allergy?

"Anyway, this morning there were little plants growing inside the bottles. They were all different, but I'm pretty sure one was the black grass."

Anaya saw Dad nodding patiently. "I'd like to look at those plants if you still have them," he said. "But I think it's more likely the seeds got blown into the water, or fell from overhanging vegetation."

"It came with the rain!" hollered Ralph Jenkins from his seat.

"How do you explain the rest of the world, then?" someone shouted back.

"It rained all over the world!" Fleetwood boomed out, and Anaya looked at him in surprise. Tereza actually held her hand over her face in embarrassment.

"It was on the—on the news, remember?" Fleetwood said,

stammering a bit now. "They had satellite pictures, and it was all cloud, and it rained pretty much *everywhere* on the planet over a three-day period, so . . ."

He trailed off, but he was right. Anaya remembered watching the news with her parents, and the weather guy had mentioned it. How unusual it was.

She watched her father's face. She could tell he was thinking hard. It looked like he was going to speak, but one of the councilors bent over her mic and said, "I think we can discuss these very interesting theories after the meeting, but we have some other important business to address. We need volunteer crews to keep the grass under control. . . ."

"I can't believe you," Tereza whispered to Fleetwood, her face still flushed. "You actually think someone made it rain all over the world?"

"Hey, I'm not the only one. On the internet—"

"Fleetwood, we've talked about this. *Ev-er-y-thing* is on the internet."

"We can *control* the weather now!"

"Oh boy." Tereza looked at Anaya, shaking her head.

Anaya smiled back weakly, but she couldn't dismiss it. Dad didn't—she could tell by the serious look on his face.

"The Chinese have this whole government department in charge of the weather," Fleetwood was saying. "They can *make* it rain."

"So you think it was the Chinese," Tereza said.

"I just said it's maybe possible, theoretically, to make it rain all over the planet at once."

"Okay," said Tereza, "so how did they deliver all the seeds? A million airplanes?"

Fleetwood looked deflated. "Yeah, I guess we would've seen the planes on our radars and stuff."

"Cloaking technology," said Tereza, slipping her hand into Fleetwood's.

Fleetwood grinned, and winked at Anaya. "Yeah. Maybe."

Anaya laughed, feeling some of the anxiety leave her shoulders. It did sound pretty far-fetched.

Tereza kissed Fleetwood on the cheek. "Maybe it's not even a country doing this. Maybe it's a secret organization called SLORK or something—"

"And an evil dude with scary glasses," said Anaya. "Biding his time in his underground lair with his supermodels and personal chef."

"And pet Komodo dragon," Fleetwood added, then sneezed.

Tereza sneezed, too, and laughed. Then she sneezed again, and kept sneezing.

Anaya was suddenly aware of all the other people sneezing, from every part of the hall. It sounded like some kind of malfunctioning engine. People held their elbows and tissues to their mouths. There was something scary about it, like everyone had suddenly lost control of their bodies. She looked at her father up front, and saw him sneezing, too.

Inside, the light had changed somehow. Anaya tilted her face up to the open windows. The air glittered with dust or *something*. She was pushed along with the tide of people heading for the doors.

Outside, all around the sides of the parking lot, grew black grass. The very tallest stalks looked different, and it only took Anaya a second to understand why. Just yesterday, the flowers on the tall central stems were still tight black buds.

Now they were wide open.

To Anaya they looked a bit like black sunflowers. The centers bristled with pale pollen. A horn honked at her. She stepped out of the way of a car trying to leave the parking lot, windows rolled up, the driver jerking with sneezes.

Anaya walked closer to the black grass, staring up at the flowers. The breeze rustled the stalks together. Maybe it was the unpleasant scraping sound, or the big facelike flowers, but Anaya had never felt so keenly that the grass had an intelligence.

With a faint creak, one of the flowers tilted its head skyward. The long black stem arched and swelled. The flower trembled and then snapped forward. With a loud pop that made Anaya jolt, a thousand tiny grains of pollen exploded through the air.

A second pop made her turn as more flowers released their mist of pollen. Everywhere, the flowers arched and recoiled as their pollen shot through the air like fireworks.

The parking lot was chaos now, people shouting and sneezing and hurrying to their cars. Doors slamming. Cars starting. Horns blaring.

Overhead, the air was heavy with pollen, the sunlight illuminating the golden grains as they danced and swirled higher in the heat of the afternoon, and Anaya thought, *That is one of the most beautiful things I've ever seen.*

Across the parking lot, she caught sight of Seth and Petra. They weren't sneezing at all.

And neither was she.

IT WAS WEIRD for Petra, stepping inside Anaya's house after so long. But right away she remembered the frayed mat, the homemade shoe rack, the wall-mounted coat hooks in the shape of elephant tusks. And the familiar, faintly spicy fragrance of the house itself. She used to spend so much time here, and with a pang she realized how much she missed it.

"Thanks for bringing them over," Mr. Riggs said, looking at the bottles of water she carried. "Come on into the kitchen."

Her father sneezed again. On the way over, it hadn't been so bad inside the car, with the windows rolled up. The pollen had swirled against the windshield, forming little drifts against the wipers. Even the short dash from the car to the Riggses' front door had made her dad's eyes and nose stream. But she herself was absolutely fine, and she had no idea why.

Mr. Riggs said, "Cal, we've got plenty of allergy meds."

Her father nodded gratefully. "Yes, please. What do you have?"

When they walked into the kitchen, Anaya was already popping a pill from a blister pack. "Might I recommend ten milligrams of cetirizine?" she said.

"You certainly know your pharmaceuticals," Petra's father chuckled.

"I'm kind of an expert," Anaya replied, offering him the pill with a glass of water.

Petra didn't laugh. So typical of Anaya to show off how clever she was. She loved being smart. Whenever the teachers returned tests, she'd always smile, and leave her paper faceup on the desk so everyone could see her marks. If someone answered a question wrong in class, she'd do this little headshake, and then lift her hand really high. Petra got good marks, too, but she wasn't so obnoxious about it.

"Do you want some antihistamines, too?" Anaya asked her.

"I'm good."

She noticed Anaya wasn't sneezing at all, and seemed kind of smug about it. Her face also looked less pimply and puffy than usual. You could almost notice how pretty her mouth and eyes were—which irritated Petra even more.

She set her bottles down on the old wooden table, and saw Anaya watching closely, enviously even. Inwardly Petra smiled. Did *Anaya* have any strange plant specimens? No. Had *Anaya* figured out the seeds must have come with the rain? No. *Take that, smart girl.*

"So, let's see what we've got here," Mr. Riggs said, bending close to the bottles. "This growth all happened overnight?"

"Yes."

"Okay. I'm just going to dump out the water," Mr. Riggs said, taking one of the bottles to the sink, where a colander was waiting.

"Oh!" said Petra. "Do you mind saving it? It's just . . ."

She snuck a glance at Anaya, who raised a curious eyebrow. Petra didn't care what she thought. She *still* wanted the water to wash with, even if weird stuff had grown in it. She couldn't bear the idea of losing it.

"Right, sure," said Mr. Riggs.

He put a big pot under the colander, and drained the first bottle. He brought the colander back to the table, lifted out the two black stalks, and placed them on a plastic cutting board. Everyone crowded around.

"Okay, this is definitely the same grass we've got everywhere. What's impressive is the seeds germinated in water and didn't rot. These dudes are very adaptable."

"They don't look very healthy, though," Petra said. "In the ground, that stuff grows four feet overnight."

"True," Mr. Riggs said. "He definitely prefers a terrestrial home. Okay, next."

He drained the second bottle. Inside was the plant with the bat-shaped leaves, which were plastered against the plastic sides.

"You want a pair of chopsticks?" Anaya said.

"Good idea," her father said. "I don't want to tear them."

Using the chopsticks, Mr. Riggs delicately gripped the plant and eased it out through the neck. Seeing it spread flat on the cutting board, Petra was surprised how big the leaves were. All this, just overnight, in the darkness of the medicine cabinet. She looked at their fine black veins, the tiny hairs.

"The leaves are quite fleshy," Mr. Riggs said, handling them gently. "Perfectly symmetrical. And see." He touched a small bulge in the plant's center. "I think this might be a flowering stem beginning here. It reminds me of a water lily."

"Same black color as the grass," Petra said. "You think they're related, Mr. Riggs?"

"Possibly. Let's have a look at this last one."

At the sink, he poured out the third bottle and returned with the colander. Resting on the bottom were the three black peas. Petra frowned. The tiny shoots looked longer than they had inside the bottle.

"These guys," Mr. Riggs remarked, "look a bit like very tiny bulbs."

"Does that mean they're flowers?" Petra asked.

"Could be. A flower bulb usually has multiple roots at the bottom, though. These guys just have a single shoot growing from this bud here, right at the pointy end." He picked up one of the bulbs. "They're very young. The shoots are still undifferentiated."

"Undifferentiated?" she asked, and was sorry she did, because Anaya answered.

"They haven't started forming leaves or branching off yet."

Petra caught Mr. Riggs give his daughter an approving nod, and tried not to roll her eyes.

Her own dad asked, "Have you seen anything like this, Mike?"

"No. And it's hard to know what this one's going to become."

As he held it close to his face, Petra saw a bead of fluid leak from the bulb onto the pad of his thumb.

"Huh," Mr. Riggs said, setting down the bulb and sniffing the liquid. He rubbed it between his fingertips, then frowned. Abruptly he stood up and hurried to the sink.

"Dad?" Anaya said worriedly.

Mr. Riggs turned on the tap and held his hand under the water.

"That has a nasty sting to it," he said over his shoulder. "Don't touch it."

"Let's take a look," Petra's dad said.

When Mr. Riggs turned, Petra could see the angry blisters on his fingertips.

"Hard to tell if it's an allergic reaction, or an acid burn," her dad said.

She looked back down at the bulb, and gave a cry as its shoot twitched.

"Holy crap! It just moved!"

"I saw it, too!" Anaya said.

Their eyes met, and for just a second it was like they were friends again.

"You sure, Petra?" her dad asked.

"Yeah! It was like it just . . . grew. Does it look a little longer to you guys?"

She didn't know much about plants, but you weren't supposed to be able to *see* them growing.

"Anaya," Mr. Riggs said, "could you get some ziplock bags and wet paper towels to pack these things up? Put on gloves before handling the bulbs."

"Sure thing."

"Thanks for bringing these, Petra," Mr. Riggs said. "This is incredibly useful." He pointed at the bulbs and the bat-leafed plant. "I haven't seen reports of these varieties yet." He shook his head. "Three new plant species in one sample of rainwater— seems like quite a coincidence, doesn't it?"

"So, you think it's possible?" she asked him. "The seeds were actually in the rain?"

"Hard to dismiss," Mr. Riggs said.

Petra cut a sidelong glance at Anaya. She couldn't help gloating. Maybe she was the first person to come up with the idea— the first person who wasn't crazy, anyway.

"So, hang on," said her father. "If the seeds were all delivered together, it means someone's doing this, right? Bioterrorism?"

Mr. Riggs nodded gravely. "I'll be calling the Ministry."

Petra watched Anaya packing the plants into ziplock bags. "Is it safe for me to keep washing with the water? Because of the seeds, I mean."

Mr. Riggs considered her question. "Well, it hasn't hurt you so far. But probably best not to." He held up his red fingertips. "You don't want anything like this getting on your skin or eyes."

"Okay." She nodded, trying to hide her disappointment. "So, what happens next?"

"I'll transplant these seedlings at the farm," Mr. Riggs said, "and grow them in controlled conditions. We need to know what else we're facing."

SETH BROUGHT THE tractor around in a one-eighty turn, still a little sloppy, but he was definitely getting the hang of it. In the late-afternoon light, row by row, he cut down the new crop of black grass. Even after the burn, the very next morning the field had bristled with new stalks. Today they were as tall as Seth.

When he'd visited Mr. Antos in the hospital earlier today, Seth had promised him he'd keep the grass under control.

"Thanks, Seth," Mr. Antos said. "But this is ridiculous. Why am *I* still here?" He turned to his wife, who had just had a coughing fit. "*You* sound worse than me, Marta."

"You're *in*side," his wife told him in annoyance. "And on oxygen!"

Seth could tell her new allergies infuriated Mrs. Antos, even if everyone on the island was suffering equally.

"Still," Mr. Antos said stubbornly. "I'm fine. I don't know why they're not releasing me."

Mrs. Antos blew her nose and glared at the tissue. "The doctors said your lungs were scarred—and I believe them. I only got a couple of mouthfuls, and that smoke *seared* all the way down my chest."

"They want to keep you in a few more days," Seth said. "Just to be safe."

Mr. Antos gave a mighty sigh, which started him coughing. "I want to get back to the farm."

Seth wanted him back, too—and he was surprised by how much. A father was not a difficult thing to imagine, even if you'd never had one. Seth had spent a lot of time watching other people's fathers. From a distance: a dad smiling and calling good-bye as he dropped his kid off at school; a dad lifting a boy onto his shoulders; a dad frowning when his daughter dropped her ice cream, then buying her another one.

Until now, Seth had never thought he might have a father of his own. It scared him, hoping for something.

So here he was, cutting down the black grass, getting sunburned on his bare arms, feeling the hot rumble of the engine beneath him, hearing the blades whirling—and loving it. Mrs. Antos knew how to use the tractor better than him, but she was sticking indoors mostly. Like everyone else now.

Except him and Anaya and Petra. He remembered how, outside the community center, everyone else had been sneezing like crazy, and the three of them had met each other's eyes. No one said anything, but it was like for that one second, they were all communicating, and an electric thrill had gone through him.

Seth brought his attention back to the plowing. He'd keep the farm in good shape until Mr. Antos came back. Then maybe they could make another start later in the summer. They'd have discovered some new herbicide by then, and everything would be back to normal.

At the far end of the field, he made another turn, nice and tight this time, and headed back in the direction of the farmhouse. Mrs. Antos was hurrying down the porch steps, waving at him, and sneezing and dabbing her eyes with a tissue. He brought the tractor to a jerking halt, stalling the engine.

Hopping off, he ran, and he knew he was running toward bad news.

CHAPTER SIX

"AND WE'RE DONE," ANAYA said.

She hit *Send,* and the last of the yearbook files were on their way to the printer. It was after school on Monday, and she and Tereza had stayed late to make their deadline.

With the pollen still flying outside, half the kids and teachers had been absent today. Crumpled tissues littered the hallways and overflowed the garbage bins. Finding toilet paper in the washrooms—rare at the best of times—was now impossible. Snuffling, coughing kids slumped around the halls like zombies.

"Another year of precious memories," Tereza said sarcastically, blowing her nose yet again. "Thanks for doing those last layouts. My eyes are literally streaming. You're way better with the computer anyway. You saved the day."

"No problem," said Anaya.

"I woke up with my eyes glued shut," Tereza said.

"Same," said Fleetwood, who was slumped in a chair, waiting for them to finish.

"I know that one," Anaya said.

She felt almost guilty, because her allergies had really eased up. Hardly any sneezing or nose-blowing. This morning, when she'd looked in the mirror, she didn't feel the usual pang of disappointment. Her face was hardly puffy at all and she didn't even *sound* like she had a cold. Today in class, when she'd answered a question, her voice sounded normal. A couple of kids had actually turned around to see who was talking.

And her skin! There were way fewer pimples. Finally, all those gross creams were starting to work, just like Mom promised. She decided she was almost—not quite, but almost—a little bit pretty. It was a lovely warm feeling.

She'd even done gym today. For the past three years, she'd hated gym. Today, though, she'd done indoor laps and squats and wall push-ups, and hadn't even needed to use her puffer. What was most amazing was the high jump. Usually she just crashed through the bar, but this time she cleared it, even after Mr. Hilborn raised it twice. It was like she'd finally figured out how to use her legs. They felt *strong* as they pushed her into the air. Afterward in the changing room, Anaya had poked her thighs with her thumb. Normally, they were a bit squishy, but today they were *hard*.

Despite everything happening in the world, today had felt like a good day. And now here she was, a seasoned yearbook pro, basking in Tereza's praise and friendship. But her thoughts kept turning to Petra and Seth, like she wished they were hanging out with her, too.

It had been so strange, having Petra in her house last Friday. A couple of times during the visit, she'd almost forgotten they weren't friends anymore, but then she felt guilty and angry all over again. Mostly sad, though, at how she'd lost a best friend.

She shut down the computer. "Did you guys hear about Mr. Antos? He had a heart attack Friday."

"Is he going to be okay?" Fleetwood asked.

Seth had told her about it earlier today. She'd found him sitting alone in the stairwell, his sketchbook closed in his lap, an uneaten sandwich in his hand.

"They don't know. He's still in the ICU."

"Those friggin' plants," Tereza murmured, and it was the first time Anaya had seen her look genuinely worried. Normally, all she had to do was raise an eyebrow, say something witty, and scary things evaporated.

"They're going to figure it out," she said, wanting to reassure her friend.

"Your dad know anything about those new ones?" Fleetwood asked.

She'd already told them how he was studying the seedlings from Petra's water bottles. After he'd transplanted them at the farm, they'd started to grow. Over the weekend, Anaya had seen them inside their terrarium.

"The ones that looked like little peas, they're becoming vines. Dad thinks they're developing little clusters of berries, and there's these tiny bulges along the stems that have acid in them."

"Same stuff that burned your dad's fingers?" Fleetwood asked.

"Yeah. And the other one's definitely an aquatic plant. Dad put it in some water. There's a flower bud that's about to open. And they noticed that the water's changed."

"What do you mean, changed?" Tereza asked.

"It's become a tiny bit more acidic. Like the plant's changed the water's makeup."

"All these plants come from the same place," Fleetwood said. "I told you. It's some kind of bioweapon. We've got to figure out how to kill these things."

Tereza's gaze drifted to the window. "Not looking forward to going out there."

Outside, pollen glittered in the air. Beyond the school field, the black grass grew tall, but the field itself was still green.

Anaya said, "It's just so weird there's no black grass on it."

Fleetwood said, "Maybe the earth's too packed down or something."

"We should take a sample," Anaya said. "I'm serious. If the grass isn't growing there, maybe there's a reason. Like, a chemical reason, in the soil. My dad was telling me about it."

"You mean something that stops the grass growing?" Fleetwood asked, interested.

"Yeah. Maybe it'd help them make an herbicide or something."

She was still irked that Petra had brought Dad those new plants—and she was not willing to be outdone, especially in the realm of botany.

"I'd like to see you ask Mr. Hilborn," said Tereza.

"Let's not bother," said Anaya, feeling reckless. "Let's just do it right now."

"I'm in!" said Fleetwood.

"We don't even have a shovel," Tereza said.

"I know where to get one," Anaya said.

She took them down the hallway to the custodian's closet, which was often ajar after school, when they were doing their daily big clean. Inside, Anaya found a shovel and snatched it, as well as a garbage bag.

"Criminal mastermind," Tereza whispered to her.

Outside on the school field, Anaya headed to the far end. "Here."

Eagerly Fleetwood plunged the shovel into the earth.

She opened the garbage bag wide so he could dump the soil right in.

"How much?" he asked.

"A little more."

The shout reached them from across the field. "Hey! What're you doing?"

"It's Hilborn!" said Tereza, glancing back over her shoulder, and giggling uncontrollably.

"We're good," Anaya said.

Fleetwood dropped the shovel and Anaya tried to lift the bag but it was really heavy, so she just dragged it after her. Fleetwood reached down and picked up the bag, so they could all run faster.

"Hey!" Mr. Hilborn called out again, but he didn't give chase.

Anaya cut through the trees and down to the road. Fleetwood had to pause and have a sneezing fit. Tereza was wheezing, but still giggling.

"That was great," she said. "Come on, we'll walk you home."

On either side of the road, the black grass grew high from the ditches, making a dark canyon. People couldn't cut this stuff down fast enough. The stalks rustled in the wind, scraping against one another like eerie radio static.

"Thanks, guys," Anaya said at the foot of her driveway.

"It was awesome," Fleetwood said, heading off. "I've wanted to dig a hole in that field for a long time."

Anaya dragged the bag up the driveway and left it near the garbage bins. She was surprised to see Dad's pickup, and hurried inside.

"Hey!" she called out. "I brought you something!"

Dad was in the kitchen, cutting mushrooms and peppers for dinner. She told him how they'd dug up a soil sample from the school field. "I was thinking there might be hostile allomones, stopping the black grass from growing."

"Great minds think alike," he said. "I just told my guys to start collecting samples from any clear pastures."

He gave her a smile, but he looked preoccupied.

"Everything okay?" she asked.

"Oh, it's just annoying. The Ministry doesn't want me growing the new plant specimens at the farm."

"Why not? How're we supposed to know—"

"They want their team in Ottawa to handle it."

She frowned. "That's stupid. You should be the one doing it, right here, where it grew!"

Dad shrugged. "They're probably right. They have better equipment out there. I just hope the plants survive the journey."

But she got the sense there was something else bothering him, something he wasn't telling her. As they made dinner, he was unusually quiet, and it started to freak her out. She was glad when Mom came through the front door, bringing with her the comforting whiff of diesel and leather.

She kissed Dad, then sneezed a bunch of times.

"It's not bad when I'm in the air," she said, her voice hoarse. "But when I land—*wham*—it hits me all over again."

Mom's nostrils were chafed from all the blowing. Her beautiful tapered face was puffy around the eyes.

Mom took out her phone and started swiping. "You'll want to see this," she told Dad. "I took this on the way home."

"There's something I need to tell you guys first," Dad said, handing her a glass of red wine. To Anaya's surprise, he handed her a small one, too.

"What's up?" she asked nervously.

"This stays in the house," Dad said, "but the government's declaring a state of emergency in a couple of days."

The words *state of emergency* settled like a brick in Anaya's stomach.

"So, they think someone definitely bioengineered this stuff?" Mom asked.

"That's the current theory," Dad said. "So far, no one's reported sightings of the other two plants, the vine or the water lily. But it's only a matter of time. Mostly, though, the government's worried about the food situation."

Anaya had seen the news reports, the videos and social media posts. Everyone had. But she'd always assumed things were under control.

"Is it really so bad?" she asked.

"Not yet," Dad said. "In the southern hemisphere, they aren't as hard hit because their crops were already fully established before the grass showed up. But it still destroyed a lot of their harvest. Up here, it's pretty terrible. If our crops fail, then we're looking at a real global shortage. Wheat, corn, rice, barley, soy . . . all the grains."

"We have reserves, though, right?" Mom asked.

"Months, not years. Remember the drought two years ago?"

Dimly Anaya remembered stories about a wheat shortage, and food prices going up. But to her, food came from supermarkets, and they always looked full.

"World reserves were low *then*," Dad said. "Less than twenty percent. That meant if all production stopped, the world had only seven months' of grains total. This would be much worse."

Anaya was aware of her mother watching her, concerned. She felt a tremor of fear move through her stomach. She took a sip of her wine and grimaced at its sour taste.

"We'll be okay here for a while," Dad said, "but in poorer countries, if this goes on much longer . . ."

"Famine?" Anaya said.

He nodded. "Without grains, you don't have livestock feed. And without good grazing pasture, there's nothing else for cattle or pigs or chickens to eat."

"Geez, Dad, you're making it sound like doomsday!"

"Sorry." He gave Anaya a big hug. She pressed herself against his warm chest. "I just didn't want you guys to be surprised when you heard it on the news. It's going to be okay. We're going to figure this out."

"Okay. You're going to want to see this even more now." Mom picked up her phone. "I took this today over Cordova Island."

Anaya leaned in to see. Mom often shot photos from the cockpit—sometimes interesting clouds, or the light on a mountainside, or a city poking up through low fog. It always amazed Anaya that Mom could take photos *and* fly the plane.

"There's that little lake at the northeastern end," Mom said. "You know the one?"

"More like a marsh, right?" Dad said.

Anaya knew about Cordova. It was a small island at the top of the Gulf Islands Archipelago, and the entire thing was a provincial eco-reserve. No one lived there—no houses or electricity, just a dock and a small cabin that botanists and conservation groups could use when they visited. She'd gone with Dad once when she was little, but she couldn't remember much, except for endless trails, and plants that all looked the same and had names that tangled in her head.

Mom scrolled to the next picture. "So, there's this little island in the middle of the marsh, and I bank right over it on my route. All last week, whenever I looked down, I saw the black grass growing on it. But today, look."

Mom swiped to the next picture. It was a close-up, a bit blurry. Mom zoomed with her fingers. "See that?"

Anaya frowned. "Is that the black grass?"

It was definitely tall grass, but it had a yellow tinge and looked droopy.

"Those guys do not look healthy to me," Dad remarked.

"That's what I thought," Mom said.

"It's dying!" Anaya said.

"Withering, anyway," said Dad. He gave Mom a big hug and a kiss on the mouth. "You are an amazing airborne asset!"

"Darling, such sweet talk!"

"This is huge," Dad said. "No one's seen this stuff dead yet. Not a single report. So we definitely know it encountered something antagonistic. Might be another plant, or"—he nodded at

Anaya—"it might be allomones in the soil. I need to get there right away. I'll know more once I have samples. I'll check the other eco-reserves up there, too."

"I can come, if you need help," Anaya offered.

"I'll take Amit. Should only be a few days."

She hated the idea of Dad leaving, even for a couple of days, with things getting so serious. But she also wanted to be *doing* something—especially if she could be part of the team that found a way to kill the black grass. Amit was one of Dad's colleagues from the experimental farm, but she knew for a fact he was hard hit with allergies.

"I can help," she insisted. "I'm not even allergic to the stuff!"

"I know, but—"

"I bet I can work harder than you guys!"

Dad smiled. "Maybe so, but you're staying here. If you want to help, I know Vicki could use an extra shovel, taking more samples around the island."

Anaya sighed.

"Hey," Dad said, "this is good news. Cordova Island might be the break we've been hoping for."

"HOW MANY CANS of chickpeas do we need?" Petra asked, watching her mother add two more to their near-overflowing shopping cart.

"Never hurts to stock up."

It was the way her mother lowered her voice just slightly that put Petra on alert. She caught herself dropping her own voice.

"You mean, like for an emergency?"

Her mom sneezed, then waited till they were past Mrs. Mingo, who was wearing a dust mask, and peering over her glasses at the organic soups.

"We're an island. If there are any interruptions in services, we're especially vulnerable."

"Interruptions in services? Like—"

"Anything. Power, water, food, medicine. A lot of people are off work because of severe allergies, and complications."

Petra knew from her dad that the little island hospital was already overloaded. For most people, it was like having a really bad cold, or the flu. But some people had much more severe reactions—lung infections, or life-threatening asthma attacks—and needed to be transferred to Victoria or Vancouver—where the hospitals were also packed.

Her mother coughed hard for a few seconds. "I just think it's best to be prepared in case things break down."

"Mom, you're freaking me out."

She had a sudden image of her mother standing at the front door with a shotgun, warding off scavengers and starving neighbors.

"I'm a worst-case-scenario kind of person."

You sure are, Petra thought, but for the first time she wondered if it wasn't because her mother was a killjoy but because she was trying her best to keep people safe.

When they'd arrived at the supermarket, the parking lot was mostly empty, as were the sidewalks in town. A few people hurried from their cars into the shops, sneezing, covering their faces. A lot of people wore masks—a very common sight since the pollen started flying. Petra had even seen a few people with those scary heavy-duty things with the canister filter. Like in pandemic movies.

"All righty," her mother said, checking the list on her phone, "could you go get some ibuprofen? And allergy medicine, if by some miracle they have any. I'll meet you at the checkout."

Petra headed over to the pharmacy. Shopping with her mother never put her in the best of moods—she never saw her other friends with their mothers.

She scowled. And gym class today—what a disaster. Beaten in high jump by Anaya. When had she gotten so fit? That was definitely a sign of the apocalypse. And even worse was when Rachel had said, "You know, Anaya's skin has really cleared up. She's pretty."

At the pharmacy section, Petra's eyes glided across all the prescription drugs behind the counter. None of them could cure her water allergy. That rainwater had been her one big hope, and now she was too scared to wash with it. Maybe that lab in Vancouver could still make a pure version for her, but so far she hadn't heard any word back. Dad said every lab was overloaded since the plants had appeared.

She noticed Seth Robertson staring at the shelf labeled ALLER-GIES. It was completely empty except for a single crumpled box of Reactine that had been ripped open and emptied—just for that added touch of end-of-the-world frenzy.

"We can't keep it in stock," Petra heard the masked pharmacist snuffle at Seth. "Guardian Drugs might have something."

"I tried them already."

"We're supposed to get some more in tomorrow. But they said that yesterday, too."

"Okay, thanks."

Seth turned and saw her. He gave a shy smile, and started to leave. With surprise, she realized she didn't want him to.

"Hey, Seth."

He looked startled by the sound of his own name. He wasn't the kind of boy she usually found cute. His body was a bit strange, but he had a good face, and he looked just a tiny bit like Garrity on that TV show, who was a weirdo but also kind of hot in a crazy, intense way.

"I didn't think you had allergies," she said.

Along with her and Anaya, he was the only other person at school who wasn't sneezing his nose off.

"Yeah, I'm okay," he said. "It's for Mrs. Antos. She's pretty bad."

Petra reached into her pocket and passed him a box of Reactine. "Here. It's almost full."

Seth stared at it like she'd just handed him a bar of gold. "Where'd you get this?"

"My dad works at the hospital. Take it already. Before someone sees and starts a riot."

Seth slid it inside his hoodie. "Thanks. You just carry around your own stash?"

She shrugged. Everyone thought being popular came easy to her. But handing out allergy pills like gummy bears was one way of making sure people kept liking her. Because at the back of her mind was the worry that if her water allergy got worse, her skin would get worse, and then she wouldn't be pretty anymore. She loved being pretty. And not just because it made her popular. Being pretty was like armor—it was the only thing between herself and her fears. Fear of people thinking she was stuck up and icy. Fear of someone stabbing her in the back again. Fear of what the future held for her.

"How's Mr. Antos?" she asked Seth.

He shook his head. "Not great. I'm going to see him later. His whole family's coming over from Vancouver."

From her dad, Petra knew he'd had a heart attack, a bad one—maybe because of the damage to his lungs.

"I hope he gets better soon."

"Thanks. Me too."

His eyes looked a little red, and she wondered if he'd been crying. She thought it was pretty sweet, how much he cared about the Antoses, when he'd only lived with them a few months.

An awkward silence hovered between them. For the life of her, she couldn't think of what to say. This hardly ever happened.

"So, you don't have allergies either," he said.

"No. Well, except the one I got a while ago. Water."

She almost regretted telling him—it was kind of nice having someone on the island who didn't know about her allergy. But he didn't look at her with pity, only interest.

"So no swimming," he said.

She thought it was strange that was the first thing he said, as if he knew how much she missed it.

She shook her head. "I used to practically live in the community pool. I did all the lessons, and got all the way up to bronze. I had this plan to become a marine biologist, swimming with sharks and stuff."

She stopped herself. She hadn't talked about that, or with such enthusiasm, for a while, and she worried she sounded like a dork.

"That really sucks." The way he said it made her feel like he truly meant it. "You must still dream about it. Swimming."

She felt the tiniest bit uncomfortable, like he'd just looked inside her.

"All the time."

He shrugged. "Maybe you'll get to swim again someday."

She let out a sigh. "Wow, that'd be great. Anyway, I should get going. My mom's waiting."

"See you," he said.

"Yeah, bye."

She walked off, thinking of the dream she'd had just last night. How she'd been moving through the water, so fast and excited.

SETH SAT IN the hospital waiting room, watching TV. The volume was turned low, but he didn't need sound to know what was going on.

Farmers staring out at blighted fields. Forests of black grass where their crops should have been.

Cows and sheep, their faces streaked with blood from trying to graze on the spiky grass.

A huge bonfire, somewhere in the world, somewhere poor, spewing yellowish smoke over a village.

A makeshift tent filled with coughing people on stretchers.

More headlines scrolled across the bottom of the screen:

New Herbicide Fails in Plant Trials, Says FDA . . . World Economy Shrinks as Workforce Hit with Allergies . . . Environmental Group Blames Climate Change for . . . UN Appoints Bioterrorism Unit to Investigate . . .

By now Seth had heard almost every kind of theory. At least twelve different terrorist groups had said they'd bioengineered the black grass, but couldn't prove it, and no one really believed them anyway. Other people were blaming aliens. A religious group was saying it was a sign of the apocalypse and we should all prepare for the end-time.

Seth's eyes dropped away from the television to Tomas, Mr.

Antos's grown-up son. He'd just come over from Vancouver with his wife and little boy, who sat on the floor, sifting through a box of grimy waiting-room toys.

Tomas was big, like his dad. Seth hadn't talked to him much, or his sister, Angela, who'd also come over. Angela was in the ICU now with Mrs. Antos. Only two visitors at a time were allowed, and Seth was still waiting his turn.

"It's bad in Vancouver, too," Tomas said to him, coughing into his elbow. "Even right downtown it finds places to grow. Stanley Park is completely overrun."

Seth nodded awkwardly. He'd just met Tomas and Angela for the first time today, and he felt like a fake. They'd smiled kindly at him. They'd shaken his hand and sincerely thanked him for saving their father from the fire. But Seth caught something puzzled in their expressions, like they couldn't quite understand why he was here at all. Why their parents had decided to bring a foster kid into their house.

Staring at the television, he wanted something nice to think about, so he angled his thoughts back to Petra and their conversation in the supermarket. He was still amazed she'd even said hi to him. It was about as likely as having a slice of pizza with a supermodel. She had a really pretty mouth. Her lips were so full that, even when they were closed, there was this tiny little diamond-shaped gap right in the center. He couldn't help thinking about kissing it—and that made him feel incredibly nervous. As if she'd ever kiss him.

But she'd seemed kind of nervous, too. Her eyes had darted all over the place. Every time he saw her at school, she was always surrounded by good-looking friends and seemed super confident and composed and, well, terrifying. But maybe that was just practice. He liked how eager she got when she was talking about swimming. He knew what it was like to dream about something you couldn't have.

Mrs. Antos and Angela came out of the ICU, and Tomas and his wife went in. Mrs. Antos played with her grandson, and Seth was afraid to ask her how Mr. Antos was doing because Angela was still sniffling.

When finally Tomas and his wife returned, Seth said, "Is it okay if I go see him?"

"The nurse said that was it for today," Tomas replied. "He's pretty out of it anyway."

"Oh."

"Sorry, Seth."

Back home he retreated to his room. He heard them all downstairs talking, and the little boy crying, and then someone else crying—he thought it was Mrs. Antos this time—and he didn't feel he had the right to go down there. He wasn't a real part of the family. He looked out at the fields, and saw the new growth of black grass, already peeking up from the earth.

He got out his sketchbook, and realized he hadn't drawn anything in it for over a week. He was about to open it when Mrs. Antos knocked on the door.

"Dinner's in a bit," she said. "Why don't you come down?"

"You sure?"

"Of course." She sat down on the chair. "I'm sorry you didn't get to see him. I know he would've loved to see you."

"When's he coming home?"

"Not for a while. The doctors say his heart was badly damaged."

Seth felt all the breath leaving his lungs, until there was nothing left. He counted out the seconds of total emptiness.

"Seth," Mrs. Antos said.

He looked at her, waited. It was easiest to just wait and listen.

"When he comes home, he won't be like he was. He won't be able to take care of this place."

"Sure he will," Seth said. "I can help out now. You guys taught me a lot of things."

"You'd be a wonderful help, but . . ."

He hated the word *but* almost more than anything. It got slipped in anywhere, and it meant something was about to be taken away. Still, he tried.

"I can do the heavy stuff Mr. Antos used to do. You guys just tell me what to do. You won't believe how hard I can work."

She looked at him, and he knew that look. He'd seen it with the nicer social workers, the ones who probably shouldn't have been social workers because they cared too much, and what they saw hurt them too much. It was sadness and pity, and he hated it.

"We're probably going to sell the farm," she said. "So we can buy a condo in Vancouver and be near our kids."

Their kids.

He watched her, knowing what was coming next, and he made himself leave his body a little bit, so it wouldn't hurt as much.

Her eyes were wet. "I am so sorry, Seth, but we won't be able to take care of you. Gregor's going to need a lot of taking care of. I had a chat with the social worker and she thinks it's probably best if you're with a family a little younger—and a little healthier."

"Yeah," he said.

"You've been a wonderful addition to our family, and we want you to keep in touch."

"Definitely," he said. He was staring at her big hands that could move anything. He should've known in the end they'd just move him, too.

"Nothing's happening right away," she said. "It'll be at least a few weeks. I'm sorry, Seth. Come down for dinner, okay?"

She left him alone. He looked at the sketchbook, still on his lap. Lately he hadn't felt like he needed to open it. It had been okay to leave the things inside. Now he wanted to let them out.

All these things he'd seen in dreams. It was weird how they somehow gave him a sense of home. They were still here waiting for him to come back. He grabbed a pencil and started sketching on a fresh page. His drawing had kept him going—not just for months but for *years*.

He'd keep drawing up here in his room, until it was the Antos family that seemed like a dream, and these sketched images were everything that was real.

That night when he fell asleep, he flew. Again.

He saw the ground dropping away beneath him: trees, yard, house, school, mall, roads—none of it mattered.

The landscape he wanted was the sky.

He wasn't scared to angle higher, so all he could see was blue. He wasn't afraid to go faster, even when he passed into cloud and felt the mist on his face and heard the whistling in his ears. Cloud, cloud, light, cloud, light.

How he loved this part, even the faint throb behind his eyes. The speed really was incredible. He was going *somewhere*. He hurtled forward. From the corner of his eyes, he saw not outstretched arms, but the shimmer of feathers.

CHAPTER SEVEN

WHEN HER ALARM WENT, Anaya slapped it silent, then dragged herself out of bed. The smell of coffee and toast lingered in the quiet house. Mom had just left, and Dad had gone even earlier. He'd woken her to say good-bye before setting off for the eco-reserves by boat with Amit. He'd sat on the edge of her bed with his warm earth smell. She'd told him she was going to miss him, told him to be safe, and he said he'd be back in a couple of days, and not to worry. She felt miserable when he left, but she'd drifted back to sleep anyway.

On her way to the bathroom, Anaya glimpsed the latest crop of black grass, already four feet tall on the front lawn.

"Hate you," she muttered.

She dressed for school and went downstairs. She microwaved an apple, poured some almond milk into a bowl of gluten-free granola, ate.

Don't worry, Dad had said. How could you not worry when terrible bioengineered plants were taking over the planet? She dropped her apple core into the compost, and saw the bag was almost overflowing. Knotting it, she carried it out through the back door.

The bins were against the wall, around the corner from the driveway. Anaya dumped the compost into the stinky green bin and clasped the lid. From the garbage bin next to it came a dry rustling sound, like something scratching inside. When the bin shuddered, Anaya stepped back. Probably a squirrel in there.

When the sound came again, it was more like a snake's hiss. There weren't rattlesnakes on the island, she knew that much. She grabbed the rake leaning against the wall. With the tines, she carefully flipped open the lid.

Gripping the rake in both hands like a baseball bat, she retreated a few steps, and waited for something to jump out. When nothing appeared, she whacked the side of the bin. After waiting a few more seconds, she stepped closer and peeped inside.

In an explosion of hissing and whirling, a long, dark snake churned frantically against the sides, trapped. With a cry, Anaya kicked the bin. It toppled into the driveway, spilling a thick tangle onto the asphalt.

It took her several seconds to realize it wasn't a snake.

It was a black vine twisted into knots, and still moving. Anaya brought down the rake's sharp teeth on it, severing the vine again and again, until it stopped writhing.

Panting, she shoved the tangled mess away from her. She bent closer, and with a chill realized it looked a lot like the vine Dad had been growing on the farm. Same color. Same little bulges along the stem. Only this vine was much bigger and longer.

Had it grown from the water puddled at the bottom of the garbage bin? From a careful distance, she bent to look inside. Light slanted through a crack in the plastic bottom. Anaya spotted the vine growing through it. Growing out? Or growing in?

She walked around the outside of the bin, and followed the vine down the driveway. It was very well camouflaged against the asphalt. She figured she must be tracing the vine to its source, because it was getting thicker. Then she stopped and stared.

It had grown from the bag of soil she'd taken from the school field. She'd left it propped against the wall because Dad said someone from the farm would swing by to pick it up. It looked a lot fatter than she remembered.

A single thick vine had grown from the top of the bag, and split into three. One had grown down the driveway and into the garbage can, and the other two . . .

The other two vines had climbed halfway up the wall of the house. Dangling from one of them was a kind of wrinkly sac. Anaya stared at it. It looked a bit like those bulges she and Dad had noticed at the lab, only much bigger.

Right above the sac was a sprig of dark berries. They were small and smooth, and Anaya was startled by how she wanted to pluck one. She could almost feel the firmness of it against her tongue, and imagine its taste singing through her mouth. She took a step closer, hand outstretched.

A tiny bird landed on the vine, and cocked its head at the berries. It took one in its beak, and tugged. The berry didn't want to come off. The bird was perched atop the wrinkly sac.

As Anaya watched, the bird plucked harder. The berry popped off, and at the exact same moment, the sac opened like fleshy lips. Before the bird could spread its wings, it tumbled inside.

Anaya made a small, startled grunt. The sac shook as the bird chirped and struggled, but the space was too narrow for it to open its wings. An odd cloying smell reached Anaya's nostrils. Already the wet lips of the sac were closing.

From inside, the bird's muffled shrieks suddenly stopped.

A terrible smell of something rotting came from the sac.

Anaya stepped back, breathing hard.

Her gaze slithered back down the vine to the bag of soil.

Heart pounding, Anaya opened up the bag and looked inside. The soil trembled. A tiny hole, like the one a clam makes in the sand, appeared. Some grains of earth slipped into it. Anaya caught another whiff of that same sweet perfume, only stronger.

Her mouth was dry with fear as she got the rake. Lightly she tapped the soil with the end of the handle. The entire bag shook violently as a hole opened up in the middle. The handle of the rake fell deeper inside, and a fleshy mouth clamped shut around it.

With a holler, Anaya pulled back on the rake. In a cascade of soil, the bag tipped over, and a huge, wrinkly sac tumbled out. It was a dark purple, and still clamped around the handle, trying desperately to devour it.

NEAR THE SCHOOL, Petra passed an orange-vested work crew with chain saws, hacking down the black grass alongside the road. She cut through the tall cedars that bordered one side of the playing field, and recognized the gawky outline of Seth Robertson, leaning against a tree.

She started to change course—she'd talked to him just yesterday and didn't want him to think she was a stalker—but he turned and saw her. His smile of greeting was so eager and genuine, she couldn't help feeling touched. He waved.

"Hi," she said, walking over.

In his cupped hand were some berries. He popped one into his mouth. There was a dribble of juice on his chin. She didn't want to embarrass him by pointing it out. And seeing it made her less nervous somehow. Like she could just be herself. Which was such a relief.

"Are those blueberries?" she asked.

"Don't know."

She laughed. "How can you not know?"

He shrugged. "They're really addictive. I saw a bunch on my way to school." He nodded at the tree. "There's some here, too."

Petra looked and saw a sprig of berries growing from the trunk at eye level. She frowned. Did berries grow right from the bark? They were a deep purple, so dark they were almost black. They did look awfully good.

She reached out for one, and noticed that they weren't growing from the tree at all. They came from a vine that snaked cleverly through the crevices in the bark. With a chill, she realized the vine was the same disconcerting color as the black grass—and the other plants that had grown in her bottles.

"Stop eating them!" she told Seth. "They might be poisonous!"

"Hey, look!" someone called out near the school. "A deer!"

Petra turned. A fawn had wandered into the middle of the school field. It bent its dappled neck and began eating grass. It wasn't the first time. Lately, they'd gotten pretty bold. Mr. Hilborn always drove them off, but Petra felt sorry for them. There was so little proper grass now.

Against the back wall of the school, near the picnic tables, Petra saw a bunch of kids watching the deer. The smokers. They were pretty much the only people who lingered outside these days. She recognized Jen Richards, and Tereza, who did yearbook with Anaya, and her boyfriend, Fleetwood, who looked an awful lot like Jefferson, the cute, shaggy guy on that surfing show.

"Oh my God!" Tereza cried out suddenly, dropping her cigarette and running into the field.

Petra's gaze whipped back to the deer. Its rear half had *disappeared* into the earth. Pawing frantically at the grass, its neck and shoulders straining, it struggled to haul itself out of the hole. Its eyes were huge, and white with shock. A terrible high-pitched squeal welled from its throat as it slipped back even deeper.

"We've got to help it!" she gasped, and she was already running, Seth right behind her.

She reached the deer first. It was still flailing, trying to climb out of the hole. But the sides of the hole weren't dirt. Petra stared in incomprehension.

"What is that?"

The walls of the hole were slick and faintly purple, with a fleshy rim around the top that was starting to flex and slowly contract. Petra couldn't see the deer's hindquarters because the hole narrowed and curved at the bottom. A sickly perfume wafted up.

She thought she heard a faraway voice shouting, "Don't move! Guys! Stay still!"

"Let's pull it out!" panted Tereza, who'd just arrived with Fleetwood and Jen.

The deer suddenly collapsed, legs twisted under. It wailed piteously from the bottom of the hole. The smell of garbage cans on a hot day rose up. Then the top began to contract, like a set of hideous lips mashing together.

"Don't move!" came the shout again, louder now, and Petra

wrenched her gaze away to see Anaya hurrying toward them along the very edge of the field. In her hands was a chain saw.

"Don't move!" she bellowed. "The field's not safe!"

SETH WATCHED ANAYA crossing the field, one careful step at a time.

"The ground could cave in!" she cried.

Seth stared at the sealed-over hole, which was shuddering as the deer kicked from inside.

"What *is* this thing?" he heard Petra shout, like it was all Anaya's fault.

"A plant!" Anaya said.

"A *plant*?" Tereza looked like she was on the verge of panic.

"It just ate a freakin' deer!" Fleetwood said.

"There could be more of them!" Anaya yelled. "Lots more!"

Seth wished she hadn't said that. Tereza and the others looked even more freaked out now. His own heartbeat was loud in his ears. He tasted the berry juice in his mouth and felt a weird rush of energy.

"Hey! What's going on?"

Seth glanced back to the school. Mr. Hilborn was doing his angry gym-teacher walk toward them.

"What're you guys doing to my field now?" he hollered.

"Mr. Hilborn! Stay there!" Anaya shouted. "Please! It's not safe!"

He kept coming. "What's with the chain saw, Miss Riggs?"

From behind Anaya, a large, orange-vested worker came stomping after her, glaring.

"Hey, young lady, I need that chain saw back right now!"

Seth turned to Anaya. "You know how to use that thing?"

"Of course I do," she said.

That was good, Seth thought, because he had an overwhelming sense that something terrible was about to happen. And the loudest thought in his head was: *Keep them safe. Anaya and Petra. Keep them safe.*

"Stop!" Anaya shouted to the worker, and then to Mr. Hilborn. "There's things *under the ground*!"

"Nobody run," Seth said to the other kids, and hoped they'd listen.

"If it can eat a deer, it can eat us!" Tereza said, and grabbed Fleetwood's hand.

"Is that another hole?" said Mr. Hilborn, squinting in annoyance, or maybe it was confusion, as he kept coming. "What've you guys—"

The earth opened under him. He fell down to his armpits, scrabbling at the ground. Then his head kicked back as he was pulled completely out of sight.

Seth looked at the others, and could tell Tereza was about to bolt. He saw it in her eyes. Anaya must have seen it, too, because she said, "Tereza, don't!"

It all happened in a matter of heartbeats. Tereza ran for the school. Fleetwood charged after her, calling, "Tereza, this way, it's safer!" then veered off toward the road. Seth wasn't sure Tereza had even heard him because she didn't stop or change course. After four strides, Fleetwood looked back over his shoulder, shouted at Tereza again, and then the earth swallowed him whole.

"No!" Seth heard Anaya gasp. She dropped the chain saw and chased after Tereza.

"Tereza, stop!" she bellowed.

Seth was about to sprint after her when Petra snatched up the chain saw and ran in a different direction.

"Petra!" he shouted.

She kept going. He looked at Anaya running, and Petra running. How could he keep them both safe?

He took off after Petra. Six strides ahead of him, she plunged through the earth, down to her shoulders. Seth threw himself to the ground and reached out. Her hands clasped his.

"Pull me!" she wailed.

"I'm trying!" he hollered. He kicked himself into sitting and leaned back with all his weight. His muscles felt strong—but not strong enough. Petra sank deeper, pulling him with her.

He could've let go, but he didn't.

He clenched his teeth, and let himself fall into the hole with her.

CHAPTER EIGHT

ANAYA CAUGHT UP TO Tereza and grabbed her arm with both hands, just as the earth collapsed. Tereza plunged feet first, dragging Anaya after her, headfirst.

In a cascade of soil, Anaya skidded down the slick purple funnel, and jolted to a stop, upside down. Her head and shoulders were wedged between the plant wall and Tereza's ankles.

Through the narrow gap between their bodies, she got an upside-down view of Tereza shouting for help at the circle of cloud-streaked sky. They must've been over six feet under. From outside she heard some muffled shouting and a few high-pitched shrieks.

"Can you jump?" she hollered at Tereza.

Anaya winced as her friend's knees banged against her ribs, and her shoes knocked her skull. But their bodies were too tightly jammed together for Tereza to make a proper jump.

"Help!" Tereza yelled again.

No one was coming. Anaya felt something cobwebby against her cheek. From the slick plant wall, long silver hairs lifted and brushed against her. In revulsion, she tried to jerk her face away. She couldn't even use her hands: one was pinned uselessly near the top of her skull, the other at her hip. She blew hard at the little hairs. Tiny pores perforated the plant wall, and through these pores now came a pale mist.

"What's that smell?" Tereza demanded.

It was sickly sweet—the same as the smell from the bag of soil in her driveway. The top of the plant quivered and started to close, its fleshy lips compressing.

"No!" Tereza wailed. "No, no, no!"

"Tereza!" Anaya shouted. "Just climb over me!"

The circle of sky shrank. It was getting darker. The cloying smell intensified. Tereza yanked her feet free and planted one in Anaya's armpit, the other on her backside.

"Go!" Anaya grunted.

"I feel so weak," Tereza said, and her voice sounded dopey.

"Just jump!"

What was taking her so long? Instead of pushing off, Tereza sagged listlessly against the wall.

Anaya pulled down her knees and wrenched herself in so many directions she was amazed she didn't tear every muscle in her body. But the funnel walls had a surprising amount of give, and she elbowed and kicked her way upright. Now she and Tereza were squished together face to face. Her friend's eyes had a strange, unfocused look.

With a wet smacking sound, the top of the plant shut completely and they were plunged into darkness.

"Your lighter," Anaya said. "Grab your lighter!"

"Can't reach it." Tereza's words were slurred.

Anaya's hands dived into the tight pockets of Tereza's jeans until she found the lighter. She pulled it out and dragged her thumb over the wheel. A flame blossomed in the darkness.

Tereza's head lolled and knocked against Anaya's shoulder.

"Tereza, wake up!"

"Yeah, I'm awake," Tereza said, blinking.

In the flickering light, the walls trembled, then glistened. From all the tiny pores, moisture beaded and formed little rivulets.

Cutting through the sickly perfume was the acrid smell of burning hide and rubber. Anaya looked down and saw a puddle forming at their feet. Smoke curled from the bottoms of their shoes.

"Oh my God," breathed Anaya. *Acid.* "Tereza, don't touch the walls!"

Which was impossible, since there wasn't room to move without brushing the walls. Already she heard hissing from the back of her own shirt. She tried to pull clear without pushing Tereza into the opposite wall.

She held the lighter as high as she could against the closed top of the sac. The hottest part of the flame was at the very tip—someone had told her that long ago. There was a wet crackling, and a smell like a candle burning the inside of a jack-o'-lantern, only not as nice.

The plant trembled, making both her and Tereza bounce against the walls. Fabric hissed as it touched, and she heard her friend cry out.

"My hand!" Tereza said, holding it in front of her face.

Anaya saw the blistered fingertips. She wondered how long their shoes would last. The foul smoke welling up from below thickened.

Come on, come on! She glared at the scorch marks fanning out across the top of the plant. Hot liquid dripped down onto Anaya's outstretched hand. She sucked in her breath, waiting for the pain. But it didn't come.

With a great spasm, the top of the plant opened. Anaya squinted in the sudden light, and looked anxiously at Tereza, who was staring numbly at her blistering hand.

"Tereza, I'm going to get out, then help you! Okay?"

Tereza said nothing. Anaya pocketed the lighter, bent deep at the knees, and jumped. She didn't know where this new strength came from, but she went much higher than expected, head and shoulders clearing the rim. Her arms shot out, and she dug into the grass. Her legs still hung down inside the plant and she heard the acid hiss on her jeans, felt a wetness on her legs. But no pain at all.

The plant made a gulping contraction, trying to swallow her back down. She held tight and dragged her entire body out.

Instantly she scrambled around and stretched out both hands for Tereza.

"Grab hold!" Her friend still looked confused, and Anaya didn't know whether it was the pain or the weird perfume.

"Tereza! Now!"

Her friend reached up and Anaya grabbed her hands and pulled. Her arms had never been strong, and Tereza was a dead-weight, too dopey to help.

"My feet are burning," Tereza said with eerie calm.

Anaya knelt so she could lean back and use her own weight. She pulled with everything she had, but she knew it wouldn't be enough.

"GET OFF ME!" Petra shouted, batting Seth away from her head.

How was she supposed to climb out of this thing with Seth sprawled all over her like a bony overcoat? She'd lost her grip on the chain saw, and it was now somewhere down at her feet, but she couldn't even see it because of Seth squishing against her, and all the dirt everywhere.

"I'm trying to get you *out*!" Seth shouted back.

"Then why'd you jump *in*?"

It smelled like cheap air freshener down here. Suddenly it was darker.

"It's closing!" he yelled. "Climb over me. Like a ladder!"

He made it sound easy, but it wasn't, the way she was mashed between the wall and his body.

"Hurry!" he told her.

"Okay!" She grabbed hold of anything she could—his hood, his hair—and dug in with her feet. Perched on Seth's back and shoulders, she made a grab for the closing rim, but the fleshy lips clamped shut fast, and they were plunged into darkness.

In panic, she thumped her fist against the top. It was like hitting a gym mat: it dented slightly, but was very firm. With her fingernails, she tried to dig into the seam where the lips met. How could a plant be so freaking strong?

"I can't make it open!" she shouted.

"You're kind of crushing me," Seth grunted, smooshed against the plant wall.

Still piggybacked on him, she plunged a hand into her pocket and dragged out her phone. The flashlight beam lurched around the inside of the plant. Its walls were slick, and Petra realized her own hands were wet. The reek of burning plastic rose from her phone. It was melting beneath her fingertips.

Without thinking, she dropped the phone. It tumbled to the bottom of the plant, but landed so its light still blared up at them. She looked at her wet hand in panic. There were little bits of plastic melted to it, but she didn't feel any pain.

"I think it's acid!" she cried.

Seth pushed himself away from the plant wall, and she tumbled off his back.

"It's all over my face!" Seth said.

Petra's shirt hissed as it touched the plant wall, and then she felt a cool wetness against her skin. But still no pain.

"You okay?" she said, looking at Seth's pale face in the ghastly light from the phone. She couldn't see any blistering.

"Think so."

She looked down at a puddle forming at their feet, smoking around their shoes. Her phone was nearly submerged. Its light flickered. And there was the chain saw. She bent down awkwardly, reaching for it. It was wet, and already pockmarked by acid, but the feel of all that solid metal in her hands was very reassuring. She grabbed what was left of the starter handle. She hoped the cord was still all right.

"What're you doing?" Seth asked in horror.

"What d'you think? I'm going to cut us out of this thing!"

"There's no room. You'll rip us to pieces!"

She passed him the chain saw. "Hold this a sec. I need another piggyback!"

"You're crazy. Do you even know how to use it?"

"Yes!"

It was almost impossible to move in the cramped space, but she managed to climb up onto Seth's back. He passed her back the chain saw and gripped her tight around the legs. She pulled the starter cord at the same moment her phone's light blinked out. In the darkness, the roar of the saw was deafening, and she swayed unsteadily, saw held high, then regained her balance.

Petra stabbed straight up. The blade dug in. The plant was too thick for her to cut across, so she pulled the blade out and stabbed up again. She tried to cut a square, like she was carving a pumpkin, and a big chunk fell down. A crooked patch of daylight flared overhead.

She'd cut through! She could see again! She slashed away at the top, enlarging the hole. The whole plant was shaking now like a bouncy castle.

"Petra!" Seth was shouting. "I can't—"

He toppled, and she toppled with him, the blade still whirling. She managed to kill it just before landing on top of Seth.

Smoke rose from her ragged clothing. She looked at her hands and arms, but didn't see any blood or blisters. And still no pain. But her heart raced, as if the true horror of the situation had just struck her. She'd fallen into this *thing*. This giant mouth filled with acid. It wanted to *melt* them.

She untangled herself from Seth, who looked at her and said, "Are you okay?"

He sounded a long way away. Her mind was empty except for two echoing words.

Get out.

Later she wouldn't be able to remember this. She was all animal instinct. She struggled up. She'd cut the plant into weeping ribbons that hung down into the pit, and she used them now to haul herself out. Her ruined shoes skidded off the slippery walls.

She clawed her way out to the grass, then turned and reached back.

"Saw!" she barked to Seth.

She might need it again. He passed it to her, and she clutched it to her chest, looking around the field, feeling like she'd just arrived in a very dangerous new world.

HEART HAMMERING AT his ribs, Seth hauled himself out.

"Don't move," he told Petra. He didn't want her going anywhere and falling in again.

And Anaya, where was she? He turned and caught sight of her, shouting and crying as she tried in vain to pull someone from a hole. She teetered on the edge, about to fall.

He raced over and grabbed her shoulders, steadying her.

She gasped, "Help me!"

He reached down and grabbed Tereza's other wrist. Together he and Anaya heaved her out onto the ground. Tereza's shoes had melted around her feet, and there were weeping red blisters all over her arms and face. Her clothing smoldered.

"She needs help!" Anaya hollered, waving her arms toward the school, where a big crowd had now gathered outside the doors.

A couple of teachers were commando-crawling across the field toward them.

Seth heard sirens in the distance. The same orange-vested

worker was still frozen in place, saying, "What do I do?" to his fellow workers, who watched from the field's edge, not daring to come closer.

Seth's eyes skittered to the place where Mr. Hilborn had gone down, and saw the top of the plant clenched shut like a disapproving mouth. Not far away were the exposed tops of two other pit plants, shuddering. From inside both came muffled shouts.

"Fleetwood and Jen!" Anaya said.

She started to move but Seth caught her arm. "No! It's not safe!"

"We've got to help them!"

She didn't understand. She thought he was just being selfish, but all he was thinking about was her and Petra, as if they were family.

"Petra!" Anaya shouted. "We need the saw!"

But Petra was limping away from them, toward the school, like she was in a trance. The chain saw was clenched tight against her chest.

"Petra, stop!" Seth shouted. She'd go down again.

He scrabbled up and ran after her. When he put his hand on Petra's shoulder, she whirled to face him, hand clenched around the starter cord, like she was ready to let rip.

"We need it!" he said urgently.

After a second, she pushed it into his hands, then sat down on the grass and started sobbing. Seth wanted to comfort her, but there wasn't time. At least, she was staying put. That was good.

Carefully he retraced his steps, then crawled over to Anaya, who was already at the first plant, holding a lighter to its wrinkly top.

"You know how to use it?" she said, nodding at the chain saw.

He shook his head. He must be the only person on the island who didn't.

"Here, keep burning it with this," she told him.

He passed her the chain saw, and she crawled to the other hole. He flicked the lighter, but worried the flame wasn't searing the plant enough. With both hands he tried to pry apart the seam at the top. It was so strong. Behind him, Anaya's chain saw kicked to life.

"Help!" came a muffled voice from inside his own plant.

"I'm getting you out!" Seth shouted.

"It's burning me!"

Without thinking, Seth sank his teeth into the plant's flesh. He worried it like a dog, tearing, until a chunk came off in his mouth and he went down for another bite. It tasted sweet, like the rind of a watermelon.

Behind him he heard voices, and glanced back to see that Mr. Gault, the geography teacher, had reached Tereza. He was using his windbreaker as a stretcher for her.

Seth bit the plant again, and felt it wince. He ripped out another chunk, and made a small hole. Clenching the lighter, he plunged his hand into the hole, flicked the flame to high, and started to burn the inside of the plant.

"I'm so sleepy," came Fleetwood's faint voice.

"Stay awake!" he shouted.

He moved the flame back and forth against the plant flesh, until with a great spasm, the lips parted. Fleetwood swayed against the wall, not noticing that his clothing was smoldering. His pupils were huge.

"Grab my hand!" Seth told him.

Fleetwood put a floppy, blistered hand in his. A teacher was suddenly beside him, grabbing at Fleetwood's other hand. It was Ms. McIntyre, the history teacher. The moment she grabbed Fleetwood's hand, she winced, but didn't let go.

"Watch out!" the teacher told Seth after they'd hauled Fleetwood to safety. "He's covered in acid!"

"I need help!" Anaya was shouting.

Seth rushed over. Anaya had sliced open the other plant with the chain saw, and deep inside, Jen Haines was curled unconscious. Liquid lapped against her body, and a terrible hissing and smoke rose up from her clothing and hair and skin.

Seth jumped in. Acid splashed around his feet as he heaved Jen up. Many hands reached down for her. They grabbed at her head, her sleeves, under her armpits, and hauled her out onto the grass.

When Seth clambered out, people were talking to him and asking him questions, but he could only look around him, stunned. Firetrucks in the driveway, ambulances, and an RCMP cruiser. Red lights swirling. Firefighters made their way across the field, testing the soil ahead of them with poles. A hole yawned open, and a firefighter almost fell in.

Against the school was a huge crowd of kids now, and almost all of them had their phones out. Some were talking into them, others were filming.

Two firefighters with gloved hands used a crowbar to pry open the plant that had eaten Mr. Hilborn. With difficulty, they pulled him out.

Seth looked at Anaya, and then Petra, still sitting on the grass, arms wrapped around her knees, rocking back and forth. They were safe. Both of them were safe, and completely unharmed.

Just like him.

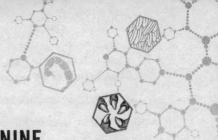

CHAPTER NINE

"WHEN CAN WE GO home?" Anaya asked.

The blood pressure cuff deflated around her arm, and Mr. Sumner noted the figures on his pad. "We want to keep you guys a little longer. You seem fine. Which is a miracle. But the doctor just wants to make sure there's no delayed reactions."

"Did you call my parents?"

Her phone had been melted by the acid goo inside the pit plant.

"No answer from your mom," Mr. Sumner replied.

"She must be in the air."

"And your father's went straight to voice mail."

Dad had warned her this would happen. Coverage around the islands and eco-reserves was always patchy. She swallowed, wishing she could hear their voices. Dad needed to know about these pit plants. What if there were more of them where he was going?

"Can you keep trying, please?" she asked Mr. Sumner.

Enviously she watched as he went to Petra and kissed the top of her head.

"Okay?" her father asked, and Petra nodded mutely.

Mr. Sumner glanced over at Seth. "We called Mrs. Antos," he said. "She'll be over soon."

"Thanks."

Seth crouched forward in a chair, bony arms and legs jutting from his hospital gown. Anaya looked away from all the red scars on his bare arms.

The hospital was crammed, and all three of them had been put in the same room. A single bed, two armchairs, and a television mounted high on the wall, silently playing a daytime soap that nobody had bothered to turn off.

Her memory was all choppy. She couldn't even remember changing into the hospital gown. She barely remembered how they'd gotten here.

At school there had been lots of voices, and gloved hands on her, and water sluicing over her. She hadn't wanted to let go of the chain saw. They kept telling her to let go. She remembered Petra screaming at them not to pour water on her, and in the end they'd dumped some kind of powder all over her. Another thing she remembered: Tereza being lifted into the back of an ambulance. There were only three ambulances on the whole island, and they were all lined up on the school driveway.

"Is Tereza okay?" she asked Petra's father.

In the doorway, he turned. "She's comfortable now, but they're transferring her to Vancouver. Fleetwood, too."

"But they're going to be okay?"

"They were pretty lucky, really."

She was aware he hadn't answered her question.

"What about Jen Haines?"

But he was already gone. As the door closed behind him, noise swirled from the hallway: sneezing and coughing, talking and crying.

"I think Jen might be dead," Seth said. "I saw the firemen working on her, and she wasn't moving or anything."

"Maybe she was just unconscious." Anaya tried not to think about how patches of Jen's hair had melted. "That gas, it puts you to sleep. Did you guys smell it? It was like really bad perfume. It made Tereza super dopey."

Petra didn't say anything. She hadn't talked much at all.

Seth said, "Fleetwood was really out of it, too. It's like they drug you first so you don't struggle as much when the acid comes. But it didn't work on us. Not the gas, not that acid."

Anaya had worried that when people saw her, unharmed, they'd think she'd saved herself first and let Tereza get really hurt. But she *had* to climb out because Tereza couldn't.

"You were brave," Seth said to her, as if reading her thoughts.

"You too."

Most kids didn't even know Seth's name and thought he was just some weird loner, but he was a hero. She felt suddenly self-conscious in her stupid hospital gown. She worried it might gape open. She wished she'd shaved her legs. She sat with them tightly crossed.

"Does your dad know about these plants?" Seth asked her.

"I don't know. Maybe. We saw those tiny little ones, but—"

"Little ones?" Petra asked, sitting up on the hospital bed.

"Yeah, those little black peas from your water bottle!"

"What're you talking about?" Seth asked in confusion.

"Those tiny peas? They grow into those huge pit things?" Petra demanded.

Anaya nodded. "I saw a big one at my house. It sent out a giant vine with these weird little sacs that trap animals, and sprigs of berries—"

"What did the berries look like?" Seth interrupted.

"Like blueberries, I guess, only smaller and darker."

She saw Seth and Petra exchange a look. "What?"

"He ate some," Petra said.

"You did?" Anaya heard the amazement in her voice, but right away remembered the hungry rush of saliva in her own mouth. She'd wanted those berries, too. "They lure animals, and then the sacs open up and trap them. But the biggest traps, those ones grow *under* the soil."

"What kind of plant *does* this?" Petra muttered angrily.

"A bioengineered one," Anaya said.

"Whoa, wait. Who said?" Petra asked.

"My dad." She probably wasn't supposed to tell, but that was yesterday, and everything felt different now, and much worse. "That's what all the scientists are thinking."

"Wow," Seth said. "Those things are killers."

"Where did you guys see the vines?" Anaya wanted to know.

"Growing up the trees beside the field."

Anaya nodded. That made sense. "The bulb grows underground, sends out vines . . ." She was thinking aloud, trying to order her jittery thoughts. "The vines grow high and get sunlight, and those little sac things eat small animals—and maybe that's all energy to feed the bulb underground. It gets big and—"

"And just waits there," said Petra. "For us."

Anaya's skin prickled. "*That's* why the black grass wouldn't grow!"

Seth looked at her, shaking his head. "What?"

"The pit plants won't let it! They must send a signal to the black grass to stop it from growing there."

"Signal?" Seth asked.

"A chemical signal in the soil." Anaya's thoughts were racing now, tumbling over one another. "All those other places it doesn't grow . . . pastures, school field—oh my God, the playground by the marina. Those pit things are growing wherever people walk!"

"YES, ANYWHERE THE black grass doesn't grow!" Petra told her mother urgently. "You've got to close it off!"

She was making the call from the nurses' station, phone

pressed to her ear, a finger plugging the other so she could hear Mom above the noise.

"She's sure about this?" Mom sounded frazzled, and there was plenty of noise at her end, too: shouting, and the urgent *blurp* of sirens.

"Yes!" Petra didn't trust Anaya as a friend, but she trusted her as a brain. "They grow underground so they can trap people!"

"All right. I've got to go. I'm so glad you're all right. I love you, Petra."

She felt a lump in her throat. "You too."

She swiped her eyes with a tissue so no tears got on her face, and headed back to her room. They'd given her socks the same gross color as the gowns. The stink of singed shoe rubber was still trapped in her nose. On her arms were patches of that weird powder the firefighters had dumped on her to neutralize the acid. Which she didn't need at all, but they hadn't listened to her. Her skin looked dry and scaly. She wanted to go home and clean up properly. Her father had said he'd try to find her some hypo-allergenic lotion, but he was too busy.

The moment she walked into the room, Anaya asked, "Is she going to close all the parks and playgrounds?"

"And the pastures, yeah, as soon as they can."

Anaya exhaled in relief and slumped back in her chair. "Thanks."

Petra's eyes drifted to the television. She felt like a sleepwalker. Her brain wasn't working very well. For a few mindless seconds, she watched a ridiculously good-looking man and woman argue silently.

Seth asked, "Where did you guys learn to use a chain saw?"

Petra shrugged. "Most people on the island know."

Anaya said, "Didn't you get a ribbon in that log-cutting competition, in grade six?"

"Second place."

"Your mom taught me, too," Anaya said.

"Oh, right." Petra didn't really want to be reminded of the days when they hung out all the time.

"I think it was the same camping trip she acted out how you survive a bear attack," Anaya added.

Petra couldn't help smiling at this. The memory was comforting. It seemed like such a long time ago.

"So, how long have you guys been friends?" Seth wanted to know.

"Um," said Petra, not knowing what to say next. She glanced at Anaya.

"That was a while ago," Anaya said, sounding like she'd been the victim of a terrible injustice.

Which was so unfair! Petra could tell Seth was looking at her, waiting for more of an explanation.

"It wasn't my fault, okay?" she said. "We just don't hang out anymore."

Anaya sniffed. "You dumped me."

That was such a lie. "I didn't *dump* you!"

It was ridiculous even to be talking about this right now. In a hospital. In disgusting green gowns. When people had just been melted by plants.

Anaya said, "You started hanging around with Rachel and all those guys. And you stopped inviting me because I wasn't pretty enough."

Petra's heart pounded with indignation. "No, Anaya, that is *not* why I stopped inviting you. I stopped *inviting* you because you told people about my *tail.*"

She hadn't uttered that word in a long time—and it was probably a mistake. But it was out and actually she felt relieved, letting it hang there, stinking, in front of Anaya. See what she said now.

"Um, what?" Seth said, looking totally confused.

"Tell him," Petra said with a shrug.

She loved seeing Anaya squirm. Anaya's eyes fell to her knees. She crossed and uncrossed her legs. She always got to play the wounded bird: the tragic, smart, good girl rejected by all the pretty, mean girls because she was homely. It was all a big fake.

After a while, Anaya said, "Okay, I did tell, but only *after* you dumped me."

"Before." She looked at Seth. "I was born with this weird little tail, a couple of centimeters long. The doctors removed it. Anaya was the only person I ever told, and she promised she'd never tell anyone. Then, at lunch one day, in front of *everyone,* she goes, 'It's so weird Petra's allergic to water when she's half reptile.' And

then people asked what she meant and she pretended to look all guilty."

"You had a *tail*?" Seth asked, looking at her intently.

"You don't need to look so *fascinated*, Seth. Lots of people have them!"

"Not *lots*," Anaya muttered.

Petra rounded on Anaya. "And then you told Sal Nuñez how the tail was a foot long, and when the doctors hacked it off, it flopped around on the floor for a few seconds."

Seth saw Anaya smile to herself. Petra punched her on the arm.

"Ow!"

"*And* you also told Barb Mueller I kept it in a jar under my bed!"

"Because you didn't invite me to your birthday party!" Anaya said.

"Yeah, because you told everyone I was a freak! And by the way, you didn't invite me to *yours* either."

Anaya was looking at Seth now, shaking her head. "It's because I got ugly after my allergies."

"I didn't dump you because you got ugly, Anaya. I dumped you because you were a jerk!"

Petra remembered everything. Where everyone was sitting at the lunch table. What they were wearing. The egg-salad sandwich half eaten in front of her. Anaya had told everyone about her tail—and Petra had been so shocked she hadn't denied it. It would have been so easy. All she'd needed to do was lie; it wasn't like Anaya had pictures or proof or anything. But she'd just sat there in silence, so everyone knew it was true. Then she'd gone to the bathroom and cried.

People talked about it afterward for a long time, and it was terrible. But eventually they forgot. What Petra couldn't forget was Anaya's betrayal—and the fact she *never* apologized. So Petra started making mean comments about Anaya being a snotty mess, and that was the final nail in the coffin of their friendship.

"Hey," Seth said, looking past them. "We're on TV."

It took Petra a couple of seconds to understand what she was seeing. It was phone footage of their school field. The image was shaky and pixelated as it zoomed in on the three of them with Tereza, Fleetwood, and Jen off to the side. And right in the middle, the struggling deer.

Petra ran to the television and turned up the volume.

The camera jerked over to Mr. Hilborn, flailing in a pit plant. Shouts and screams came from offscreen.

An unseen news anchor was saying, "Again, we warn viewers some of these images are disturbing. This is Salt Spring Secondary School, where earlier today several sinkholes opened up, swallowing first a deer, and then a man we assume was a teacher from the school. . . ."

It was like watching one of those joke hidden-camera videos, the way Mr. Hilborn got slurped up so suddenly, arms waving. She worried she might start laughing—it was like a cartoon—

and then realized she was shivering so hard her teeth were chattering.

"Maybe turn it off, Seth," she heard Anaya say.

"No," Petra said. "I want to see it."

The fact was she couldn't remember very much. Her short-term memory had been yanked out like a flash drive.

The news announcer was saying, "You can see some of the students on the field running in panic. . . ."

Like a stranger, Petra watched herself run clumsily with the chain saw and topple into a sudden hole. Seth struggled to pull her out, then went down after her.

She felt dizzy as the camera ricocheted around the field from one person to another as they got swallowed up.

"According to local authorities, these sinkholes are actually underground plants that seal their victims inside. . . ."

On-screen, a whirling chain saw blade came jabbing up through the earth, over and over. And then Petra watched herself come scrabbling out, smoldering.

"Some of the students—we can't release their names as they're minors—escaped uninjured, and, as you'll see, went on to heroically free the others. . . ."

"We're heroes," Seth said dully.

Petra didn't want to look anymore. Right now, on the screen, she was sitting by herself on the field, doing nothing while Seth and Anaya helped free Tereza and Fleetwood and Jen. She'd completely fallen apart. Her cheeks burned with shame.

Seth started clicking channels. On the next three, it was just the usual stuff: people renovating houses, and calling out answers on game shows, and telling each other to drop their guns. But then Seth clicked again, and she was back at the school field, watching it all over again.

"Turn it off," Anaya said. "It's making me feel sick."

The television went dark. And then finally Petra asked the question that had been banging around inside her head, like a wasp against a window.

"So, why didn't the three of us get hurt?"

"WE'RE THE SAME," Seth said.

He didn't know why he said it out loud. He usually kept things to himself. But with these two, he felt a closeness that was new for him. Anaya and Petra felt *important*. On the school field, he wasn't being a hero. He just didn't want anything bad to happen to them.

"How do you mean, *same*?" Petra asked, her face wary.

"Well, we're not like anyone else," he said. "None of us is allergic to the black grass. We didn't get knocked out by the sleeping gas. Or burned by the acid."

Anaya said, "Maybe it's just a fluke. We can't be the only ones."

He glanced back at Petra, who sat very still, looking down at her hands. Her fingernails pressed so hard into her skin that they left red marks.

"I shouldn't have washed with it," she said. "The rainwater I bottled. Maybe that's why I'm different." She looked up with panicked eyes. "I even drank a little!"

Seth tried to sound reassuring, like one of his social workers. "Well, I didn't drink any of the water, so—"

"Yeah, but what about those berries!" Petra said. "How many did you eat?"

"I don't know—"

"Maybe they changed you, too!"

He remembered the rush of power he'd felt after eating them. They'd definitely made him feel stronger and faster.

"Okay, hang on," Anaya cut in. "I didn't eat berries, or drink the water. So it can't be that."

"Then why're we like this?" Petra demanded.

Haltingly, Seth said, "I didn't just mean how we are with the plants. There's other stuff. It's like you were born with a tail, and I was born with . . ." He wasn't quite ready to say the word "wings" to them yet, so he pointed at the scars on his arms. "I had surgery when I was about three. I had all these bony growths."

That was the term he'd heard his social worker use once, to explain the scars to his new foster parents.

"They grew out a couple of centimeters, and they were kind of bendy." He paused. "But they weren't bony at all. They looked like feathers."

"Whoa," murmured Petra.

"And they cut them off," said Anaya.

He nodded, watching their faces closely.

"Well, okay," said Anaya. "That's pretty unusual. But I wasn't born with a tail or feathers or anything. Even if I were, I don't see what that's got to do with being immune to the plants."

Seth didn't know any better way to explain himself.

He wished he could tell them: *You feel sort of like family.*

He wished he could tell them: *Last night I had a dream. I was flying, and when I came down low over the earth, I saw both of you. And we were all something different and extraordinary.*

CHAPTER TEN

SLAMMING THE CAR DOOR shut, Anaya glared up at their house. Black vines had now snaked high up the wall, jagging in all directions.

Mom swore under her breath. "All that came from one plant?"

"I should've killed it right away," Anaya muttered.

Under her coat, she was still in her hospital gown, wearing borrowed sneakers.

"Come inside," said Mom, sneezing. "I need some allergy meds. And you need rest."

"I've been sitting around all day."

Seething, she marched up the driveway. After she'd discovered the pit plant in the bag of soil, she'd just run for the school, to warn everyone. Now she needed to destroy this thing.

Half covered by dirt, the wrinkly pit plant lay on the driveway. The head of the rake still jutted from its fleshy lips. Anaya pulled, and the wooden handle came out, shorter now after being melted inside the thing's guts. She gave the plant a kick. It shuddered, and she kept kicking with her strong legs. It felt good.

"Anaya!" her mother said, hurrying closer. "Be careful."

"Stay back," she told Mom. "It might splatter."

She gave the plant one more big kick. It had grown since this morning. From its bottom sprouted the thick vine that had spread everywhere—into the garbage can, and forking up the wall of her house. She lifted the rake over her shoulder and brought the teeth down with all her might. The metal punctured the thick flesh. She wrenched the rake out and struck, again and again. Goo splattered her coat and smoked, burning holes. A spray of liquid harmlessly hit her face and eyes, and she just wiped it away. The plant quivered, gaping wetly. When Anaya finished, the thing looked like a huge smashed purple pumpkin.

Panting, she stepped back. The asphalt smoked lightly from the spilled acid. Overhead she heard a bird give a startled squeak, and she looked up to see a sparrow gobbled up inside one of the vine's wrinkly sacs.

These things were still alive! Anaya's gaze lowered to the pulpy mess on the driveway, and the thick central vine. It twitched. She brought the rake down on it until it was completely severed.

The echoing clang of the metal against the asphalt rang in her ears for a moment, and then it seemed unnaturally silent. She heard a faint creak from the vines, and saw a sprig of berries sag, and one of the eating sacs droop a little. All of it looked withered suddenly.

"I want it off the house," she said, and grabbed one of the vines on the wall.

138

This was *her* house. This was where she slept at night. Wasn't it enough she had to put up with the black grass taking over her lawn, sucking the light out of their windows, and the entire freaking sky? She wasn't having this stuff on her house a second longer.

Mom came and took hold with her, and together they tugged. It was like dragging off ivy or Virginia creeper, with all their little suckers. A small, wrinkled eating sac ruptured and spilled out the half-digested remains of a squirrel.

As they kept going, Anaya felt like it was getting easier to rip off, like the stuff was losing its grip. Up high, the vines snapped and tumbled down to the driveway in a black tangle. But that still left plenty higher up, spread out across the wall and roof. Little brittle pieces wafted down.

"We're going to need the ladder," Anaya said, but finally fatigue hit hard. She felt hollow with hunger.

"Inside now," Mom said firmly. "We'll do the rest later."

Anaya let herself be led into the kitchen. She sat down and started to cry. Mom hugged her until she stopped. They both went upstairs to change into fresh clothes, and afterward Mom started a meal for them. Anaya realized she had no idea what time it was. In the hospital, the clock had barely seemed to move. It was just past five o'clock.

She tried again to call Dad, but his phone was still out of service. She wanted to warn him about the pit plants, to tell him everything that had happened.

She and Mom ate in front of the TV. The news played the video from the school field again. Anaya could barely watch, but her mother did, and afterward turned to her with wet eyes and hugged her some more.

"Thank God you're all right," she said. "I am so proud of you. You helped so many people."

"Seth did, too."

The truth was, she didn't feel proud of herself right now. In the back of her mind, what Petra had said in the hospital—all that stuff about her tail—gnawed at her. Because she'd been telling the truth.

Petra hadn't betrayed her. Anaya had been the disloyal one, telling everyone about her tail. She did it because Petra was getting so pretty, and Anaya wanted to keep her a weirdo like her, so they could stick together. But what she'd done was a terrible thing, and it had lost her the best friend she'd ever had.

On the TV, more news stories were coming in. There was footage from a farm in Bellingham. A cameraman walked through a pig shed. All the pigs were pressed against the walls, squealing in terror. In the middle of the floor were three big holes and inside each, the sealed lips of a pit plant that had just eaten something.

Anaya put down her fork and swallowed queasily. Mom had her arm around her shoulders and she didn't want to move.

There was video from Naperville, Illinois, of a field pockmarked with holes. Six soccer players had fallen through during afternoon practice.

140

"Try Dad again," she asked Mom.

Mom dialed, then shook her head.

"What if something's happened to him?"

"Your dad is a very careful man, Anaya."

She kept thinking of him walking along, the ground opening under him. What chance would anyone have? Anyone who wasn't immune to the acid, like her, or Seth, or Petra.

"Who would create things like this?" she said, with a rush of anger.

Mom just shook her head.

"Are you scared?" she asked Mom.

"No."

It was too quick.

"I'm really worried about Dad."

Mom gave her a squeeze and kissed the top of her head. On TV, people protested outside government buildings, demanding to be told the truth about these plants.

Then the TV went dark—and all the lights in the house, too.

The dishwasher made a few last quiet sloshes and then silence filled the house.

"I WANT TO stay!" Petra said.

"Did that streetlamp just go out?" Mom said, glancing in the rearview mirror.

Petra hadn't noticed. They were on the road to the ferry terminal, and judging by the traffic, lots of people had the same idea. The last boat for Victoria left in twenty minutes, and Mom wanted her on it. She was going to stay with Aunt Grace until things *settled down*. Those were Mom's exact words. Like it was just slightly *inconvenient* that plants were melting and eating people.

"You guys aren't even coming," Petra said.

"They need Dad at the hospital, and I'm run off my feet here."

It was true. The RCMP was overwhelmed with emergency calls, fencing off trails and parks, helping farmers close their pastures. School was canceled. People were told to stay indoors.

"I'm good with a chain saw!" Petra said.

"You're getting on that boat."

It was weird: She should've been happy to get off the island, to a city where things must be safer. All that concrete. But Petra didn't want to go. It wasn't about missing her parents, or her friends. It was Seth and Anaya. It didn't feel right leaving without them. And this surprised her. Seth, with those strange scars on his arms, and the slightly scary, intense look in his eyes. Anaya, who'd stabbed her in the back all those years ago—and even today hadn't even said *sorry*. But the fact was: they made her feel *safer*.

Mom's cell phone trumpeted, and she picked up.

"The whole island? Okay, I thought something was going on . . . yeah, I'll be there as soon as I can."

"What's going on?" Petra asked.

"Power's out."

"Why?"

"They don't know yet."

Uneasily Petra looked out at the twin beams of their headlights, glittering in the mist. And then the road heaved up and hit them. Her cry was stifled by the airbags exploding against her face.

"Are you okay? Petra?"

"Uh-huh."

Dazed, she turned and saw Mom, smooshed up against her own airbags. The car was tilted down at a crazy steep angle.

"Road must've collapsed," Mom said.

The white airbags glowed with light, which confused Petra, until she realized it must be their own headlights, reflected back through the windshield.

"You all right, Mom?"

"I can't move my feet." She grunted with effort. "I think they're caught. You try to get out."

Petra smelled gasoline. She popped her seat belt, but the door only opened an inch before hitting something that wouldn't budge.

"Mine's blocked, too," Mom said, and swore. "I've told the budget committee this road needed . . ."

Petra sniffed again. Something that wasn't gasoline.

"Mom, I don't think we're in a hole!"

The airbags blocked her view through the windows. She reached over to Mom's belt and yanked out the Swiss Army knife. Snapping open the biggest blade, she plunged it into the airbags. Air hissed out. Now she could see through the windshield.

In the glow of the headlights, Petra caught sight of slick purple flesh. The walls of the pit plant trembled and contracted, dripping with acid. The disgusting perfume smell was quickly overpowered by the stench of melting tires.

"We're inside one of them!" she cried.

The walls of the plant tightened, trying to swallow, and the car sank deeper with a sudden jerk.

"Back doors!" Mom said.

Petra twisted around. Through the rear windshield she saw the moon, and the left door was still above road level.

"Go!" her mom cried.

This was one time Mom wasn't going to boss her. Petra squinted below the steering wheel. Mom's boots were crimped in the mangled metal. Dark liquid lapped against the soles of the boots, sending up nasty fumes.

She grabbed her mom's right leg and pulled, but her foot wouldn't shift.

"I'm going to undo your laces," she said. "Mom?"

Mom's eyes looked a little glazed. The sleeping gas! Petra slapped her.

"Mom! Stay awake!"

A flashlight beam suddenly skittered around inside the car. From overhead came the sound of people shouting.

"It's one of those things!"

"There's two people in there!"

"Does anyone have a winch?"

Petra crammed her torso into the small space beneath the steering wheel. The acid was searing the plastic and metal—and rising quickly, right over the soles of Mom's boots.

"You're gonna need to slide your feet out," she said, hoping Mom was still awake.

Her fingers fumbled with the laces. *Crap.* Double-knotted. How typical of Mom. The car lurched to one side, and more acid seeped into the car, flowing over the laces of the boots— and Petra's hands. She smelled seared leather and knew she didn't have much time before the acid burned through to Mom's skin.

She grabbed her mom's knife and slashed the knot apart—and then the acid did the rest. The other laces shredded like wet toilet paper. She loosened both boots.

"Mom! Pull your feet out! Pull!"

She felt her Mom trying weakly, and then slid her hand into the right boot and yanked until the foot popped free. Then the left.

"Keep them out of the acid!" she yelled.

Mom nodded but Petra could tell she was pretty out of it.

Grunting, she pushed Mom around in her seat and shoved her toward the back. It was like trying to move a bag of sand.

"We're getting out, Mom. Come *on*!"

The back door of the car opened, and someone leaned in and handed her a rope with a loop at the end. Petra slid it over Mom's head and under her arms.

"Hold on, Mom! They're gonna haul you out."

The people on the road pulled, and Petra pushed her mother through the rear door. Now it was Petra's turn. Without warning, the car jerked lower. The door slammed shut.

Her heart beat so hard in her throat she thought she'd choke.

"Hurry!" the people outside shouted.

She opened the door—only a few inches before it jammed against the glistening wall of the pit plant. Petra made herself as skinny as possible and wiggled through the opening. Hands reached down from the rim of the hole and grabbed her. She was yanked roughly up and onto the asphalt, beside her mother.

"Are you okay?" Petra asked, looking at Mom's feet. Her socks were a bit singed, and Petra hurriedly peeled them off. "The acid didn't get your feet, did it?"

Mom shook her head groggily. "I'm good. Thanks."

Petra glanced back at their shuddering car, now sunk completely beneath the road. Cars were stopped in both directions. The road to the ferry had been completely wiped out.

Mom squeezed her hand. "My brave girl," she murmured.

Then Petra did something she hadn't done in ages. She hugged her mother very tightly and for a long time.

SETH COULDN'T SLEEP. He was still too amped up by everything that had happened. The school field, the hospital, all the stuff on the news—and then the power going out.

He wondered if Petra or Anaya could sleep. He'd actually been sad when he was released from the hospital and had to go home with Mrs. Antos. He wished he were still in the room with the girls, just the three of them. They had so much more to talk about.

He sat up in bed and switched on the flashlight Mrs. Antos had given him. His watch said a quarter to four. He was hungry— he hadn't eaten much of his dinner. Grabbing his sketchbook, he quietly headed downstairs.

He poured some cereal into a bowl. The milk in the fridge was still cool. He left the flashlight on and, as he ate, he sketched. He sketched what he'd seen in his last dream, and thought about Petra and Anaya. He wished he'd had the courage to tell them what he'd seen. Maybe it would be easier if he drew it. He hoped he'd have the courage to show them next time. With a pang, he wondered when that might be.

At his last foster home, Mrs. Walsh had looked through his sketchbook one day while he was at school. When he came home, she was sitting in the living room with it on her lap. She asked if he wanted to talk about the things in there. Like she was one of his therapists.

He'd asked for the book back. It was private. She wanted to know what he liked so much about those images. He asked for the book again. She asked him if he had a lot of nightmares and was drawing his bad dreams. When he stood up, she shrank back in the chair, and he was surprised because all he'd done was stand up. Did he look scary? But she was scared of him. He'd snatched the book and gone upstairs.

Not long after that, the Walshes said they were rethinking their "lifestyle choices" and thought Seth would find a "better fit" elsewhere.

Anaya had caught a glimpse of his drawings, that day in the stairwell. She hadn't seemed horrified or disgusted. She'd even asked for some of his stuff for the yearbook. Still, he'd never risked showing it to Mr. and Mrs. Antos.

If you drew creatures with wings, you would probably show them flying. And if you drew creatures with teeth, you might show them eating. And then you'd have to think about what kinds of things they might eat, or who they might eat.

He thought about Petra and Anaya and how they used to be best friends. It had really surprised him, Anaya telling everyone about Petra's tail and hurting her feelings. Seth had never had a best friend, but he was pretty sure if he did he wouldn't risk losing the friendship. He didn't understand people very well.

The pleasant clicking of Maddox's toenails on the floor preceded the dog into the room. Seth patted his warm head, glad of the company. He gave the dog the rest of his cereal. Maddox gulped it down happily and then went off to sniff other things.

Seth sketched a little more. From the cellar came a sharp yelp, and then the sound of Maddox growling. Seth stood, a cold sweat prickling his forehead. He snatched up his flashlight, and then the drip torch he'd brought inside yesterday, just in case.

"Maddox," he said as he made his way down the steep stairs. "You all right, boy?"

His flashlight beam skittered off the shelves where the Antoses kept all their preserves, then found Maddox. The dog was hunched, hackles raised, growling at a small hole in the dirt floor.

"Maddox, get back!"

The floor caved in, and Maddox pitched forward into the maw of the pit plant. Seth lunged and grabbed the dog around the middle, pulling him back. Maddox's front paws looked a little singed, but he was all right. "You're okay, boy."

Seth played his flashlight beam on the pit plant. It trembled impatiently, hungry. Seth wanted to light it up with the torch, right now, but he worried he might start a fire in the house.

He spotted a thick black vine growing over the shelves of bright preserves. The sight of the dangling berries made his mouth water, and he tried to ignore it. He followed the vine up as it branched across the wall and disappeared into the corners of the ceiling.

The vines were growing through the house! He needed to tell Mrs. Antos. He was surprised all the noise hadn't woken her up already.

"Come on, Maddox!" he panted, hurrying up the steps. Maddox squeezed past his legs and ran ahead, limping on his injured front paws.

When Seth reached the top floor, Maddox had already pushed his way into Mrs. Antos's room. He was barking. A wave of sickly sweet perfume hit Seth as he entered.

"Mrs. Antos?" Even now he felt a bit shy just barging into her bedroom.

He heard no reply, and played his flashlight over the bed.

He stared and stared, trying to understand what he was seeing.

CHAPTER ELEVEN

ANAYA DREAMED SHE WAS sniffing a flower and not sneezing at all. But she didn't like the scent, or the way the petals tickled her nose.

When she woke up, it was pitch-dark, and the unpleasant smell was still there—and terribly familiar.

She tried to sit up, but it was like someone had tucked in the covers too tightly. Her arms were pinned to her sides.

Something thin poked shyly up her nose, and she yelped. She jerked her head away, tried to yank her arms free. The thin, poky thing plunged deeper and Anaya gagged. She thrashed, kicking against the covers. Across her body, she felt things snap, and suddenly she could pull her arms free.

She grabbed at whatever was inside her nose and ripped it out. "Mom!"

That terrible perfume—it was the same as inside the pit plants. Anaya grabbed the flashlight on her night table and raced down the hall into Mom's room. It reeked of sleeping gas.

Anaya gasped. Mom's entire body was crisscrossed with black

vines. They grew across her face, covering her mouth. Two twitching tendrils had grown right into both nostrils.

Anaya seized the tendrils and tugged. They slid out a little bit, then snapped. Mom made an awful wet choking sound. There must still be stuff caught farther back.

Anaya peeled the vines off Mom's mouth, parted her lips, and shone the flashlight inside. At the back of her throat was a dense tangle of vines, big as an egg.

She slid her hand inside Mom's mouth. Her fingertips dug into the knot, getting a good grip. She pulled. With a wet smack, a long, glistening tangle of vines came out. Mom coughed several times and gave a big sigh, but still didn't wake up.

"Mom!"

Anaya shook her. The perfume had knocked her out cold. Anaya rushed to the window, tripping over a thick vine that had grown across the floor. Mom needed fresh air. Who knew what this stuff did if you breathed it for too long?

She pulled back the curtains and nearly screamed because the window was webbed with vines, blocking the predawn sky. She tried to open the window, but the vines had welded it shut. There was a smaller window with only a couple of tendrils across it, and Anaya forced that one all the way open. Cool air streamed into the room.

In the bathroom, Anaya got a mug of cold water, ran back, and splashed it onto Mom's face. Gently Anaya slapped her cheek, then harder.

"Mom!"

Finally, she twitched, and her eyes opened slowly. She stared at Anaya blearily, then sat bolt upright, spluttering.

"What the heck?" she croaked, spitting out bits of vine.

"The vine was growing down your nose! It was strangling you!"

Mom looked wildly around the room. Snapped tendrils littered the bed sheets. A thick, corded vine ran down the bedpost to the floor and disappeared into a crack in the baseboard.

"That grew just overnight?" Mom gasped.

"We should've pulled it all down yesterday!"

Or maybe, Anaya thought, it was from an entirely different pit plant outside their house. Seething, she jumped off the bed and grabbed the vine near the wall. She leaned back, grunting and swearing and yanking with all her might. Mom's hands seized hold just behind her own and together they pulled. Finally, it snapped.

Anaya fell back on the floor, panting. "We've got to warn Dad!"

"I know." Mom grabbed her phone, dialed, and swore. "Still out of service. I'm calling Diane Sumner at the RCMP. Go pack a bag."

"Where we going?"

"I'm getting us a plane, and we're going to go find your dad."

"Good!"

In her bedroom, she snatched some clothes off her messy floor, sniffed to make sure they were cleanish, and threw them into her backpack. There was a sharp knock at the front door. She raced downstairs just as Mom was opening it.

It was an unfamiliar woman dressed in a navy-blue suit. The crest on her lapel made her look like a government official. Behind her, an RCMP cruiser idled on the road.

"Lilah Dara?" the woman asked, looking straight at Mom.

Anaya had never seen her mother's face go so pale.

"Is Michael all right?" Mom blurted, her voice cracking.

Anaya's stomach flipped over.

"Michael?" the government woman said with a frown, then looked suddenly apologetic. "Oh my goodness, your husband. He's absolutely fine, as far as I know. That's not the reason I came."

"Thank God," Mom said, sagging against the doorframe.

"I'm so sorry. I did that very badly," the woman said. She was about Mom's age, with a big freckle on her left cheek, curly shoulder-length hair, and quick, intelligent green eyes. "My name's Dr. Stephanie Weber. I'm a scientist with the Canadian Security Intelligence Service. And this must be Anaya, yes?"

Anaya nodded weakly, so relieved that Dad was okay.

"What's this about?" Mom asked.

Dr. Weber said, "I've come because of your daughter."

WHEN PETRA ENTERED the doctor's lounge of the island hospital, Anaya and her mother were already sitting around a coffee-stained table with Seth Robertson. Anaya's mom had her hand on Seth's shoulder and was softly saying how sorry she was about Mrs. Antos, and Seth just nodded mutely.

Petra already knew what had happened. After she and her mom had escaped from that giant pit plant, the RCMP had been swamped with emergency calls from all over the island. Seven people had died. Three who'd fallen into pit plants. Four who'd been strangled by vines while they slept—like Mrs. Antos. And then came the call that a scientist had arrived on the island and was looking for her and Anaya and Seth. Someone from CSIS.

This must be her, the one in the blue suit, standing to greet her. Her smile made her look a bit like Jezebel on that reality cooking show, but when she stopped smiling, she looked more like Chelsea on the space-station show—except for that fetching little mole on her cheek.

"You must be Petra. Thank you for bringing her, Sergeant Sumner," she said. "I'm Dr. Stephanie Weber, and this is Carlene Lee." She pointed to a woman with hair that had been bleached too many times. "Carlene's a social worker with child welfare."

Petra supposed she must be here for Seth. Petra met his eye and gave him a sympathetic smile. She couldn't imagine what it would be like to find someone strangled in their bed.

"Please, sit down," Dr. Weber said. "I didn't want to start until you were all here."

Petra took the seat next to Seth. The way he'd talked at the hospital yesterday had freaked her out a bit, all that stuff about his feathers, and the three of them being the same. Still, she was startled by how glad she was to be back in the same room as him and Anaya.

Dr. Weber got right to it. "We saw the video from the field incident. You three were completely unaffected by that plant. The corrosive enzyme. The sleeping gas. There's no other case where people just walked away. I also noted, from your hospital records, that none of you are allergic to the black grass pollen."

"You've read their hospital records?" Mom asked sharply.

Petra rolled her eyes. Mom was very big on privacy rights. She didn't seem to realize that no one had privacy anymore. No one even *wanted* it. You could probably find everyone's hospital records on social media.

"Yes," said Dr. Weber. "I requisitioned them as a matter of national security. As of now, we're in a state of emergency."

Petra's mother looked grim, but not surprised. Had she already known? That would explain the shopping cart overflowing with chickpeas.

"And not just here," Dr. Weber continued. "Worldwide, we've got millions of people with severe allergic reactions to these plants. Acute asthma, bronchitis, pneumonia, sometimes fatal. We don't know the long-term effects of exposure. A lot of our population is literally suffocating. That's just from the black grass. And now we have an even more aggressive species."

"We know, believe me," Mom said a bit impatiently. "And I've got an island to take care of, with only four officers. So what does this have to do with our kids?"

Dr. Weber looked directly at Petra, then Seth and Anaya. "There's clearly something very unique about you three."

Petra shifted uncomfortably. She was sounding a lot like Seth, talking about how they were all the same.

"Your bodies have incredible natural defenses against these plants," Dr. Weber continued. "If we can figure out what it is, we might be able to make a vaccine so others won't be harmed either."

Petra saw her mother exchange looks with Anaya's.

"So you want to run tests on them?" Petra's mother asked.

"Yes," Dr. Weber replied.

"Shouldn't you guys be worrying more about killing this stuff?"

"Believe me, Sergeant Sumner, the military is taking care of that. But we also need to protect ourselves in the meantime. Especially since we're dealing with organisms that aren't from this planet."

A deep silence expanded through the room.

"For real?" Petra exclaimed.

"I thought it was bioterrorism," Anaya said.

Dr. Weber shook her head. "We're not ready to tell the public yet."

"You're saying these plants are *aliens*?" Anaya said.

157

Petra swallowed. Once you heard that word, you couldn't just *un*hear it. It ricocheted all over the place. She looked around: the chairs, the table, the grimy floor. These things were as solid and normal as ever, but they now existed in a world that also included alien life.

"The term we use is cryptogenic," Dr. Weber said. "Meaning: of unknown origin."

"You know for sure?" Anaya's mother asked, leaning forward in her chair.

"We ran DNA tests," Dr. Weber said. "And there's nothing like these plants on Earth. Not even close."

"How?" Seth said. "How'd they even get here?"

"We don't know for certain. Somehow, the seeds entered Earth's atmosphere."

"Like on a meteorite?" he asked.

"Possibly."

Petra frowned. "Wouldn't they just all burn up, entering the atmosphere?"

"Maybe not," Anaya said. "Dad told me about the Murchison meteorite in Australia. It had organic compounds on it. Amino acids." She looked at Dr. Weber. "Right?"

"Yes. The building blocks of life. A big enough meteorite shower could've scattered seeds worldwide."

Petra didn't remember hearing anything about a meteor shower. Wouldn't that have made the news?

"No," she said. "Those seeds were in the rain."

"That's another theory," said Dr. Weber. "And the favorite right now. I'm more focused on protecting people from the plants than figuring out where they came from. Which is why I'm interested in you three, and finding out if we can make other people immune."

"What kind of tests would you do?" Anaya's mother asked.

"Blood tests primarily, allergy tests, some low-dose medical imaging. Since they're minors, we need your consent."

Dr. Weber was already taking forms from her attaché case, and passing them around.

"Seth," Carlene Lee said, in the most soothing voice Petra had ever heard. "You have no guardian at the moment—"

"What about Mr. Antos?" he asked, sounding surprised.

"He's too ill right now. He's agreed to surrender his guardianship."

"Oh."

"So technically you're a ward of the Crown. Do you understand what that means?"

"Yep."

Seth's voice was numb, but his eyes were wet. Petra felt her heart clench. She'd seen his eyes in the supermarket that time, and knew how much he cared about Mr. Antos.

"So I'll be acting as your temporary guardian, Seth," said Carlene. "I don't work for CSIS. I'm here to represent *you*. Nothing happens if you're not comfortable. Okay?"

Seth just nodded, his face hardened.

"So I need to know if you're okay with these tests, and if—"

"I'm good."

"Thank you, Seth," Dr. Weber said gently.

Petra watched her mother carefully read the paperwork. She always read things before signing. She even read the stuff on the internet before she clicked.

"You all right with this?" Mom asked her.

She nodded. "Yeah, I don't mind."

"You're a medical doctor, I assume," Anaya's mother asked Dr. Weber.

"Yes, and a biochemist. I have a team in Vancouver."

"Vancouver?" Petra said in surprise.

"The hospital here doesn't have the diagnostics we need."

"How were you planning on getting them over there?" her mother wanted to know.

"The same helicopter I came in. It's waiting on the pad."

"You mean right now?" Petra asked. She hadn't expected it to be so soon.

"That's why we asked you to pack a few things," Dr. Weber said.

"No," Anaya said, looking anxiously at her own mother. "I mean, I want to help, but we need to find Dad first!"

"Ah," said Dr. Weber with an understanding nod. "We're very aware of your father's work. He's out collecting soil samples at the eco-reserves, right?"

"We haven't heard from him since he left," Anaya said. "Yesterday morning."

"We might be able to reach him from the base," said Dr. Weber. "They have more powerful equipment."

"Can't you send a boat out for him?" Anaya asked. "What if he's hurt?"

"Anaya, there are people all over the country who need urgent help right now," said Dr. Weber.

Petra could tell by Anaya's eyes that she wasn't ready to give up yet.

"Yeah, but he's collecting soil samples that might kill the black grass, and the other plants!"

She was starting to cry now, and her mother put an arm around her. "I'm sure he's absolutely fine."

"I know how important your father's work is, Anaya," Dr. Weber said. "Most likely you'll only be at the base two nights, three at most."

Anaya still looked miserable, but she nodded.

"I'd like to come as well," Anaya's mother told Dr. Weber.

"I completely understand. But the helicopter only carries five passengers."

Petra quickly did the math. Her, Seth, Anaya, the doctor, and the social worker. No mothers. She glanced at Mom and was startled by the pang of alarm she felt.

Dr. Weber looked sympathetically at both mothers. "I can

arrange for another helicopter to come and collect you and your partners. As soon as possible. With luck, even later today."

"And I'll be with them the whole time," Carlene chimed in. "Until a parent is present."

Petra caught Mom giving Carlene and Dr. Weber her sternest RCMP look.

"Your facility, where is it, exactly?"

"The military base off Stanley Park. Deadman's Island."

Petra almost laughed out loud. The name didn't exactly inspire confidence, but she remembered the park from their visits to Vancouver.

"And it's completely secure?" Mom asked.

"Absolutely," said Dr. Weber.

"What do you think, Diane?" asked Anaya's mother.

"They'll be safer over there, for sure."

"I agree," said Anaya's mother.

Petra watched their mothers sign the forms.

"We're very grateful," said Dr. Weber, gathering the paperwork and slipping it into her case. "Oh, one last thing." She produced two specimen jars and slid them toward the moms. "If you wouldn't mind just spitting into the jar, we'll be able to check your DNA as well, to see if there are any hereditary factors. Thank you. All of this will be a huge help in countering the invasion."

The word caught Petra totally off guard. "Invasion?"

"That's exactly what this is," Dr. Weber told her.

"You make it sound like it was planned," Seth said.

"Planned or not," said Dr. Weber, "our planet's being colonized."

Petra heard a helicopter's rotors start to turn, somewhere outside. Dr. Weber's phone pinged. She glanced at it and then stood. "We need to go."

THE HELICOPTER MADE a sudden sideways dip, and Seth felt Petra tense beside him. She looked a bit green. He hoped she wasn't going to throw up. Next to her sat Anaya, who didn't seem bothered by the turbulence. He knew her mom was a pilot, so she was probably used to this.

Opposite them were Dr. Weber and Carlene Lee. Over the years, Seth had met lots of social workers and was good at sizing them up fast. Carlene was one of those super-efficient ones. Her smile was frequent but a bit chilly. She'd had her job long enough to keep herself at a good distance.

They bumped again, but Seth didn't mind. He'd never been in a helicopter—never been on an airplane either—and he loved it. The way it had just lifted straight off the pad like an elevator, then nosed forward. It reminded him of his dreams, the way he sometimes soared through the sky.

Invasion.

When Dr. Weber had said that word, it was like the

temperature in the room plunged. He'd seen the shock on everyone's face. It sounded like a war. He wondered why he didn't feel more frightened. Nothing seemed real since he'd found Mrs. Antos, cocooned by vines. Definitely he would've been more scared without Anaya and Petra here. He felt calmer just being with them—and Dr. Weber.

At the meeting, he'd liked the way she talked directly to him and the girls instead of to the mothers. He liked all her facts. He'd only known her a couple of hours but he already trusted her.

Seth gazed out the window. Below, the Vancouver airport looked normal enough, until he noticed the sinkholes in the runways. A jet jutted out of a huge crater, its left wing snapped against the tarmac. Over neighborhoods, Seth saw streets turned into canyons by the tall black grass. Roadblocks were everywhere, pit-plant holes in the parks and golf courses. Charred sinkholes in the asphalt and sidewalks. Hardly anyone outside. Even from up here, he could see pollen glittering in the air.

As they passed over downtown, the streets were nearly deserted. Some of the tall buildings looked like they had cracks in them—until Seth realized they were vines, crawling their way up the glass and steel.

Stanley Park bristled with black grass. Its open fields were cordoned off with yellow tape. A lone bicyclist in neon-green racing gear pedaled madly around the seawall, head to his handlebars.

The helicopter made a smooth turn, and Seth got his first glimpse of Deadman's Island. Jutting into the harbor, the military base was connected to the park by a skinny road that was gated, and guarded by two armed soldiers.

As the helicopter descended, Seth saw teams of masked personnel cutting down the black grass along the base's fenced perimeter. In a cratered field, a bulldozer was dragging something dark purple and boulder-sized out of the ground. In the center of the base were some wooden barracks, several old brick buildings, and a bigger, more modern one.

The helicopter settled on the pad, and the co-pilot got out and opened the doors. Dr. Weber guided them to the modern building. Even on the short walk across the tarmac, the doctor and Carlene Lee started sneezing. Inside, it smelled like a hospital.

"The entire building's climate-controlled, so it's pollen-free," Dr. Weber said as they made their way down a corridor with lots of windowless doors.

"I'll show you where we're staying," Carlene said. "It's a small apartment. It's really nice."

"Do we have our own bedrooms?" Petra asked hopefully.

"Seth does, and me. You and Anaya are sharing."

Seth caught the dismay in Petra's expression.

"What?" Anaya asked.

"You're so messy. Do you still snore?"

Anaya shrugged. "Guess we'll find out."

They turned a corner, and up ahead, Seth glimpsed a tall man with buzzed gray hair. His uniform had lots of colored bars on it.

"Ah," said Dr. Weber quietly, "you're about to meet Colonel Pearson."

The colonel stood peering through a long observation window at a shooting range. Inside, soldiers milled about, buckling on body armor, handling various lethal-looking weapons.

As the colonel turned to greet them, the deep lines in his gaunt face seemed to tug down the sides of his mouth.

"So. These must be the Miracle Three."

Dr. Weber introduced them all by name and then said, "The colonel was kind enough to offer my team a home here on his base."

"I wanted more weapons, but they sent me a scientist instead," the colonel said drily.

"And if my work's successful, Colonel, you'll have soldiers who are immune to the plants they're fighting."

The colonel just grunted and spoke into the intercom on the wall: "Go ahead."

At the back of the shooting range, a thick plastic curtain parted, and Seth saw a row of three pit plants, tipped against the wall like giant rotting potatoes. He'd never seen them from the outside before—only the *inside*. Their flesh was wrinkly, and from the bottom of each sprouted a thick black vine that had been hacked very short.

"Where'd you get them?" Petra asked.

"There's no shortage. We're still bulldozing them out of our fields," the colonel said. "Don't worry, Dr. Weber, we've saved enough for your science experiments."

"I appreciate that," she replied.

As Seth watched, a soldier opened fire with a machine gun. The pit plant swallowed every bullet. When the shooting ceased, another soldier went over and poked the top of the plant with a stick. The fleshy lips sprang open, still very much alive and ready to eat.

"I'm not sure you can kill them with bullets," said Anaya.

"Maybe not," agreed the colonel. "But we'll find a way."

The soldiers crouched behind a low wall of sandbags. One of them pulled the pin from a hand grenade.

"Those things are full of acid!" Petra warned the colonel.

With excellent aim, the soldier lobbed the grenade right inside the open pit plant, then ducked behind the sandbags. The pit plant snapped shut its lips, then exploded. Bits of plant splattered everywhere, including the glass observation window, right in front of Seth's face.

"I call that dead," Pearson said, looking at the pulpy mess where the pit plant once rested.

Right away Seth saw the acid fuming on the walls and floor. Even the glass was smoking. One of the soldiers stood and hurriedly pulled off his helmet. The top was smoldering. He held it up to the window for the colonel to see. The acid had burned a small hole clean through.

Pearson said calmly into the intercom, "Everyone out of there until we get the hazmat crew to clean up. Then we're going to try the flamethrowers."

"Be careful," Seth said. "The smoke might be toxic. Just like the black grass."

"We'll take precautions," the colonel said, walking away.

"He doesn't seem very happy we're here," Seth said quietly, when the colonel was out of earshot.

"Don't worry about the colonel," said Dr. Weber. "He's a good man, and he wants to kill these things as quickly as possible. We're both trying to save lives, but I'm not sure he sees the value in what I'm doing. So, are you three ready to begin?"

CHAPTER TWELVE

WITH ALL HER ALLERGIES, Anaya was used to getting pricked with needles.

"What're you going to do with all this?" she asked, looking at the vials of her blood on the lab counter. It was enough to feed Dracula and everyone in his castle.

Dr. Weber smiled. "It always looks like a lot. First order of business is your genome."

"My DNA," said Anaya.

"Right. A complete map. It could really open some doors for treatments."

Anaya knew this was important, but it felt wrong to be *here* when Dad was out *there,* with murderous alien plants. *Cryptogenic plants.* If Dr. Weber thought that word was any less scary, she was wrong.

"Can you try and call my father soon?"

If she couldn't look for him herself, at the very least, she needed to make sure he was safe.

"I already sent in the request. They said they'll keep trying until they get through."

That was something. "Thanks."

Next, Dr. Weber dripped two beads of pit-plant acid onto the underside of her wrist. Anaya had absolutely no reaction. They fitted a mask over her face and sprayed in the perfumed mist from the pit plant and vines. She didn't fall asleep, or get dopey. When Dr. Weber swabbed the inside of her nose with a liquefied version of the smoke from the black grass, she didn't even sneeze.

Dr. Weber shook her head. "It's incredible that someone with so many allergies isn't allergic to these plants. Let's do a quick physical."

Anaya changed into a gown, and Dr. Weber listened to her heart and lungs, checked her blood pressure, probed her stomach.

"You're very healthy," she pronounced.

Anaya laughed. "I think you're the first doctor to say that to me. It's weird, but since the plants came, I've felt way better."

"Your other allergies have eased up."

"Yeah. My asthma, too. And"—she blushed because it suddenly seemed so frivolous—"my acne's really cleared up. And I feel stronger. Especially my legs."

"I was going to ask if you were a runner. Your toenails are pretty beat up."

Surprised, Anaya looked down. How could she not have noticed this? Some of her toenails were black, like she'd dropped something heavy on them.

"Must've happened on the field," she mumbled, frowning.

"They're quite sharp," said Dr. Weber. "If you didn't bring nail clippers with you, I can find you some."

Anaya stared down in embarrassment. The nails of her big toes were jagged and longer than the others. They looked like claws.

"YOUR AQUAGENIC URTICARIA," Dr. Weber said as she probed Petra's stomach through her gown. "Have you noticed any changes over the years?"

Petra didn't feel like talking about her water allergy right now. She was weary of tests and questions. She'd been stabbed and dabbed and misted. And the whole time, Carlene Lee was hovering, taking notes and asking her if she felt comfortable. She just wanted to go back to the apartment and crash.

"Not really. Except for that rainwater, you know, from that big rain before the plants appeared—I didn't get any reaction from that. I washed with it."

Dr. Weber was writing on the pad. "That's very interesting. If the seeds were in the rain, they might've changed the chemistry of the water. You can sit up now."

"Can you make me some?" Petra asked.

For a moment, Dr. Weber looked surprised. Then she nodded. "Ah, the water. Well, if we know the exact makeup of a solution, we might be able to synthesize it. We'll look into it."

"Thanks," said Petra, breathing out in relief. "It would just be so good to wash properly."

"I can believe it." The doctor looked at her legs and frowned. "How long have you had that rash?"

"Where?" Petra asked in surprise.

"There's quite a bit of scaling on the back of your thighs."

Anxiously Petra reached down and touched her skin. Both legs were extremely rough. She twisted around and flexed her leg so she could see.

"Oh my gosh!" she cried. Over the years, she'd had all kinds of rashes from getting wet, but none quite like this. It was really red and scabby.

"Is it itchy?" asked Dr. Weber.

"No." It looked hideous. "I can't believe I didn't notice this."

"I can get a dermatologist to consult with us."

"Do you think it's the rainwater? Because I've been washing with it?"

Dr. Weber shook her head. "You just washed your face, yes? And no reaction there. So no, I don't think this could be some delayed reaction."

Dr. Weber bent to look, then pulled on blue gloves. Petra thought this was a bad sign. When people put on gloves, it was because they thought they were going to touch something really gross.

"You know, I don't think it's a rash at all. It's more like a membrane. . . ." Dr. Weber took a pair of tweezers from a tray. "It pulls away quite easily and . . ."

"What?" Petra said, alarmed by the pause.

"The skin is smooth underneath. Remarkably smooth."

Petra touched the spot, and let out a sigh of relief. It did feel amazingly smooth. Then she looked at the long patch of skin dangling from the doctor's tweezers, and shivered. It looked like something a snake had just sloughed off.

"DO YOU REMEMBER having them?" Dr. Weber asked Seth, nodding at the scars on his arms.

He wasn't used to people asking about them. "I was just little, but yeah."

"Your records say the growths—"

"Feathers," Seth interrupted. The other doctors always referred to them as growths, and he'd never argued because he didn't want people to think he was weirder than he already was. But he felt like he could tell the truth to Dr. Weber.

He held his arm out. "I looked at pictures of bird's wings. They have around ten primary flight feathers." He touched the scars on his forearm. "And then up to twenty secondary feathers." He pointed at the scars on his upper arm, which were closer together. "The pattern's the same."

When Dr. Weber smiled, her eyes crinkled up in a friendly way. "All right. Feathers. And yours grew to ten to fourteen millimeters in length?"

"They seemed longer." Maybe they'd just felt bigger to his three-year-old fingers.

"My little boy was born with exactly the same thing."

Seth's pulse quickened. "Really?"

"When I first saw them, I said the same thing you did. *Feathers.* Little feathers growing from his arms."

Eagerly Seth asked, "What do they look like now?"

But he saw the change in Dr. Weber's eyes, and understood that look: something you'd lost and were never getting back.

"He would've been the same age as you. But he had a lot of health problems when he was born. He only lived five months."

Seth felt the air leak from his lungs. "Oh."

"It's a very rare condition. Doesn't even have a name. But there are others who have it."

"How many?" No one had told him this before, never. The idea there were others like him—just the *idea* he wasn't alone—was so exciting he could barely wait for Dr. Weber's answers. He had so many questions.

"Several in this country—elsewhere in the world, too, apparently. All the same age as you, more or less. Amazing thing, isn't it?"

Amazing thing. He'd never heard it described like this. The few times his doctors or social workers or foster parents mentioned it, they treated it like something freakish.

"And the others, did any of them get—" He stopped himself. Had they all died, too?

"Wings?" she asked. That kind smile again. She shook her head. "They all had their feathers removed when they were young. Like you."

"Oh," Seth said.

"Are they tender?" she asked, gently touching two of the scars with her fingertips.

"No," he lied instinctively, and then: "A bit."

"For how long?"

"A couple of weeks. Since the big rain."

She sat back in her chair and looked at him. He knew she was about to speak, and he knew exactly what he wanted to hear. It was something he'd wanted for so long, but hardly dared hope for.

She said, "Unless I'm very much mistaken, your feathers are growing back."

CHAPTER THIRTEEN

"THE HELIPAD COLLAPSED," ANAYA'S mom told her over the phone. "Not long after you guys took off. There was a huge pit plant under it."

Anaya suppressed a shudder. "How long till they fix it?"

She was back in their little apartment after the day's tests, looking out the window, with her back to the others. She was trying to be brave, but she wanted Mom *here*. It hadn't been easy, getting on that helicopter without her—but she'd managed it by telling herself Mom would be joining her very soon.

"They're looking for a new landing site," Mom said, "maybe in the parking lot, but they've got to make sure it's safe first."

Beyond the high fence of the base, Anaya could see across the harbor to downtown Vancouver. Thin strips of oily smoke rose between the tall buildings. Why were there fires? Broken gas lines? Shorted power lines? A few helicopters buzzed past.

"Where are you now?" Anaya asked Mom.

"Home. The power's still out, but there's water, and I can use the barbecue."

"How'd you get home from the hospital?" she asked, worrying about the pit plants.

"I got a stick and slammed it into the ground before I took a step. Everyone's doing it now."

"You've got to keep the vines off the house, Mom."

She caught herself looking around the window frame and floors, checking for cracks.

"Don't worry. I'm sleeping at the Morrisons' tonight. I think it's a good idea if we take shifts. They've also set up a shelter in the community hall for people who live alone."

"Have you heard anything about Tereza?"

"She's at Vancouver General. She's in the burn unit, but she's going to be okay. Fleetwood, too."

Anaya closed her eyes and let out a big breath. "That's so good." All day Tereza had been in her thoughts. "And the others?"

There was a slight delay before her mother said, "Mr. Hilborn died, and Jen Haines is still in a coma."

A shadow of terror crept toward her, like something waiting at the edge of a dying campfire. She smelled the inside of the pit plant, felt its slippery flesh, the reek of burning clothing and hair. These things killed. These things were everywhere.

"Mom, have you heard from Dad?"

The question had been looming, unasked, over their whole conversation. She'd been afraid to ask, afraid of hearing no. She'd tried Dad herself, just before calling Mom, and got the usual message: *The customer is not available at this time.*

"Not yet," Mom answered.

The phone here was old-fashioned, with a curly cord that connected the handset to the base. Anaya kept twisting the cord around her index finger, until it was so tight the fingertip was red and swollen.

"Where do you think he is now?"

She remembered those little lodges on the eco-reserves. That's where he'd sleep, with all the chinks between the timbers, the black vine slipping through at night, exhaling its terrible perfume and stretching toward the sound of gentle breathing.

Mom said, "I don't know, but—"

"Maybe he's already on his way home, right?"

Two days he'd been gone now, traveling by boat from one eco-reserve to another. Anything could have happened to him. A water accident, or falling into one of those plants.

"Sweetheart. Don't cry."

"I wish he were back."

"Everything's going to be okay," Mom said, which was what moms were supposed to say—but right now it didn't make her feel one bit better.

She felt a hand on her shoulder and turned. Carlene gave her a professionally supportive smile. Behind her, Seth and Petra were watching.

"I should go," she told Mom. "There's only one phone here."

"Okay, sweetie. I'll see you soon. I love you."

"Love you, too."

She wiped her eyes, and dragged a tissue from her pocket. It reminded her of how little she'd had to blow her nose lately. How much she'd changed in these past days.

To her complete surprise, Petra came over and gave her a hug. She relaxed into it gratefully. When they were little, they were always slinging their arms around each other. All that had ended a long time ago. It felt good to be hugged now. She squeezed back, and then Petra pulled away and went over to the phone to call her own parents.

"I'm going to have a shower," Anaya said to no one in particular.

She grabbed the toiletries bag from her suitcase, then locked herself in the bathroom. It was good to be alone, and be done with all the needles, and masks, and beeping things attached to her. For today anyway. Dr. Weber had said there'd be an MRI scan tomorrow morning for all of them. Painless, she'd promised. You just lie still inside a metal tube with headphones on.

When she peeled off her jeans, she was embarrassed by how hairy her legs were. She didn't remember them being like this during her examination. It couldn't have grown in just a couple of hours, could it? She swallowed back her unease. She'd shave right now in the shower. Pulling off her socks, she grimaced at her hideous toenails. She poked the big one. It wasn't sore. Just long and thick. And it had a wicked point.

She suddenly remembered that kangaroo video Fleetwood had shown them—it felt like a thousand years ago. The shape and color of the kangaroo's claw were a bit like her own toenail.

Her unease ignited into panic. Was something wrong with her body? Dr. Weber had said she was very healthy, but maybe she was just saying that. She stared at herself in the mirror, trying to reassure herself. Her face was clear, and she'd barely gotten used to that: looking at herself and thinking she might be a little bit pretty. Was she going to lose that so quickly? The thought came with a flare of anger. She couldn't get all hairy and weird with kangaroo toenails right now.

From her toiletries case, she dug out her clippers. When she tried to cut the toenail, she couldn't squeeze down hard enough. The nail was too thick. On the second try, she pushed down with all her might, and the clippers snapped into pieces and clattered across the bathroom tile.

The black toenail didn't even have a scratch on it.

PETRA KNOCKED ON the bathroom door, bobbing up and down impatiently.

"Anaya," she whispered to the door. "I really need to go."

The shower wasn't even running. What was Anaya doing in there?

From behind the door: "Can't you use the other bathroom?"

Geez, way to treat someone who just gave you a hug when you were crying.

"Seth's in it, and he'll probably stink it all up. Please."

"Okay," Anaya said. "Hang on."

Petra heard a click and entered hurriedly, just as Anaya disappeared behind the shower curtain. Petra tugged desperately at her jeans, and dropped down onto the seat at the exact moment the shower came on.

She was glad of the noise, and gave a long sigh of relief. She hadn't realized how long she'd been holding it. It just snuck up on her suddenly when she was on the phone with Mom.

She glanced around the bathroom in disapproval. Anaya had already messed it up pretty well. The shelf was crammed with all her stuff, and the back of the toilet, too. She wasn't sure which towels and washcloths had already been used. How could it be so hard to keep things tidy?

From behind the shower curtain came the sound of vigorous splashing.

"Don't get me wet," she called out to Anaya.

"I'll be careful. Are your parents okay?"

"Yeah."

"It sounds pretty bad on the island," Anaya said.

"They're telling people to stay inside, but there's been a bunch more accidents with the pit plants. They're everywhere, and the roads are mostly shot. There's supposed to be a new helipad set up by tomorrow morning, though."

She listened to the sounds of Anaya in the shower and felt a familiar stab of longing. To feel water rushing over her. Except for that glorious big rain, it was a sensation she hadn't had for years. Not awake, anyway—only in her dreams.

She checked the backs of her thighs, and felt the new patches of skin. Was it even smoother than her old skin? It looked and felt firm and healthy, but she hoped the rest of her wasn't going to molt like this. It was freaky.

She shifted to grab some toilet paper, and winced. Her backside hurt. Probably all those uncomfortable chairs today. She gave her tailbone a gentle poke, and her breath caught in her throat. Instinctively she pulled her hand away, but then forced it back. What she touched felt like the tip of a little finger, jutting out. It was thin but firm, with a knuckly bit.

She jumped to her feet, legs shaking. She twisted and flexed but couldn't see her tailbone, and the mirror above the sink was mounted too high.

She took little gulps of air. "Anaya. Can you—come out here?"

"What's wrong?"

"I need you to look at something." It was hard to keep her voice calm when she wanted to scream.

"Pass me a towel?" asked Anaya.

She snatched a bath towel from the pile and pushed it through the curtain. A second later Anaya emerged, wrapped up, looking a bit alarmed.

Petra wasted no time. She turned around and touched the place. "What is *this*?"

"Well, it's just like a bit of . . . um, it's grown out from—"

"Is it a *tail*?" She forced the words out through gritted teeth.

She heard Anaya take a breath. "Um, well . . ."

"Just say it!" she hissed.

"I guess, yeah. Yes."

Petra swallowed. Her head felt like a radio playing all the stations at once. She'd been too young to remember the tail she'd been born with. But the moment her fingers touched it just now, she'd known it could only be one thing.

"Why would it start growing again?" She pulled up her jeans. First, these weird patches of snake skin, and now . . .

"Don't freak out," Anaya was saying.

She whirled to face her. "I have a *tail*!"

Anaya patted the air with her hands. "Maybe they just grow back a little sometimes. Anyway, you got your last one snicked off, right? They can do it again."

"Is it really gross?"

"If you hadn't told me, I wouldn't even have noticed."

She tilted her head. "You're lying."

"Just a bit." Anaya winced apologetically. "It's just a tiny . . . cute little tail."

Petra gave a snort of laughter, and couldn't stop. It was insane to be laughing right now, but it felt good. It helped beat back the panic bashing around inside her head.

Anaya held her by the shoulders. "Are you okay?"

Still giggling, she could barely get the words out: "Think of . . . the fun you'll have . . . telling everyone at school."

Anaya's entire body suddenly seemed to deflate. Her shoulders sagged and her head drooped.

"I'm sorry," Anaya said. "Really sorry. It was such a rotten thing to do."

Petra was silent for a moment. She'd been waiting to hear those words for so long.

"Why'd you do it?"

Anaya covered her face with her hands. "I was jealous, because you got so pretty. And you can do that pouty thing with your mouth."

Petra felt her cheeks flush. "What're you talking about?"

"You know what I'm talking about," Anaya said. "The puffy-lip thing."

"The what? Seriously, I . . ." She trailed off. What was the point of lying? "Okay. Look, it took me a long time to practice that."

"I knew it," Anaya said behind her hands.

Petra made a grunt of impatience. "You think it was so perfect for me? I'm allergic to the one thing humans most need to survive! I was freaking out. I had to go see a counselor! I would've traded being pretty for just being *normal*."

184

She wasn't sure if this was entirely true, but it came out in a rush. Anaya looked genuinely surprised, then nodded, like she was seeing something for the very first time.

"Okay. But I could see you getting friendly with Rachel and all of them, and I was worried you were going to dump me. So that's why I told people about the tail."

"Not the best way to stay on my good side."

"I know, it was so stupid. Forgive me?"

She wasn't sure if she could trust Anaya, but she wanted to. And it wasn't as if she herself had tried to save the friendship. "When you told everyone, at first I was mostly just really hurt. And then I got angry, and wanted to hurt you, so I started ignoring you, and saying mean things behind your back."

"Can we be friends again?" Anaya asked, peeping out between parted fingers.

Petra couldn't help laughing. "I've never had a friend as good as you. So yes, we'll be friends again. As long as you invite me to your birthday party." She let out a breath. School and birthday parties seemed like a very long time ago.

"I think I have a claw," Anaya said suddenly.

Petra choked back another laugh. "Is this a joke?"

"Look." Anaya lifted her foot onto the rim of the bathtub. Petra bent closer. The nails of both big toes were black and pointy—and very thick.

"You sure you didn't eat any of those berries, or drink the rainwater?"

Anaya shook her head. "And my legs are really hairy." She parted her towel and showed her an unshaven part of her leg. It looked pretty thick.

"Maybe you just haven't shaved in a while," she said.

Anaya looked dubious. "I can't remember it ever being this thick. I'm pretty freaked out."

"Me too." Petra shivered. "There's something happening to us. We're changing."

SETH SPRAWLED ON the sofa, paging backward through his sketchbook.

Everyone else had gone to bed, but he couldn't sleep. His mind and body were jittery, and if he didn't do something, he'd just pace. Every once in a while he'd pull back his sleeves and look at the raised scars on his forearms.

Over the years, he'd had dreams where he'd watched feathers poke through. Even when he was little, though, he never really thought he'd actually grow wings. It was just a story he told himself. It made him feel better, like the drawings.

He looked at his sketchbook. He'd created a lot of winged creatures over the years, all different kinds. Some he'd seen in his dreams, some he invented. Would he actually grow wings? If he did, what would they look like? Most important, would they take him into the air?

His heart raced. *Slow down.* Dr. Weber had only told him his feathers were coming back. That was all. Feathers did not necessarily mean wings.

He gave a start when a door opened and Petra and Anaya emerged from their bedroom. Both looked surprised to see him. He closed his sketchbook.

"We couldn't sleep either," Petra whispered.

"We got hungry," Anaya added.

The two of them crossed to the kitchen area and started opening cupboards. They definitely seemed friendlier with each other now. Anaya waved him over. Gratefully Seth joined them. The kitchen was well stocked with cereal, cans of soup, boxes of pasta. In the fridge was a selection of ready-made meals, like the ones they'd heated up for dinner.

Seth wasn't hungry, but he grabbed some cans of ginger ale and sat down at the table. Anaya was rummaging around inside a cracker box with her hand. Petra scowled and called her a pig, then set out plates for cookies, a big bunch of grapes, and a brick of cheese.

"I used to eat a ton of cheese," Anaya said, sighing.

Seth was about to ask why she stopped, when Petra told him: "Lactose-intolerant."

"*Everything*-intolerant," said Anaya.

"These are gluten-free," Petra said, shoving another box of crackers toward her.

Anaya wrinkled her nose. "They look gross." She nibbled one. "They taste gross, too. I'll stick with the grapes."

Seth cracked the tab on the ginger ale and took a slurp. The two girls were lost in their own thoughts—and they didn't seem to be pleasant ones. There were worry creases in Petra's forehead.

"My feathers are growing back," he blurted out.

He was surprised they didn't look more startled. Maybe they simply didn't believe him.

"Dr. Weber said so. She's seen it before. Her own son had it, too."

"My tail's started growing back," Petra said.

Seth felt an electric jolt go through him. "Really?"

"And Anaya's toenails have gone weird."

"Like claws," Anaya added.

"Weird stuff's happening to all of us," Petra said.

He nodded eagerly. "We're not like other people."

"Yeah, I think we've all realized that by now," Petra replied.

His hands were shaking a little bit. From fear, from excitement. He knew there might never be a better time to tell them. His thumbs crinkled the can of ginger ale.

"I think what's different about us, well, I think it started even *before* the plants arrived. Do you guys ever—?" He stopped himself. For the first time, he felt like they liked him. That he had *friends*. He didn't want to wreck it.

"Ever what?" Anaya said.

"Just tell us, Seth!" Petra said, less patiently.

"Do you guys ever have weird dreams where you're going somewhere? Fast. And it's really exciting . . ."

He watched them. Petra's eyes skittered around the room, like she was trying to chase something down. Anaya stared hard at a spot on the table.

"And sometimes you have a headache, but then it goes away like—"

"Like water spraying from a hose," Anaya said. "Just gushing out of you."

Seth felt the hair on his neck lift. "Yes!"

He'd never thought of it like that, but that was a really good description.

"And I'm flying," he said.

He'd never told anyone this. Not his foster parents. Not kids at school. Not his social workers—*especially* not the social workers. He sealed his dream memories in the vault of his sketchbook.

Nervously he looked at Anaya. Petra still hadn't said a word.

"I'm not flying in mine," said Anaya. "I'm running. And jumping. I can jump over all sorts of things. And there's always somewhere I'm supposed to be going."

"This is crazy," said Petra.

"What about you?" Seth asked her, even though he already knew the answer.

"I swim."

His entire body was trembling now, like he had a fever. He said, "I saw you in my dream the other night. You were swimming. And, Anaya, you were running." He swallowed. "And none of us looked like ourselves."

A long silence stretched out.

"So, what did we look like?" Petra asked.

He grabbed his sketchbook from the sofa and opened it on the kitchen table.

"There," he said, pointing to the sketches he'd made after the dream.

He watched Anaya's face as her gaze flowed over his drawing. She lingered on the claws and the powerful legs. He saw her touch the top of her own thigh, like she was testing the muscle there.

"It's beautiful," she said.

Petra's face was pale and taut, as if she were chilled to the bone.

"Why would you even *think* these were *us*?" she said angrily.

"Well, um," he stammered, "I said we didn't look—"

"No, these are just stupid monster pictures, Seth. Anyone can have weird dreams."

He didn't know what to say, she seemed so furious at him. He felt a hot tingle behind his eyes, and worried he might cry.

"I'm going back to bed," Petra said, and stalked off.

Seth swallowed and went to the fridge, just to open the door and rummage around for a second. Had he wrecked everything? When he turned, Anaya was paging backward through all his winged creatures. He let her.

"Is this what *you* look like in your dreams?" she asked.

He shrugged. She didn't seem angry like Petra, but he didn't know how much more he should say. She probably thought he was crazy now. "Sometimes. Some of it I just make up."

She paused and frowned at something at the bottom of the page.

He followed her gaze. It was just a doodle, really. A curling vine with little bulging sacs, and sprigs of dark berries.

Just like the black vines.

His mouth went dry.

"When did you do this?" Anaya asked.

He said, "At least six months ago."

CHAPTER FOURTEEN

"ANAYA, WAKE UP, PLEASE."

She opened her eyes and saw Carlene Lee standing beside the bed, smiling apologetically. Across the room, Petra was sitting up, looking bleary.

"What time is it?" Anaya asked.

"Seven o'clock," Carlene told her. "Dr. Weber wants to go over your test results."

"Is something wrong?" Petra asked, and Anaya felt her own heart give a thump.

"I'm sure she'll explain everything," Carlene said. "She's waiting in the living room. I'll just put out some breakfast things."

She closed the door behind her as she left.

"Well," Petra said, "the good news is I don't think I can get any more freaked out."

After Seth had shown them his dream drawings, it had taken Anaya forever to get back to sleep. She didn't know what to think. The one that was supposed to be her didn't look like any creature she'd ever seen. It was weirdly human and feline and kangaroo-like, and altogether otherworldly. Petra's, on the other hand, resembled some kind of ferocious reptile. Anaya could totally understand why she'd stormed off in a fury.

They were things from a comic book. They should have been easy to dismiss. But she couldn't. And that picture of the black vine—if Seth was telling the truth, he'd drawn it months before they'd ever appeared on Earth. Which was beyond creepy.

Anaya looked at her friend, saw the shadows under her eyes, and the fear inside them. For so long she'd thought Petra led a charmed life, and Anaya had never let herself imagine what it must really be like for her: how scary her water allergy must be. And now this.

She gave Petra's hand a quick squeeze. "Maybe Dr. Weber has some good news for us."

"She'd better. I've got a ton of questions."

Hurriedly they pulled on their clothes. They entered the living room at the same time as Seth. He had bed head, and wore his usual jeans and hoodie. In the living room, Dr. Weber sat in an armchair, a file folder on her lap. She looked like someone trying very hard to appear relaxed and normal.

"Sorry for the early wake-up, guys," she said. "Take a seat."

Anaya tried to guess what she was about to tell them. The doctor's cheeks looked a tiny bit flushed. Carlene finished setting out some boxes of cereal and cartons of juice on the kitchen table, and now sat down in a nearby armchair and tapped her pen against her clipboard, before stopping herself.

Anaya's stomach jittered nervously.

"We have your DNA results back," Dr. Weber said. "And we've found—"

"Before we begin," Carlene interrupted, "I need to say that medical results should only be discussed in the presence of the children's legal guardians."

"Yes, I apologize," said Dr. Weber, "but we haven't been able to arrange transportation for the parents yet."

"Is it possible to delay this conversation until—"

"Just tell us!" said Anaya. "Please!"

Carlene asked, "Are you all comfortable hearing these results without—"

"Yes!" said Petra.

"I'll note that, then," said Carlene, prissily jotting on her clipboard.

Dr. Weber leaned forward slightly in her chair. "We've analyzed your DNA, and there are sequences in your genomes that we've never seen before."

"That's what you were hoping for, right?" Anaya said. "The things that make us immune to the plants."

"Absolutely," Dr. Weber said.

"Great," said Anaya.

"What surprised us was the sheer *number* of unusual sequences in your DNA."

Anaya shifted uneasily in her chair. "*How* many?"

"Millions. In fact, only half of your DNA is familiar to us."

"Familiar?" Petra said.

Dr. Weber's index finger traced the edge of the file folder, back and forth. She said, "Only half is identifiable as human."

"Whoa," said Seth quietly.

"So, what's the other half?" Anaya asked.

"I think," Carlene Lee said, "that this conversation is upsetting—"

"Shush!" Anaya told her.

"The other half," Dr. Weber said, "is highly irregular, but there are quite a few sequences we've only seen in one other place."

"Where?" Seth asked.

"The cryptogenic plants. The black grass. The pit plants and their vines."

Anaya had the strangest feeling she'd floated free of her body and was watching all this from overhead.

"I told you!" Petra cried, her voice panicky. "The water and those berries messed us up!"

"Petra," said Dr. Weber calmly. "There's no way washing with the rainwater or eating the berries could have altered the DNA in every cell of your body."

"So, how else did it get in there, then?"

"Well," said Dr. Weber, "first of all, believe it or not, humans and plants share a lot of the same DNA. You might not have known this, but humans have sixty percent of the exact same DNA as bananas."

"Okay," Anaya said, "but how did alien—I mean, *cryptogenic*—plant DNA get inside us?"

"It was there to begin with," Seth said.

Anaya looked over at him in surprise. He'd said it with perfect calm, sitting very still and intent on the sofa.

"What're you talking about?" Petra demanded.

"Dr. Weber," said Carlene Lee, "I must recommend we stop—"

"Shut up, Carlene!" Petra snapped.

"Seth's correct," Dr. Weber said. "You were all born with it."

Anaya sat there, empty and wordless, feeling like her mind had been blasted clear by a gale-force wind. She didn't know if she was beyond surprise, or simply not surprised at all.

Dr. Weber continued. "Half your DNA is human and absolutely from your mothers. We know that from the samples they gave me yesterday. And, Seth, I'm sure your portion of human DNA is also from your mother."

"So the other half . . . ," Anaya began, and didn't finish her sentence.

No one had to.

"YOU'RE SAYING WE'RE *aliens*?" Petra demanded.

Dr. Weber cleared her throat. "Petra, that's not the language we'd use to—"

"Right, whatever! You're saying we're *cryptogens*!"

"No. Only half your DNA is cryptogenic."

"Oh, *phew!*" She gave a strangled laugh. "Only *half.* That's great!"

"This is extremely hard to hear, I know," Dr. Weber said.

"This is garbage!" Petra said. "I've had a million blood tests, and I bet Anaya has, too. Because of our allergies. How come no one's noticed this before?"

"Because no one's ever sequenced your DNA," Dr. Weber said. "It's completely possible your blood would present as normal."

"So you're saying our mothers were, what, *abducted*? And these . . . these cryptogens did something"—the images were so awful Petra banished them instantly—"so we were born half human, half cryptogen?"

"That is my working theory, yes," said Dr. Weber.

"No." Petra looked at Anaya and Seth, bewildered. "You guys don't believe this, do you?"

Anaya just sat there in shock, and Seth looked weirdly composed. Petra turned back to Dr. Weber.

"Your tests must be wrong. Do them again!"

"We've run them twice, Petra."

"People make mistakes all the time, okay? My dad works in a hospital and the stories he tells . . . even brilliant doctors make mistakes."

"I agree absolutely, but in this case there's no chance of error."

Petra looked desperately at the social worker. "Carlene, this is crazy, right?"

Carlene didn't even try to paste on a fake smile. She looked pale, and her eyes darted away nervously. She was *scared*.

"Only nutjobs believe in alien abduction!" Petra said. "I want to talk to my parents!"

"This is a lot to take in—" Dr. Weber began.

Seth interrupted her. "It happened to you. Didn't it?"

Petra frowned, and felt even more confused when Dr. Weber said, "Before this week, I would've denied it. But after meeting you three, and seeing the test results, yes, I believe I was abducted."

"Okay, no," Petra said. "This is—"

"What happened?" Anaya asked urgently.

"I was on a camping trip with my husband. I couldn't sleep so I left the tent to look at the stars. My husband joined me and said, 'You've been out here a long time. I got worried.' And I said, 'I just sat down.' When I looked at my phone, I saw that I'd been out there over an hour."

Petra sighed impatiently. "So you lost track of time. Or you fell asleep."

"Let her finish!" said Anaya.

"A few weeks later I discovered I was pregnant. And I gave birth to a son who had arms just like Seth's. If he'd lived, he would've been the same age. The same age as all of you. His birthday was June tenth."

Petra swallowed uneasily.

"Mine's June eleventh," Seth said.

"Ninth," said Anaya, then looked at Petra. "And you're the fourteenth."

Petra felt a tight ball of fear in her stomach. "This still doesn't prove anything! It could all just be coincidence!"

She looked to Anaya for support, but her friend's chest was rising and falling fast. When she spoke, her voice was shaky.

"Mom has this story, about how she was flying and lightning hit the wing. Everything was fine, all the controls still worked, except for the clock, which got shorted out. When she got back, they told her she was forty-five minutes behind schedule. She found out she was pregnant that month. She joked I was born from a lightning bolt."

The ball of fear in Petra's stomach spread like an octopus uncoiling. "But what about the other people on the plane? They would've noticed something, right?"

"There was only one other passenger," Anaya told her. "Your mom."

A STRANGE CALM had settled over Seth.

So many years of wondering, and feeling he was different and strange—and now finally having the answer why. He was stunned but also relieved. There was a *reason*.

"I think I've seen the cryptogens," he told Dr. Weber.

"How?" she asked, leaning forward. She looked equal parts eager and frightened.

"In my dreams. And I've dreamed that we become—"

"They're just *dreams*!" Petra said, giving him a furious look.

"I don't know," said Anaya. "He drew the black vines before he even saw them. He showed me in his sketchbook."

"Seth, may I see this sketchbook?" Dr. Weber asked.

Petra stood suddenly, fists clenched. She was shaking. "No way. I am *not* turning into one of those things, Seth!"

"This isn't my fault!" he shouted back at her. "I didn't do anything!"

With an unsteady voice, Carlene said, "I think we need to calm down and—"

"Carlene, we can't calm down!" Petra yelled. "We're *half alien*!"

"Petra," Dr. Weber said.

Just the quiet way she said it made everyone take a breath, Seth included. Petra dropped limply back onto the sofa.

"What's going to happen to us?" she asked meekly.

"I don't know yet," Dr. Weber said, "but I'm going to find out."

"I don't want any more changes," she said. "Can't you fix us?"

Dr. Weber said, "Listen to me. I'm going to do everything I can to take care of you." She looked at Seth. "All of you."

He nodded. Over the years, he'd taught himself not to trust grown-ups, but he couldn't help it: he trusted her.

"I'm going to get you guys in the MRI scanner today," Dr.

Weber said calmly. "We'll do full body scans. That'll give us an idea if we can expect any more physical changes."

"Oh my God," Petra said, covering her face with her hands.

Anaya moved closer and put an arm over her shoulders. She leaned her head against Petra's and said, "It's okay."

"Fine for you," Petra snapped. "You get to be sleek and beautiful!"

"I'm getting *claws*!" Anaya protested.

"Oh, boo-hoo! I'm turning into a *crocodile*!" She stood up. "I'm calling my parents."

"Wait," said Dr. Weber. She took a breath. "You can't call your parents yet."

Anaya frowned. "Why not?"

"Right now the only people who know about this are us, and my team. And we need to keep it that way for a little bit. You included, Carlene."

"Dr. Weber," the social worker said, shaking her head, "my job is to ensure the well-being and safety of these children—"

"And you will be, believe me."

Dr. Weber sat forward, looking solemnly at Seth, then Anaya and Petra.

"We're on a military base. If this news gets out, I'm worried you won't be safe. If Colonel Pearson learns you're cryptogen hybrids, he may only see you as enemies."

CHAPTER FIFTEEN

"DO YOU THINK THEY'RE going to invade?" Petra asked quietly.

"Haven't they already?" said Anaya.

"Only with plants."

Anaya snorted. *Only plants.* "Yeah, well, those plants are pretty good at killing people. And if the black grass keeps going, it's going to starve everyone to death."

She and Petra were waiting alone in a small examination room curtained off from Dr. Weber's lab. Through the wall she heard the *bangbangbangbang* of the MRI machine scanning Seth. They'd been taking turns so no one had to stay too long inside the claustrophobic tube. So far, she'd done two shifts. The first with her head in a weird kind of cage; the second with her torso wrapped in coils.

Petra nodded. "I guess you're right. The plants are doing all their dirty work."

"They're trying to wipe us out," Anaya said. "And we're part *them.*"

She'd taken a long, hot shower earlier, but she knew she

couldn't wash away that fact. It was inside every cell of her body, and there was absolutely nothing she could do about that.

"I just want Dr. Weber to fix us," Petra said. "I don't want to change any more."

"We might not."

Petra's eyes were darting everywhere, and Anaya could tell she was panicking. "If I change into that *thing* Seth showed us, I'll be a monster, and who could ever—?"

Love me. Anaya knew those were the unspoken words. She'd wondered exactly the same thing. Petra's whole body sagged, and she looked at Anaya with the helpless eyes of a small child.

"Your parents," Anaya told her. "Your friends. Me."

Petra was shaking her head. "I won't be *me* anymore."

Anaya took her hands. "No matter what happens, we'll still be us."

It seemed so ridiculous now, all the time she'd spent worrying about how she looked on the outside. How much pleasure she was taking in her new, prettier face. Who knew if it would even last? Even with normal people, your outside changed all the time. Maybe the *you* traveling inside your body was the only thing you had any control over.

Petra seemed a bit calmer now. Anaya was glad it was just the two of them, without the social worker hovering around, asking how they were feeling about everything. Carlene had said she had to check on her grandmother, and would be back before noon.

It was strange to think of people having normal family things to do right now: visiting a seniors' home, buying food, taking care of a child with a cold.

Anaya couldn't sit still, so she paced. She peeped through the curtain into the lab. Dr. Weber's staff were working busily at their screens and instruments. Decoding their DNA and blood. Mapping their mysteries. All the scientists had stared when they'd arrived this morning. They all knew. She wondered what they saw: kids, freaks, alien monsters? She hoped Dr. Weber was right, and they could all be trusted to keep secrets.

Dr. Weber parted the curtain and came inside the waiting room.

"How're you guys doing? Do you need more juice or snacks?"

"Did you see anything in my scans?" Petra asked, sitting up tensely.

"We're just logging images right now," Dr. Weber told her. "It's going to take time to analyze the results."

Petra sagged into her chair, foot tapping.

Dr. Weber sat down, and Anaya recognized Seth's sketchbook among her file folders. She thought, *Seth must really trust her, to let her look at it.*

"It's quite a collection of images, isn't it?" Dr. Weber said, catching her glance, and patting the cover.

Petra let out a big sigh. "Yeah. If that's me in there, someone's going to put me in an aquarium. Or harpoon me."

Dr. Weber rocked her head from side to side. "I'm not sure how much weight we should give these pictures."

"Really?" said Petra hopefully.

"I'm a scientist. I prefer MRI imagery and genetics to dreams."

"How could Seth draw the pit plant and black vine before he'd ever seen it?" Anaya asked.

"Very curious, I agree. There may be a genetic component to how we dream. Certain images, hardwired into our brains."

Anaya thought of her dreams, running and jumping. Petra's, swimming. Seth's, flying.

"Do you think each of us is a different kind of cryptogen?" she asked. "Like, a different species? One lives on land. One lives in the water. One lives in the air."

"I don't know, Anaya."

"But we're not going to turn *into* them, right?" Petra said anxiously, pointing at the sketchbook. "We're only *half* them!"

"And so far," said Dr. Weber, "your human DNA clearly has the upper hand."

"So far," Petra murmured. "But why'd they even do it? The cryptogens. Why'd they . . . *make* us?"

Anaya's mind had been twisting through this exact same rabbit warren of questions.

"You can't be the only ones," the doctor said. "My own son wasn't the only other child born with Seth's condition. I looked into it. And I'm wondering if we'd find teenagers who fit the profiles of you two as well. All conceived at the same time. It might be a sizeable sample group."

Anaya winced at her choice of words. *Sample group* was the term her father used when studying certain plants and other specimens.

With a chill of realization she said, "Are we an experiment? To see if they could live here on Earth."

Dr. Weber said nothing, but Anaya could tell by the way her eyes moved that she was thinking hard.

"To see if they could survive in our ecosystem," Dr. Weber said. "Our atmosphere. Our bacteria. Our plants."

"So we're like lab rats," Petra said.

"And maybe we didn't do so well," Anaya said, nodding at Petra. "You got allergic to water, and I got allergic to everything. Not exactly prime specimens."

"And then the big rain came," said Petra. "And *new* plants grew."

"All those seeds," Anaya said. It seemed so obvious now. "To make a new ecosystem for themselves."

Petra said, "And your allergies go away, and I can wash with the rainwater."

"We need to tell Colonel Pearson, right?" Anaya said. "Everyone still thinks it's a bunch of random plants. This is way bigger now."

"I think the military's assumed from the start those seeds didn't come alone," Dr. Weber said. "It was far too purposeful."

Anaya inhaled. "But no one knows there's hybrids like us."

"No," said Dr. Weber. "And I want to keep it that way for now. I'm worried about you three. If the news gets out, there's going to be a lot of fear and paranoia. You guys are completely innocent. You didn't ask for this."

Anaya suddenly thought of her father. Dad who wasn't really Dad. She felt all crunched up inside. Her father was one of the pillars that held up her entire life, and it had just been toppled. It shouldn't matter if he wasn't her biological father—she *knew* that—but she wished she were half him and not something else.

Dr. Weber handed her a tissue from a box, and she wiped her cheeks.

"Have you gotten through to my dad?" she asked.

"Still trying."

She pictured him on the eco-reserves, and remembered the withered black grass from Mom's photos of Cordova Island. A blighted crop.

An idea flared in her head. "Maybe they really are farmers," she said. "What if the plants weren't just sent down to kill us? Maybe all that black grass really is food to them, or a nurse crop, to make the soil ready to grow something else."

"Go on," said Dr. Weber, listening carefully.

"So if we destroyed their crop, would they leave us alone? Would they *go away*?"

She waited for someone to say something. Petra was staring at her lap, lost in thought. Then she looked up.

"And would *we* stop changing?" Petra asked.

"THINK ABOUT IT," Petra said, feeling suddenly hopeful. "None of this started until that big rain and the plants started growing. *That's* when our bodies began changing." She looked at Dr. Weber. "I know you said the plants and water have nothing to do with it, but—"

"They might be a trigger," Dr. Weber agreed. "They didn't *change* your DNA. But they might have woken it up."

"You mean with chemical signals?" Anaya said.

Dr. Weber nodded. "Everyone was exposed to the rain and the pollens, but in your case, maybe they flipped a switch."

"And if we could take all that stuff away," Petra said, "then we'd go back to being normal!"

With a sinking heart, she watched the doctor let out a big breath. "I don't know if it's that simple, Petra. But it's *possible*."

Possible was something. Possible meant *maybe*.

The picture of Seth's alligator thing slithered through her mind—and it was all she could do not to scream. She tried to slow-breathe and didn't even finish the third breath. Her whole body was contaminated. Maybe those drawings were an extreme form of what she might become, but the fact was, she was *changing*. Another big patch of skin had sloughed off her legs this morning. The new skin felt smooth, but how did she know it wouldn't turn into reptile scales? And her tail felt like it had grown a little longer.

"Can you take it off?" she blurted out. "My tail."

She'd shown it to Dr. Weber before her first MRI scan.

"I think we should wait for the results—"

"I don't want to wait!"

Dr. Weber leaned forward and took her hands. "I can't imagine how scary this is for you. And yes, surgery is an option, but I'm not a surgeon, Petra."

"There must be one here on the base, right?"

"Yes, but an army surgeon. If she sees it, our secret's out. I'm going to take care of you all, I promise."

"This is why we need to find my dad!" said Anaya. "You're spending all this time studying us, but if that soil on the eco-reserve kills the grass, then it might kill the other plants, too."

"Agreed," Dr. Weber said. "And there are teams all over the world working on herbicides. It's not just your father. But I'll put in a request with the colonel to send a team out to find him."

"Thank you," said Anaya.

"Seth should be coming out soon," Dr. Weber said. "Petra, are you ready for another round?"

She nodded. This one was going to be of her lower body—and

she was dreading what the scanner might find, waiting beneath her skin.

SETH WAS STILL in the MRI tube when it happened.

Last night the scars on his arms had been especially red and tender, and right now each one was a hot flare of pain. He wanted to move his arms, but they were pinned to his sides by the mesh they'd wrapped around his body. It was like being inside a coffin.

He looked down at his bare forearms. *Bangbangbangbangbang* went the machine, loud even through the headphones. On his left arm, some of his scars were raised like blisters. Something dark abruptly poked through the skin, and a cry of pain leapt from his mouth. It was a black, sharp-tipped quill, jutting out a couple of centimeters, trickling blood.

Another jab, and he looked over at his right arm, where a small bloodstain grew on his gown, just below his shoulder. Then the pain came fast and fierce, all up and down both arms. Blood-stains blossomed everywhere.

Feathers! It was finally happening. He was getting feathers, like in his dreams, only so much more painful. He was excited and terrified and couldn't think straight. He wanted the pain to stop. He wanted to get out of this cage.

He wrenched his arms to and fro, and felt his new quills catch on the plastic mesh—and tear it. Were they so sharp? After a few more strokes, the mesh fell away in tatters. With the machine still *bangbang*ing around him, he scrambled out of the tube.

He stood there, gasping, blood dripping from his arms, and pulled back the sleeves of his gown so he could watch the last of the quills erupt. He looked up at the window and saw the two technicians staring in shock. Dr. Weber came running out.

"Seth! Are you all right? Sit down."

Dr. Weber eased him down into a chair.

"It really hurts," he said. His arms throbbed.

"Can we get some painkillers?" Dr. Weber called over her shoulder.

She grabbed a pack of sterile swabs and began cleaning the blood off his arms.

"Careful," Seth said, "they're really sharp—"

He was too late. Dr. Weber grunted as one of the quills jabbed through the swab and left a bright-red line on her palm.

"They certainly are," she said, and continued to clean Seth's arms, more carefully.

Seth sat there, feeling like a child. But it made him calmer. He couldn't remember anyone ever taking this much care over him.

He looked up as Anaya and Petra rushed into the room.

"Oh my God," Petra breathed, staring at his barbed, blood-streaked arms.

"You okay, Seth?" Anaya asked.

One of the technicians returned with a cup of water and some pills. Seth swallowed them. His hands were still shaking. Staring at the quills, he saw downy hairs growing from their sides. The beginnings of feathers.

He looked up at Dr. Weber with sudden anxiety. "Are you going to cut them off?"

"Do you want me to?" she asked.

He shook his head.

"Then no," she said gently. "I won't do anything you don't want. If you say they stay, they stay."

Never in his life had Seth felt so grateful to anyone. For the first time, it was okay to be himself. He wasn't supposed to be something else.

"Thanks."

"They're quite flexible," Dr. Weber said. "I think we can fold the quills flat against your arm and wrap them loosely. Just so you don't cut anyone, or yourself."

"And so no one sees," he added.

"That, too," said Dr. Weber.

She got a roll of gauze and he watched as she carefully wrapped down the quills on his right arm, and taped it. She was halfway through his left when one of the technicians poked his head into the room and said, "Colonel Pearson's just come in, and he's looking for you."

Dr. Weber swore under her breath. In panic, Seth looked at his taped arms, his blood-stained gown, the red swabs scattered all over the chair. From outside came the beat of hard, official footsteps.

"Into the machine!" Dr. Weber hissed at him.

He clambered inside the tunnel and flipped onto his back, his lower half jutting out. Through the opening he saw Anaya snatch up all the blood-stained swabs and clench them in her fist just as Colonel Pearson strode into the MRI suite.

"Dr. Weber," he said.

"Hello, Colonel," the doctor replied, glancing back over her shoulder as she fussed with some of the shredded mesh. "We're just about to start another round of imaging. How can I help you?"

On the bottom part of his gown, Seth noticed a spatter of blood that must have dripped from his arm. To him it looked as bright and red as a thing could look.

He saw the colonel's eyes go right to the machine, then skip to Anaya. Between her fingers, Seth spotted some red-tinged swabs sticking out.

"It's your father," Colonel Pearson told Anaya. "We got through to him."

"He's on the phone?" Anaya asked, her voice breaking with excitement. "Right now?"

"No. About twenty minutes ago. But we taped it—we had enough signal for a video call. When you're ready, we'll play it back for you in the comms room."

CHAPTER SIXTEEN

ANAYA WAITED IMPATIENTLY AS the soldier clicked icons at his console.

"The video quality's pretty poor," the soldier apologized. "Sound, too."

Anaya didn't care about any of that. Back in the lab, she'd dragged her clothes on so fast her top was inside out. She wanted to see her father, right now. Beside her stood Petra, Dr. Weber, and Seth, whose arms were wrapped up and hidden inside his hoodie. She cast a nervous glance just to make sure no blood had soaked through his sleeves. Colonel Pearson loomed nearby in the dim comms room, watching the monitor.

It flared to life, and Anaya's heart clenched at the sight of her father's face. It was almost unrecognizable. Dirt was smeared across his cheeks and clotted thickly in his hair, as if he'd been rolling around like a crazed animal. He'd tied a cloth across the lower half of his face, covering his nose and mouth. The whites of his eyes looked enormous and wild as he shouted.

"... can't ... off!"

The sound cut in and out, and the image kept pixelating and freezing.

"Where is he?" Anaya croaked.

He was definitely outside, but it looked awfully dark for daytime. Why was he so dirty?

"Can you give us your location, sir?" the comms officer asked on the recording.

Static ate up her father's first few words, and then: "... dova!"

"Can you confirm your location, please, sir?"

"Cordova!" Anaya exclaimed. "He said Cor*dova*. It's an eco-reserve!"

Dad's face took up most of the screen, but those were definitely trees behind him. They grew so high and thick that virtually no light made it through the branches.

Dad's face pixelated again. "... lake ... can't get off!"

"There's a lake!" Anaya said, remembering. "And a little island in the middle. Maybe he's stuck there!"

"... They're everywhere!" Dad said.

Anaya's throat tightened in fear. She'd never seen her father look so desperate. *They're everywhere.* She could only assume he meant the cryptogenic plants—or was it something worse?

"... is dead!" Dad was saying.

"Sir," said the comms officer's voice in the recording, "can you please confirm: Is someone dead?"

Anaya swallowed. Did he mean Amit? She hadn't seen him in the background anywhere. Then she pointed at the screen. "What're those?"

Behind her father, two snakes dangled down, but they weren't snakes. They were black vines, winding their way in midair toward her father.

"Turn around!" she couldn't help shouting at the screen.

". . . works!" Dad was shouting now. "The soil . . ."

Something hit him in the neck with a wet splash.

"What was that?" Petra cried.

The camera shook as Dad swiped at his neck like he'd just been stung. His face creased with pain, and Anaya felt her own face crumple as she watched, helpless.

"Dad!"

She gave a yelp as the phone was yanked out of her father's hand by something unseen. Dad made a grab for it, but it was already out of reach, and rising even higher, still filming him.

". . . soil . . . it kills them!" he bellowed.

Then all Anaya could hear was the crackle of air as the phone was whipped higher still. She was trembling so badly she could barely breathe.

"What's got his phone?" Seth gasped.

As if in answer, something thin and dark jagged across the screen like a crack, followed by another and another until the screen went completely dark and then hissed with static.

"The vines," Petra said, sounding dazed. "They snatched it out of his hand."

"That's all of it," the colonel said.

Anaya forced some air into her lungs. Dad was alive. At least he was alive. But for how long?

"Something hit him," she said. "All that wet stuff on his neck. Was it acid?"

"I'm sorry you had to see that," Dr. Weber said quietly to her. To the colonel she said, "Perhaps it would've been better not to—"

"Please, can we go get him *right now*!" Anaya cried.

The colonel turned his deeply lined face to her, and she realized how weary he was. "I have a city of millions under siege, Miss Riggs, and limited resources. Right now almost all my troops are trying to rescue people trapped inside homes with plants that are gassing and strangling them. If I call off some of my soldiers, that's fewer families I can help—just to rescue a single man."

For a moment, Anaya couldn't speak. It was like he was accusing her of something terrible and selfish. Of course she didn't want other people to suffer or die! But of course she also wanted her own father saved!

"But. . . . you heard what he said! He's found soil that kills the plants!"

The colonel said, "That was far from clear to me."

"Colonel Pearson," Petra said, "if he's found something that kills—"

"If."

Anaya looked over at her friend, and saw she wasn't discouraged by the colonel's severe look.

"Okay, fine," Petra replied calmly. "*If.* But how can you not check it out? Your bullets and grenades aren't going to kill these things. Not nearly fast enough, anyway. Mr. Riggs might have the solution to get rid of the plants for good! And if he does, you'll save way more families than you can right now!"

Anaya had seen her friend act lots of times, in games and on school stages, and this was definitely one of her best performances. She watched the colonel's face for his reaction, and saw a small twitch of admiration at the corner of his lined mouth.

"Lieutenant," he asked the man at the communications console, "is the Griffon out of maintenance?"

"Yes, sir."

Anaya's heart leapt.

"Prep it," the colonel said, then turned to Anaya. "We'll take a pass over the island and try to evac your father."

"I'm going, too," she said, startled by her boldness.

She felt Dr. Weber put a cautioning hand on her shoulder.

"I can lead you right to him," Anaya plunged on. "I've *been* there."

Technically, this was true, but she hadn't been there in years, and didn't really know the geography. But no way was she letting them go without her. If Dad had let her come along in the first place, he might not be in so much danger.

"You could also just tell us where he is," the colonel said.

"I'm useful!" she persisted. "The plants can't hurt me. I can go places the soldiers can't!"

"My people are very highly trained."

"Have they been *inside* a pit plant?"

"Or cut their way *out* with a chain saw?" Petra added. "I want to go, too."

Startled, Anaya looked at Petra. "You sure?" she asked. It wasn't even her own father.

"And me," Seth said.

"You guys don't have to," Anaya said, touched by the dogged loyalty in Seth's solemn face.

"It's too dangerous," Dr. Weber said. "I can't authorize it."

Anaya expected the colonel to back the doctor up, but he wasn't even looking at her. He was looking at the three of them intently—and with far more interest than he had when they'd first arrived at the base. Anaya felt a twinge of discomfort: She wasn't entirely sure if she liked that look. It was the way someone might stare at an intriguing piece of machinery, or a weapon. But all she cared about right now was that he let them go.

"You three might be assets to the mission," he said.

Dr. Weber said, "Colonel, they are civilians and they are minors."

"I *want* to go!" Anaya insisted. For the first time, she was irritated by Dr. Weber. She just wanted to get going. Dad had been hit; he might need help *right now*!

"Carlene will flip," Dr. Weber said to Seth.

"Let her," Seth replied. "I'm going."

Colonel Pearson said, "You're free to accompany them, Dr. Weber. Your feet won't even touch the ground. You'll stay in the helicopter the whole time. It's a straightforward extraction. We'll be ready to go in half an hour."

"Thank you," Anaya said, hoping they weren't already too late.

THE SOLDIER SITTING opposite Petra was unbelievably handsome. His name tag said BROCK, which she knew was his last name, but it could also be an awesome first name. In fact, he had the same eyebrows as Brock on that ranch show she told everyone she hated, but totally did not hate, and watched secretly in her bedroom.

Looking at Captain Brock was the only way she could distract herself from the fact she was strapped into a helicopter, bumping her way toward an island thrashing with cryptogenic plants. She really, really hoped she wasn't going to throw up all over Brock.

She glanced at Seth, who actually seemed to be enjoying the ride, and then at Anaya, pressed against the opposite door. Petra wanted her to get her dad back—and she also wanted that special soil. The faster they got it, the faster they could start killing the plants. And the faster she'd stop changing. Maybe she'd even go completely back to normal. Or as normal as she got with her water allergy. Right now living with a water allergy seemed easy, compared to turning into a reptile.

Also in the cabin with them was a female soldier whose name tag said JOLIE, yet she looked anything but jolly. Petra had never seen such humorless eyes. Colonel Pearson wasn't with them, so Brock was the commanding officer. He'd made that clear before they even took off.

"You don't do anything until I tell you to do it," he'd said. "And right now, all you need to do is buckle up."

Dr. Weber was wedged between the two soldiers, and she didn't look at all pleased. Before they'd left, she'd tried to talk them out of going, but Anaya hadn't budged, and Petra wasn't letting her friend go alone. On the school field, she'd freaked out and left everyone in the lurch, and that wasn't happening again.

She shifted so her tiny tail wasn't jammed so much against the seat. She wondered how long before it was noticeable—with any luck, she'd have it hacked off by then. She squashed the thought down. Slow, deep breaths.

"This should be fairly routine," Brock said above the noise of the rotors. "Once we reach the site, we'll land if possible. If not, we'll hover. I'll rappel down, get a harness on your father"—he was looking at Anaya now—"and bring him up."

"And the soil samples," Anaya reminded him.

"No sweat," said Brock.

"My father said there were plants everywhere," Anaya told him. "It might not be so easy."

"I'm an expert gardener," Brock said with a cocky smile. "And I brought my pruning shears."

He nodded at the bulging duffel bags Petra had seen them pack at the base.

"We'll have your dad back in time for dinner," Brock told Anaya. "Don't worry, Miss Riggs."

Petra saw Anaya blush, and felt irked. The captain had barely glanced her way the whole trip. *I'm an expert gardener.* Obviously a conceited jerk. And *Brock*—what a stupid name.

"We're coming up on Cordova Island," Jolie said.

"Let's open them up," Brock said, and he and Jolie popped open both doors, sliding them flush along the sides.

Air galloped in, and the noise doubled. Below them, water flashed past, and Petra felt a surge of vertigo. Instinctively she grabbed Seth's hand. He squeezed back.

"Okay?" he asked her, looking as surprised and embarrassed as she felt.

She nodded, and released her grip. "Sorry."

"All right," said Captain Brock, "we've spotted a dock. We're doing a circle."

The helicopter tilted over, and Petra now stared straight down on a rocky shoreline. She figured if this didn't make her puke, nothing would. A single boat was tied up at a skinny wooden dock.

"I think that's Dad's!" Anaya shouted.

"Proceed northeast," Brock told the pilots through his headset. "We are looking for a small lake, with an island in the middle."

Petra stared down at a steep, rock-strewn slope. Black grass soared up everywhere there was open ground. She spotted a bony goat standing on a boulder. Then they were over thick forest. In the treetops she caught sight of dark vines, a quick flash of berries.

"I'm not seeing anything!" Jolie shouted.

Petra caught the worry lines in Anaya's forehead.

"Thought you said you knew where this place was," Brock said. He didn't sound charming anymore. He sounded testy.

"I do. It's sort of bean-shaped. I've seen pictures."

"You said you'd been there."

"It was a while ago."

"This place isn't that big. We should've seen it by now."

"It's here!" Anaya said firmly.

"One more circle of the northeast," Brock told the pilots over his headset.

Anaya shook her head in frustration. "It should be right down here!"

"Take us lower," Brock told the pilots over his headset.

Petra's stomach jumped as they tilted and swooped down. Through Anaya's open door she gazed into dark treetops.

"All I'm seeing is forest," Brock said.

"Those aren't trees," Anaya told him.

Petra blinked and stared harder. What she'd thought were branches were actually thick vines that formed a huge canopy. Her breath snagged as she saw some of them slither, growing over one another. Even from this height, she caught a faint whiff of the sleeping perfume.

"The lake's down there!" Anaya pointed at a gap in the vines, and Petra saw a quick flash of water.

"The vines must've grown right over it," Seth said. "Like they're trying to hide it."

Jolie looked at him sharply. "You're talking like they're intelligent."

"They *grabbed* a cell phone!" Petra told her.

"It's like they don't want us getting that soil," Seth added.

"These are *plants*," scoffed Captain Brock. Into his headset he said, "Okay, we're over the site. Hold here." He unbuckled himself and leaned way out the door. "We're certainly not landing, but if we torch away some of these vines, I can rappel."

"I'll burn a hole, Captain," said Jolie, unzipping a bag and pulling out a flamethrower.

"Wait!" said Seth. "It might be toxic. Like the black grass."

"We've got masks. And you guys are immune, yeah?"

"I think we should turn back," said Dr. Weber.

Anaya looked at her, shocked. "Why?"

"This is already more dangerous than we thought. I've never seen the vines growing so fast—and Seth's right. The pattern of growth suggests an intelligence we haven't seen before."

"We can't just leave her dad down there!" Petra protested.

Dr. Weber looked at Captain Brock. "Anywhere else to land?"

"Not on this island. If we want our man today, we need to cut a hole to bring him through."

"Anaya," said Dr. Weber, "I know you want your father back right now. But my chief concern is keeping you three safe. If we start a fire, we might not be able to put it out. And think of the debris that might fall on your dad. We've got gas masks. Your father doesn't."

Petra saw her friend struggling.

"On the video he had his mouth and nose covered," Anaya said. "There must be sleeping gas floating around down there. They're trying to knock him out. If he falls asleep, that's it. We can't wait any longer."

Brock passed out gas masks to the pilots and Jolie. He held one out to Dr. Weber, who reluctantly took it.

"Try and burn as little as possible," the doctor told Jolie.

"Will do," the soldier replied.

"Take us down, thirty feet above the canopy, and hold steady," Brock instructed the pilots, his voice muffled through the mask.

Nervously Petra held on as they dropped closer to the vines. Birds fluttered away from the bright clusters of berries. Two tendrils stretched and wound themselves around each other.

"Light it up!" Brock commanded.

Jolie shot out a thin stream of flame. The vines caught quickly, and a plume of yellowish smoke expanded toward them.

The helicopter banked away skittishly.

"Man, that stuff burns," said Jolie. "When it stops smoking, we can see if—whoa!"

Petra's head jerked back and hit the wall as the helicopter dropped.

Brock staggered off-balance. "Hold her steady!" he shouted at the cockpit.

"Wasn't me!" the pilot called back.

Petra peered out her open door. Cold electricity tingled across her skin. Some vines had snagged around the helicopter's landing strut.

"Look!" she shouted.

"You've picked up a couple of stragglers," Captain Brock told the pilots. "Pull up!"

The helicopter lurched sharply higher, but was instantly yanked back, knocking Petra against Seth.

When she looked outside again, she saw more vines crawling around the landing strut.

"They're dragging us down!" she yelled.

"Flamethrower!" Brock shouted at Jolie, who tossed it to him.

The captain sent a blast of fire down into the vines, and the helicopter surged forward. Petra exhaled in relief, but her breath jolted in her chest as they tipped sharply.

"Still got us!" the pilot shouted back.

Petra felt something against her shoe and cried out when she saw the vine. It had grown across the floor of the compartment, and out the far door.

"There's one inside!" she said, stamping at it with her foot.

Brock pulled a serious knife from his belt and started sawing. It took him several seconds to cut through, and then Petra and Seth and Anaya helped him peel it off the floor and fling it out.

"We're still snagged around the struts!" Jolie shouted from her open door.

The helicopter slewed in a circle, ever tighter and lower.

Petra looked out her doorway and saw that two vines had grown into the engine cowling right underneath the helicopter's rotors.

"That's not good," muttered Brock as alarms bleated from the cockpit.

"Brace!" the pilot shouted back at them.

It was all so fast. The helicopter jerked back, as if yanked from behind, then keeled over. Petra clenched her eyes and held tight.

IT WAS LIKE a fairground ride Seth had been on once, only much, much worse. The seat restraints bit into his shoulders and chest. The rotors shrieked a rusty tune of tortured metal. Branches crackled against the sides as the helicopter plowed through treetops. When it finally came to a brain-shuddering stop, the air was punched right out of him.

He choked in a breath, and started coughing. Beside him in the tilted compartment, Petra was blinking, dazed, holding a hand to the place where they'd just knocked heads. On his other side, Anaya stared confused at the branch that jutted into the cabin. He heard someone saying his name, and it took him a moment to realize it was Dr. Weber.

"Seth?" she said, looking at him in concern. "You okay?"

"Yeah. You?"

"Fine." She tilted her head at his right arm, and he followed her gaze. His sleeve had been shoved up, revealing the bandages on his arm. The tip of a feather poked through. Quickly he yanked the sleeve down. He glanced anxiously at Brock and Jolie, but they were busy with other things.

Up front, the helicopter pilot was slumped motionless against the crumpled controls. The co-pilot had unbuckled himself and was shaking the pilot's shoulder. "Berton? Berton!" Somehow, a vine had already crawled partway across the windshield.

"Do not move!" Captain Brock told them all, unbuckling himself.

When Seth looked out the doorway, he understood why. They were way up, and the helicopter teetered in the branches.

"Berton needs a medic!" the co-pilot called back to them.

"Coming," Dr. Weber said, unbuckling herself.

"Carefully," said Brock as the helicopter tilted. "Jolie, you and

I are going to balance this baby while the kids get off. Anaya, you good to climb into the tree? Go."

Seth watched as Anaya unbuckled herself and grabbed hold of the branch. There were lots of smaller branches to hold on to, and she clambered toward the trunk. The helicopter creaked ominously. Brock and Jolie took small steps around the compartment to keep it level.

"Berton's losing a lot of blood," Dr. Weber said. "His hip's crushed. We need to get him to a hospital."

"We still got a radio?" Brock asked the co-pilot.

"Dead."

Brock swore under his breath. "Seth, go! All the way to the ground if you can, and get clear."

Seth scrambled out into the tree. Anaya shifted to some lower branches to make room. Now that he was outside the helicopter, he could see how mangled it was—and how tippy. Not much was holding it up. From the engine cowling, flame licked up at the mangled rotors.

"There's fire," Seth called back to Jolie, pointing.

"Yep," she said, like this was the most normal thing in the world.

"We should keep going," Seth said to Anaya, and she nodded and kept climbing down.

He looked back to Petra, who had just stepped into the hatchway. Without warning, the helicopter dropped. Petra half jumped, half fell, and landed clumsily on the same branch as

Seth. She started to slip off, but he seized her wrist and steadied her long enough so she could get a grip.

The helicopter fell a few more feet, and Seth saw one of the mangled rotor blades come swinging toward them.

He shoved Petra's head down and ducked, just as the blade sliced over their heads with a rusty moan.

"Geez," muttered Petra. "Thanks."

And then he was climbing down as fast as he could. When he glanced up, he saw the branches bending under the helicopter's massive weight. Two black vines grew into the open door. He heard Brock shouting orders.

"Dr. Weber, go! Granahan, you too!"

"We can't leave Berton!"

With a terrible groan, the helicopter listed over. The flames burned higher. Seth turned his full attention to the tree, one branch after another, working his way lower.

A bag of gear tumbled past him, crackling through the branches.

Brock's voice again: "Granahan, get out! That's an order!"

"Something's snagged my foot!"

"Jolie, go!"

With a great snapping of branches, the helicopter dropped— and this time didn't stop. Seth hugged the trunk as its burning bulk fell past him with a roar.

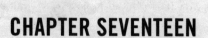

CHAPTER SEVENTEEN

ANAYA'S FEET HIT THE ground at the same moment as the helicopter, and the concussion knocked her flat. Branches and debris rained down on her.

"Run!" someone shouted from the tree.

She thought it was Brock but couldn't see him through the branches and thickening smoke. To her huge relief, Petra and Seth landed on the ground nearby.

"Come on!" Petra said, pulling her by the arm.

She stumbled over a big bag of gear. Whatever was in there, they might need it. She dragged it after her. Seth hefted up a side so they could go faster.

"Everyone get out?" she panted.

"Don't know," Seth said, stumbling on.

Behind them, an explosive clap of thunder sent a hot gale blasting past. When she dared look back, she saw churning smoke, and then Dr. Weber came through it, followed by Brock and Jolie, who was the only one without a gas mask. She was bent over, coughing.

"Go! Go!" Brock shouted—or that's what Anaya thought he said, because she was still half-deaf from the blast. They all hurried on for another minute before the captain told them to hold up.

Anaya's pulse pounded fast in her ringing ears. A single thought bounded wildly through her head.

"Which way's the lake?" she asked, looking around. During the helicopter's fatal spin, she'd lost all sense of direction.

"Hold on a sec," said Dr. Weber. "Is everyone okay?"

"Fine," she said, sinking down against a trunk.

"Where's your mask?" Dr. Weber asked Jolie.

"The faceplate got smashed when I jumped. I dumped it."

Behind them, Anaya saw the flickering glow of the fire, and felt sick to her stomach. Berton and Granahan. The two pilots.

She was sore all over, face and arms scratched to bits, but she didn't see any blood on her clothes—then her gaze snagged on her right sneaker. Her clawlike toenail had jabbed right through the canvas. She clenched the toe back inside, and hid it under her other sneaker.

She peeped over at Brock, but he was busy unzipping their one surviving bag of gear. "Let's see what we've got," he muttered.

"A radio would be good," Dr. Weber said.

The captain scowled and lifted out two shattered walkie-talkies. On the ground he set out a first aid kit, a shovel, and a chain saw. Eagerly Petra snatched up the saw.

"Does it work?" she said.

"Hand it over," Jolie barked.

Petra ignored her. She pulled the starter hard, and the blade whirled to life.

"It works!" she shouted. "That's good news!"

"Kill it!" Brock barked, and after she obeyed, he said, "You don't do anything until I say so!"

Anaya could tell Petra was going to say something snarky, so she cut in. "Are there any extra gas masks? Jolie's going to need one."

Even through the acrid smoke, she could smell the sleeping perfume. It was very strong.

"These vines pump out gas," she told Brock. "It'll knock you out pretty fast."

"We can share," Brock said, peeling off his mask and passing it to Jolie.

"They're everywhere," Anaya said, for the first time taking a good look at the trees around her. Each had at least one black vine welded to its trunk, sprouting berries and small flesh-eating sacs. "Which means there'll be pit plants, too." She nodded at the shovel. "We're going to need that to test the ground."

"Will anyone come for us?" Dr. Weber asked Brock.

"We didn't send a distress call. If we're overdue, they'll try to send someone, but only if they can spare the equipment. And only if it's still light." He checked his watch. "Two oh five. We've got about six and a half more hours of sun. Let's go get Riggs."

"Thank you," said Anaya. Her father must have heard the

helicopter—that would give him hope. But he'd probably heard the crash, too. As long as he was alive to hear it—that was the important thing.

Dr. Weber looked at her, then Seth and Petra. "You sure you three are all right? No drowsiness? You're alert?"

Seth nodded. "I'm good."

Captain Brock pulled out a compass and checked the reading. He chopped his hand in the air. "The lake's that way."

He said it with such confidence, but Anaya wasn't sure she trusted him. She didn't believe anyone could be in control down here. Aside from the crackling of the distant fire, the forest was eerily quiet: no birds, no animals scampering in the undergrowth. But the air throbbed with a thick sense of expectation, like just before a lightning storm.

"Single file," Brock said, leading the way, pounding the earth ahead of him with the shovel.

Anaya fell into line behind Dr. Weber. Petra and Seth were behind her, with Jolie bringing up the rear, holding the chain saw.

"'Your feet won't even touch the ground,'" Petra muttered into her ear. "Yeah, right."

Up ahead, Brock stumbled, and put his hand against a tree for balance.

"You need the mask?" said Dr. Weber, offering him hers.

He took it without a word of thanks, and kept going.

Anaya felt Petra touch her shoulder. "Your dad's going to be fine," she said.

"Hope so," she said gratefully.

"Remember that camping trip he took us on, when we were, maybe, seven?"

She nodded.

"I remember thinking, *There's nothing this guy can't do.* He knew how to do everything. He knew the name of every plant. And the best way to carry a canoe. My mom's a survival freak, but I felt safer with your dad."

Anaya smiled gratefully, then stumbled. Glancing down, she saw, almost hidden among the sandy earth and pine needles, a crisscross of black vines.

"Hey, there's a ton of—" she began, then gasped as one of them slithered like a snake over the top of her shoe. She kicked it back.

"What?" Dr. Weber said, turning.

"The vines, they're moving!"

Without warning, Dr. Weber went sideways, her feet whipped out from under her.

"It's got my foot!" she cried, kicking and digging her hands into the earth, trying to slow herself down.

With terrifying speed, the black vine dragged Dr. Weber toward a hole in the ground where two fleshy lips were parting hungrily.

"Nobody move!" Brock shouted, pulling the knife from his belt. He took only a single step before staggering and falling, his own foot snared.

Gripping the chain saw, Jolie ran toward the pit plant. Seth was faster. He bolted past her and threw himself at Dr. Weber's feet. Anaya saw Seth yank his sleeve up, and slash at the vine with his sharp quills.

It worked. Suddenly Dr. Weber was scrabbling backward, free. Seth leapt back from the rim of the pit plant.

"They're everywhere!" Petra cried out, hopping from spot to spot to escape the curling vines.

"We're moving!" shouted Brock, slashing through the vine around his own ankle, and standing.

Anaya ran with the others, skipping over the snaking nest underfoot. Up ahead, Brock climbed onto a large flat-topped boulder. It looked vine-free to Anaya, and she sank down with everyone else to catch her breath. Rock was good. Pit plants wouldn't grow under rock, would they?

"Enjoying gardening?" Petra asked Brock.

"Dr. Weber?" Anaya said, patting her on the leg. Her eyes looked unfocused. Anaya glanced over at the captain. "She needs the mask back. She's getting drowsy!"

"I'm all right," Dr. Weber replied, her voice a little thick.

But Brock wasn't listening. He was staring at Seth, who was hurriedly tugging down his right shirtsleeve. Anaya sucked in her breath when she saw the three feathered barbs that had ripped through the cloth, jutting out in plain view.

"What happened to your arm?" Brock asked.

"I'm fine," Seth said, turning away.

"Whoa, whoa," said the captain, grabbing him by the shoulder and pulling his sleeve farther back.

More feathers were revealed, and Anaya saw bits of black vine stuck to some of them.

"What the heck . . . ," said the captain, touching the feathers, then pulling his hand back with a hiss. He glared at his bleeding finger.

"What are those?" Jolie demanded angrily, pointing at Seth. "What's wrong with you?"

"Nothing's wrong with him!" Dr. Weber said, and Anaya was startled by the indignation in her voice. She sounded like a protective mother. "It's a congenital condition."

"He's got *spikes*," Brock said. "Let me see your other arm."

Before Seth could back away, Brock yanked up his left sleeve and revealed the careful bands of gauze and surgical tape.

"Why're you hiding them?" Brock asked.

Dr. Weber said nothing. Her head lolled forward.

"Give her the mask!" Anaya shouted. "She's going to pass out!"

"She'll get the mask when she answers my questions. Colonel Pearson know about this?"

"No," Dr. Weber said. "No need."

"Well, *I* need to know," said Brock, pulling off his mask and fitting it over Dr. Weber's face. "Do they all have spikes?"

Anaya watched the doctor take some hungry breaths. Her gaze sharpened.

"No, but they all have unique traits. That's why I brought them to the base."

"Told you," Jolie said grimly to Brock. "But everyone laughed at me."

"Laughed at what?" Petra asked.

"I said you three were cryptogens," Jolie said as she drew her service pistol.

"What're you doing?" Anaya said in horror.

"Are you?" Jolie shouted. *"Cryptos?"*

"Of course we're not!" said Petra indignantly.

Captain Brock reached out for Dr. Weber's mask. "Don't make me take this off. The truth!"

"They're hybrids," said Dr. Weber. "There's cryptogenic DNA in them, but they are absolutely not cryptogens."

"And we're *not* dangerous!" Petra told Jolie.

"Seth cut Dr. Weber free back there," Anaya said. "He saved her life!"

"Quite a secret you've been keeping," Brock said. He looked at Seth, then Petra and Anaya. To Jolie he said, "Lieutenant, holster your firearm."

"I don't think that's a good idea, Captain."

Anaya could barely breathe. Jolie's pistol swung like a skittish compass needle—to her, to Dr. Weber, to Petra—before settling on Seth.

"Look at them," Jolie said. "Not a scratch, not on any of them!"

"Lieutenant!" Brock barked. "That's an order."

A black vine dropped down between Anaya and Lieutenant Jolie, dangling about three feet off the ground. With a gasp, Anaya stumbled away. In a single motion, the vine flexed and looped itself around Jolie's neck. Her pistol clattered to the rock as both hands flew up to claw at the vine. With a sickening creak, the vine tightened, and lifted Jolie right off the ground.

Brock ran to grab her, but she was already out of reach, hoisted into the trees. He pulled his pistol, tried to take aim, and fired some shots up into the vines. Higher, more vines curled around Jolie, almost cocooning her.

Helplessly, Anaya watched as Jolie swung, kicking, and then was still. Brock swore and lowered his gun. The gas mask clattered down through the vines and landed at Anaya's feet.

PETRA COULDN'T TEAR her eyes away from Jolie, just dangling there. She felt like she'd been electrocuted. Her mind blared like a car alarm that wouldn't shut up. Those vines. They were psychotic. They could bring down a helicopter. They could strangle all of them.

Her eyes darted. Her world had gone soundless. She saw Brock putting on the fallen gas mask, then snatch up her pistol and slap it into Dr. Weber's hand, barking instructions. She saw Seth pick up the chain saw.

For a moment, she felt paralyzed—just like that day on the school field.

She forced air into her lungs and grabbed the shovel. She would not freeze this time.

"Come on!" she shouted to the others, and led the way toward the lake, banging the shovel ahead of her, blazing a safe path for everyone.

"Petra! Stop!"

It was Brock, shouting orders.

She kept going. They had to move. They couldn't stay still or those vines would come down for all of them.

The ground was getting squishy. Smelled like rotten eggs. Was the forest getting darker? She had the strangest feeling she was hurrying toward night.

A heavy hand fell on her shoulder, and Brock wrenched her around and snatched the shovel from her hands.

"You stay behind me!" he said sharply.

"We can't go any farther anyway," she said.

"What?"

"Look." She pointed at the solid wall of darkness, not twenty paces ahead of them.

"Black grass," Anaya said behind her.

With the shovel, Brock tested the ground right up to the wall. Petra had never seen it so tall, or the stalks growing so close together. Hardly any light came through the gaps. Not even wide enough to slip your hand through without getting slashed to pieces by the wicked thorns.

"We must be close to the marsh," Anaya said, pointing at the mud squelching around her sneakers.

"Stinks!" Petra said.

"Hydrogen sulfide," said Dr. Weber, lifting her mask away from her face for a sniff.

Brock walked along the wall several paces and squinted into the distance. "It just keeps going and going," he muttered. "It's like a stockade."

"Keeping us out," Seth said.

"Not for long," Brock said. "Chain saw."

Seth handed it over. Petra bet she was better with the saw than Brock, but she held her tongue. He fired it up, and got to work.

These were the thickest stalks Petra had seen yet. Brock had to lean into each one before the blade bit. The first stalk fell like a skinny tree. When he'd cut down a few more, Petra got busy, clearing the stalks out of the way. Trying not to get her hands shredded.

After half an hour, Brock had only made a narrow notch into the wall, just wide enough for him to keep working. Judging by the darkness in front of him, Petra figured there was still a ways to go.

"Blade's getting dull," he said over his shoulder, his masked face drenched with sweat.

Not long after that, the chain saw began to cough. Petra's heart sank. Running out of gas. A couple more minutes and the chain saw sputtered and died.

"Any more fuel?" asked Dr. Weber.

"Back in the helicopter," Brock said, pulling out his knife.

Crouched down, he began sawing away, grunting with the effort.

"This is going to take forever," Anaya whispered anxiously to Petra.

Seth pulled off his hoodie. He rolled back both sleeves and started unwinding the gauze.

"Seth," said Dr. Weber quietly. "This isn't a good idea."

"Secret's out now anyway," said Seth. He pulled off the last bit of tape.

Petra stared in wonder. From the outer edge of his arms, every inch or so, jutted short black quills. And growing from either side of the quills were feathery barbs. They didn't look soft and downy like bird feathers. They had an almost metallic sheen.

"Mind if I try?" Seth said to Brock.

The captain looked back in annoyance, then stood tall in surprise.

Seth spread both arms and gave them a shake, so the barbs flared. Petra gasped: It wasn't just that the feathers looked much fuller now, it was their color. They seemed to explode with deep greens and purples, more amazing than a peacock's. They were so unusual, so startling, the sight raised the hair on the back of her neck. And she saw now how very sharp the edges of those barbs were.

She felt a bit afraid of Seth. Afraid of herself, too. She saw Brock tighten his grip on his knife.

"I think I can cut through it faster," Seth told him.

Warily Brock stepped out of the notch, and Seth went in. Petra watched Seth fold his right arm close to his chest, then slash out. The tips of his feathers cut low across the black grass with a sound like a knife cleaving watermelon. Two more swipes and Seth called out, "Timber!" and turned to the side as two stalks of black grass toppled.

"Whoa," Anaya said softly.

Using both arms now, Seth slashed down more grass. It was all Petra and the others could do to drag the stalks out of the way fast enough, so he could keep working.

Light was starting to show through the gaps.

"Almost there," Seth said over his shoulder.

With five more ferocious strokes, the last stalks fell forward, opening a narrow corridor in the wall.

Petra stepped through. The ground disappeared quickly into a dark marshy lake. The water smelled so bad, it had to be stagnant. As far as she could see, the lake was encircled by the same high stockade of black grass. No wonder Mr. Riggs had said he was trapped.

Overhead, a freakish canopy of vines had grown out from the trees, blotting out the sky. She spotted the hole they'd burned earlier. Afternoon sunlight shafted down through the gloomy twilight, angled straight toward a small island in the middle of the lake.

It was a startling green because there was grass.

Real grass.

It felt like so long since Petra had seen so much of it! It grew among the shrubs and rocks and the snapped stalks of black grass—which was no longer black but a blotchy, sickly yellow. Dead. That stuff really was dead!

And on the shoreline stood a man.

"Dad!" Anaya yelled, waving her arm high. "Dad!"

He was too far away to see clearly, or hear. Only a few words wafted across to them.

". . . the water!"

"Where's his boat?" Brock asked.

Petra pointed. "There."

Out in the middle of the lake was an overturned canoe. Its green hull was low in the water, half-hidden by a cluster of water lilies. She knew Mr. Riggs was an excellent canoeist. Something terrible must've happened for the boat to flip.

"We need to watch out for those vines," said Dr. Weber, her head tilted back.

"We need to get the canoe!" Anaya said, taking off her shoes.

"Whoa, hold on!" said Brock. "Why hasn't your dad swum out to get it?"

"I don't know," Anaya said impatiently. "Maybe he's injured!"

". . . in the water!" Mr. Riggs was shouting.

"Anaya, stop!" Seth said. "He's telling us something about the water!"

"How else do we get the boat?"

Seth cupped his hands and shouted out, "What's wrong with the water?"

Petra walked closer. Despite its stench and its murky color, there was something about the water that pulled her. She felt the same electric prickle of excitement she had the day of the big rain. Muddy water squelched over the top of her shoes, and soaked into her socks.

"I can swim out," she said, but no one was listening.

"We need a boat!" she heard Anaya saying to Brock. "And I'm pretty sure you didn't bring one!"

"We had an inflatable raft in the copter," he retorted angrily. "We've lost a ton of things, all right?"

"Brock," said Dr. Weber, "there's a lot of movement up there with the vines. . . ."

"I can get it," Petra said, more loudly.

Anaya looked at her like she'd gone crazy. "What?"

Petra dipped her hand into the water, and held it up. She couldn't stop herself smiling. "No reaction. I'm not allergic."

"You sure, Petra?" asked Dr. Weber.

From the island came Mr. Riggs's voice, all the words washed away except ". . . water lilies!"

Petra kicked off her shoes, giddy with anticipation. The whole lake was safe! She didn't know how or why, and she didn't care.

"Petra, hold on," said Anaya, staring intently out into the lake, "those water lilies—"

"You want the canoe, I'll get the canoe," she said, and before anyone could stop her, she dived in.

BREATHLESSLY SETH WAITED for her to surface. Ripples from Petra's body spread out across the dark water, rocking the water lilies near the shore.

"Why isn't she coming up?" he said.

Brock cursed under his breath.

"The water lilies are moving," Anaya said.

Seth looked. She was right. They weren't just bobbing from the ripples, they were drifting toward them, twirling prettily, like they wanted to show off their cones of purple flowers. Their black leaves were very large. They reminded Seth of a manta ray's wings.

"I've seen these before," Anaya said.

"Where?" asked Dr. Weber.

"Dad's lab. They're cryptogenic."

"Fantastic," grumbled Brock.

Seth looked worriedly at the water lilies gathering around the overturned canoe.

"Petra should've come up by now."

Four lilies had drifted within fifteen feet of the shore. With a faint creak, one of the purple flower cones lifted slowly into the air at the end of a long black stem. To Seth, it was like watching a strange swan gracefully raise its head.

A rustling sound overhead snapped his gaze high. From the high canopy, vines uncoiled toward them.

"Look out!" he shouted.

One slapped against his shoulder, snaking under his arm. He slashed out with his feathers and severed it. A second vine tightened around his ankle, and Seth whirled and sliced through it before it could jerk him off his feet.

Wildly he looked around at all the dangling, writhing vines. He spread his arms, and felt his feathers flare to their full length, and it was a *very* good feeling. The small feathers were magnificent, their tips sharp as serrated knives. Never had he felt more powerful. With both arms, he scythed everything in his path, sending twitching tendrils flying.

He glimpsed Dr. Weber get snared around ankle and arm, and hoisted up into the air. Anaya crouched low and jumped after her—and Seth had never seen such a jump. She went straight up and grabbed Dr. Weber around the waist. The extra weight dragged them both down, low enough so that Seth could slice through the vine around the doctor's ankle. When she tumbled to the ground with Anaya, he slashed away the final vine around her arm.

"Stay near me!" he shouted out, because he'd cleared away all the vines near him. He turned in a slow circle, looking up, waiting for anything new that might come.

He saw Brock sawing through a vine coiled around his leg. Once free, the captain hurried toward him.

From the water, Seth heard a strange creaking noise and saw that there were even more lilies near the shoreline now—and all of their flowered heads had lifted high, glittering with sharp seeds. They didn't look like swans anymore. They looked like cobras, swaying, ready to strike.

A musical twittering filled the air, and he looked around for birds. Then he realized the sound was coming from the water lilies. A cone-shaped head arched on its slender neck, then recoiled with a chirp. Something sharp and wet hit him in the cheek. His hand flew up, and he pulled a pointy, goo-covered seed out of his skin.

"They're spitting seeds!" he cried.

Another chirp, and at the same moment, a seed smacked against his jeans and started smoking as it ate through the fabric. Acid! He didn't feel any burning on his cheek, so he hoped he was immune to this stuff, too. But Brock and Dr. Weber . . .

"Get down!" he said, and threw himself to the ground so his

body shielded Dr. Weber. She needed protection. He couldn't bear the idea of her getting hurt.

Brock's gas mask had been hit, and the acid was sizzling its way through the faceplate. He pulled the mask off hurriedly, and a second seed hit him in the neck, and a third in the stomach. He took out his gun and started firing into the water lilies. They returned fire even faster.

Two vines plunged down and swept Brock up. Seth ran to him but was too late. Shouting, struggling, Brock was whipped high into the air. He fired with his gun, to no effect, and then pulled his knife, slashing furiously.

On the opposite shore of the lake, Seth saw a shimmer of movement. Near the waterline, the ground trembled. A crack opened in the earth, and parted, revealing the slick purple flesh of the biggest pit plant he'd ever seen. Wider and wider its hideous lips spread. Black vines grew like a single tree up from the nearby earth, and they were all trembling now, as if sending signals along their length, higher and higher into the canopy, to where Captain Brock was snared.

Slowly the vines encircling Brock began to shunt him in the direction of the pit plant, and Seth realized what was about to happen.

"Brock!" he shouted. "They're going to—"

At that exact moment, Brock cut himself free. Seth breathed a sigh of relief as the captain plunged down, and cannonballed into the water. But when he resurfaced, he was hollering and flailing. "It burns!" His eyes were shut, and he was grinding a fist into his eye sockets.

Water lilies converged on him.

"Look out!" Seth shouted, and everyone else joined in, trying to warn him.

But Brock probably didn't even see the plants coming. They reared their flowered heads and let rip with their seeds at point-blank range. Brock tried to cover his head with his arms but it was no good. Eventually his arms fell limp and his head lolled back, and his entire body slipped below the black surface.

CHAPTER EIGHTEEN

THE MOMENT PETRA SLID underwater, everything changed.

All those years she couldn't swim—they just poured away. She was in and under and moving through the dark, silky water. Her sight was blurry. Light slanted down between the water lilies floating overhead. The feel of the water against her face! It was like she was eleven years old, before everything went wrong. She didn't want to surface.

She pulled again, and again, toward the tipped canoe. She felt her tiny tail twitch, as if it wanted to help steer. Were things getting clearer? Everything had been so murky at first, but now, if she really concentrated, things were more in focus.

It was a strange underwater forest. The water lily stems were like skinny tree trunks, rising from the pond's bottom. Beneath the finely veined lily pads—she could see this now—sprouted all sorts of little wavy tendrils, and some of them were wrapped around dead fish and frogs, a squirrel, and even, off to her right, what looked like a decomposing raccoon. She felt amazingly calm: this is just what these plants did. They ate things.

How long had she been under? It felt like a long time, but she didn't need a breath yet.

Up ahead was the long shadow of the capsized canoe. Below, on the lake bed, were backpacks and gear that must have fallen out when it tipped. She surfaced inside the upside-down boat, and took a breath of the dank trapped air. Light slanted through bullet-sized holes in the hull.

Treading water, Petra blinked hard. It took several tries before her eyes refocused after being underwater—and when they did, she stifled a yell.

Bobbing at the far end of the canoe was the bloated corpse of a man. A water lily grew from his gaping mouth. Even in her terror she recognized the strange bat-shaped leaves—the same as the tiny plant that had grown in her bottle of rainwater. But that baby plant hadn't had a big cone of purple flowers that now turned toward her with a menacing creak, bristling with sharp seeds.

Instinct took over. Her hands shot out, grabbed the lily's stem, and snapped it. Almost at once, the flower's head curled and dipped lifelessly into the water.

With her feet, Petra pushed the dead body outside the canoe. She heard shouting, and put her eye to one of the holes in the side. All around the canoe were lilies with their flowered heads raised. One reared back, and she heard a hail-like clatter against the hull.

These things shot seeds! A new ray of light pierced the gloom as another tiny hole slowly opened in the boat's side. She touched the still-hissing rim and rubbed the sticky goo between her fingers. Must be acid—but she felt no burning.

Slowly she rotated the canoe so she was looking back to shore. Her breath snagged. It was total mayhem. Vines were dropping from the sky, trying to snare Anaya and the others. And there was a cluster of water lilies, their flowered heads lifted high and recoiling as they pumped out seeds. Dr. Weber was being lifted into the air—and Anaya jumped to grab her. Petra had never seen anyone jump so high from standing!

As fast as she could, Petra started swimming the canoe back to shore. Water lilies brushed past; seeds hailed against the hull. She thought she heard a big splash from back out in the lake, and shouting. She kept going.

When she was near the shore, she gave the canoe a good shove to send it the rest of the way. Then she dived underwater and swam hard for land. This time when she opened her eyes, it went from blurry to clear in seconds. Her eyes ached a bit, and she got the sense she was actually *shrinking* her pupils, changing the entire *shape* of her eyes in their sockets.

She saw the cluster of water lilies that were firing at everyone. She saw the long stems that tethered these plants to the lakebed. She grabbed the nearest one and yanked. It was thick, and really anchored in the mud. With both hands she pulled, and this time the stem tore loose. She went to the next lily, and the next, ripping. Their flowered heads sank uselessly into the water.

When she'd torn out the last stem, she surfaced and waded into the shallows. Water and muck streamed off her like some swamp monster, but she'd never felt so exultant.

"I swam!" she cried out, unable to hide her joy. Then she grabbed the canoe and flipped it right side up. "Come on!" she shouted to the others. "Get in!"

ANAYA CROUCHED LOW, her face pressed against the canoe's slimy bottom. There wasn't space to lie completely flat, but she and Seth and Dr. Weber all squished themselves as small as possible. Underwater, Petra was ferrying them across the lake to the island.

Toward Dad.

Anaya stayed very still and quiet, watching water leak through the small holes in the hull. Dr. Weber still had her gas mask on, although Anaya had noticed that the sleeping gas seemed much weaker by the lake. Or maybe its smell was just overpowered by the rotten-egg stench of the water itself.

Quite a puddle had formed at the canoe's bottom. Anaya hoped they were close, but she didn't dare lift her head to check, in case the lilies started firing again. Dr. Weber had been hit twice in the legs. There wasn't time to do anything to help her right now. Anaya just wanted to get to Dad. She hadn't heard his voice in a while, and was feeling even more anxious.

Something landed on her back, and uncurled toward her arm. She struck it off with her hand and lifted her head to look. Vines dangled down all around them. Most were very still as the canoe glided past, but a few were now questing after the boat—including the one she'd just brushed off.

It came curling back toward her like a hook.

"Seth!" she hissed.

In the canoe's middle section, Seth raised himself up and slashed out with his feathered arm. The severed vine fell into the water. More came. She heard the chirp of lily seeds whistling past.

"Stay down!" she said to Dr. Weber, who was crouched at the bow.

Vines writhed all around them now, and Seth lunged to and fro, cutting them down. The canoe rocked violently, and Anaya worried they'd tip. She gave a yelp of surprise as the boat's stern lifted right out of the water, followed by the bow.

Peering over the side, she saw that vines had encircled the canoe and were lifting the entire boat toward the seething canopy. Seth pulled his arm back to strike the vine holding the stern.

"Wait!" cried Anaya, but too late.

Seth sliced through, and the stern plummeted. Anaya tumbled backward into the air, along with Seth and Dr. Weber, still wearing her gas mask. In those few seconds, she saw the lake, and Petra treading water and staring up at them in shock, and a cluster of drifting water lilies, and the shore of the small island—

Dad gazing up at them—and the only encouraging thing was that they were close to the island.

With a great splash, she hit water and went under. She spluttered up and started swimming for shore. Seth thrashed beside her, his feathered arms making him clumsy. Spluttering, Dr. Weber tried to drag off her gas mask, which was filling with water. Anaya came closer and fumbled the straps loose for her, and the doctor ripped the mask off, gasping. Anaya made a grab for the mask, but it was already sinking, and the seeds were flying everywhere, and they needed to get to land. She swam alongside Dr. Weber, trying to shield her.

Seeds stung her head and shoulder, and she kept her face low. Suddenly there was a water lily right in front of them, rearing, ready to shoot. Without warning, the whole plant got dragged underwater, and Petra surfaced in its place, standing, the lily's snapped roots hanging from her clenched fist.

"Come on!" Petra yelled, grabbing Dr. Weber by the hand and pulling her into the shallows.

Anaya staggered to her feet and slogged the rest of the way to shore. Straight ahead was Dad, urgently waving them in.

"Come away from the water! They're attracted by sound and movement."

He was completely caked in dirt, his hair a filthy, matted mess. A damp cloth was tied around his mouth and nose, and what she saw of his face looked red and blistered, as did his hands. But it was *Dad,* and Anaya felt such a flood of relief and joy. She ran and threw her arms around him.

Instead of hugging her back, her father started smearing dirt on her hair and face.

"What're you doing?" she cried.

"All over!" Dad shouted to the others, looking crazed. "It keeps the vines away. It's toxic to them! On your clothes, too, yep, and don't forget your shoes, they love ankles."

Even as he spoke, vines came curling down from overhead. Anaya didn't hesitate. She scooped up some dirt and plastered it over her upper body. When a snaky black tendril touched her dirty shoulder, it recoiled as if scorched.

They were all covering themselves as fast as they could, but the vines were quicker. Anaya saw one slyly wrapping around Petra's leg.

"Petra, look out!"

"Got it!" said Seth. He flared the feathers on his right arm, and severed the vine with one quick blow.

"Whoa!" said Dad, staring at Seth and his barbed arms.

"Hi, Mr. Riggs," Seth said.

And it suddenly struck Anaya how much her father didn't know. About the plants being invasive species from another planet. About his own daughter being *half* cryptogen.

Seth stood guard and slashed more vines while she and the others frantically covered themselves with dirt. Dad made sure

Seth was caked, back and front. A few vines hovered around Dad, darting at him like hissing snakes, but never quite touching.

Covered in dirt, Anaya looked around nervously. The vines nosed around them all for a bit and then, as one, pulled back up into the high canopy, where she could see their canoe, cocooned by vines.

"This way," Dad said, leading them quickly through the splintered stalks of black grass.

"It really is dead!" Anaya said, kicking at the stubble. It was incredibly satisfying to see it like this.

Dad brought them to a big boulder. On one side was a very small cave, maybe an old animal burrow that Dad had enlarged into a shelter just big enough for a single body. Inside, Anaya saw a backpack and some trail snacks and bottles of water.

"Are you okay?" Dad asked, looking at her closely, then at Seth and Petra. "No seeds, you're sure?" He frowned. "The water didn't burn you guys at all."

Anaya shook her head. "We're fine, but Dr. Weber . . ."

Her father grabbed the bottle from his shelter and turned to the doctor.

"Tilt your head back," he told her. "I'll sluice your eyes."

Dr. Weber's skin had erupted in a red rash from the lake water, and her eyes were nearly swollen shut.

"Thanks," she said tightly.

"Happened to me, too," Anaya's father told her. "I was in the water a lot longer. It's a severe reaction, but it gets better. I was nearly blind for a couple of hours. Who are you, by the way?"

"Dr. Stephanie Weber, Canadian Intelligence."

"What's changed the water?" Petra asked. "Is it those lily plants?"

Anaya's father nodded. "I noticed the same thing in the lab. They change the acidity of the water. They also seem to exhale methane. That's the rotten-egg smell." He looked at Dr. Weber. "Did you get hit with any seeds?"

"My leg."

"We need to get them out fast."

Anaya helped Dr. Weber pull up the leg of her acid-scorched trousers. In her calf were two red welts where seeds had burned themselves into her flesh. Only their sharp tips jutted out.

"Anaya, can you do it?" Dad asked. "My fingers are still a bit swollen. You might have to dig in a bit."

"Sorry," she said to Dr. Weber in advance, and gouged out one seed, then another, with her fingernails.

"Thanks, Anaya," said Dr. Weber, wincing.

"They germinate really fast," Dad said, and lowered his bandanna.

Anaya sucked in her breath. On his neck was a raised welt with a small black tendril curling out of it. Anaya felt a squeeze of horror. One of those plants was *growing* out of him.

"Oh my gosh, Dad . . ."

"I couldn't get the seed out. Then it sprouted. I've torn it off a few times, but it just grows back."

"Let me have a look," said Dr. Weber, peering with her swollen eyes. She prodded gently around the wound with her fingers. "It's very deep. It needs to be cut out."

"Can you do it?" Anaya asked.

"It's too close to the artery. A surgeon needs to do it."

Anaya scratched at her own neck, feeling a sympathetic itchiness.

"We'll worry about that later," Dad said, tying the bandanna back over his mouth and nose. "Here, you'll want to do the same," he said, handing Dr. Weber a strip of ripped T-shirt, sluiced with water.

"The sleeping gas from the vines, I know," the doctor said, tying it around her face.

"It was way worse in the forest," Anaya said, sniffing the air.

"I think the breeze helps clear it away," Dad said. "You guys aren't affected?" he asked, looking at Anaya.

"No," she said, and saw his puzzlement. But she wanted to put off telling him as long as possible.

"Okay," he said. "I saw your helicopter. Who else was on it?"

"Two pilots," she told him. "They died in the crash. And there were two military officers. The vines got Jolie, and . . ."

She didn't need to say any more. Her father must have seen what happened to Brock.

"Can we expect a cavalry?" Dad asked Dr. Weber.

"The captain said they might send a rescue team before night-fall. Maybe."

"Dad," Anaya asked, "what happened to you? Is Amit—"

"Dead," said Petra. "He was under the canoe."

Anaya saw Dad nod and take a breath. "When we got here yesterday morning, that wall of black grass wasn't nearly so high or thick. Only a few vines crisscrossed overhead. We took the canoe out. Halfway across we stopped to take a closer look at the lilies. I was pretty sure they were the same ones I had growing in the lab. They clustered around the boat and started shooting. I got hit a few times, but Amit got the worst of it. When he fell out, the canoe tipped and everything went in, except the back-pack I was wearing. The water got in my eyes, and I could barely see. Amit went under before I could reach him."

"So awful," Anaya said, scratching again at her neck. She must've gotten a mosquito bite.

"I made it to the island," Dad continued. "My skin was seared, and both my eyes were swollen shut. But after a few hours, my vision started to come back."

He gestured across the lake to the stockade.

"By then the wall was even thicker, and more vines were weaving over the lake."

"Incredible," murmured Dr. Weber. "They really are hiding it."

"They started coming for me then, and that's when I found out they didn't like the soil. I also figured out they were all grow-ing from one place."

He pointed across the lake to a marshy spot on the shoreline. A colossal tangle of vines, the width of a car, grew straight up, higher than the black grass, and into the trees behind it.

"It's a monster pit plant over there," Seth said. "I saw it open when the vines caught Brock. They were carrying him over to it. They were going to dump him right in."

"Pit plant," Anaya's father said. "That's a good name for them. Before we got to the lake, Amit and I almost fell into one."

Anaya could see Dad studying Seth's feathers. Worriedly she glanced down at her clawed toes sticking through her ripped socks, and tried to pull them back in, but they were too long now. When she lifted her eyes, her father's gaze met hers.

He must know, she thought.

"Dad," she said helplessly.

"It's okay," he said, and as he reached for her, she started to cry.

It was not okay. How could it ever be okay? She was not what she used to be—and never had been. From the moment of her birth, she'd been something different, and how could her father possibly accept her? But he held her tightly as her shoulders shook, and said nice things into her ear, some of the same things he'd said when she was little and sobbing like this.

Gently she pulled away and took a big breath. She felt bad for Petra and Seth, not having anyone to blubber all over. Seth was staring at his hands, scratching at a knuckle.

Dad looked at Dr. Weber and said, "What can you tell me?"

She said, "You already knew the plants were cryptogenic, yes?"

262

"Yes."

Anaya gaped. "You did? And you didn't tell me or Mom!"

"Mom knew. I didn't want to terrify you." To Dr. Weber, he said, "Keep going, please."

Anaya was happy to let Dr. Weber tell it. About how only half of their DNA was human, about how they were changing. The doctor was calm and thorough, and made it sound scientific, and somehow less personal. When, really, what could be *more* personal than the fact that your daughter was half cryptogen and you weren't even the father?

Anaya watched Dad most carefully during this last part, dreading how he'd react. Would something die in his eyes when he next looked at her? Would he be frightened of her? He listened to all of it, and then nodded and said, "Okay." He scratched at his filthy hair and squinted up at the writhing mass of vines overhead. "This is a lot." He tried to grin. "Quite a day." He took her hands in his. "As far as I'm concerned, not one thing has changed. You're my daughter. That will never stop."

She smiled, grateful and so relieved, and tried hard not to start crying all over again. She scratched at her neck. The other side was itchy now, too. There must be tons of mosquitoes here.

"We have a lot to talk about," Dad said. "But right now we need to get this soil off the island. It works!"

"It really kills the plants?" she asked.

"You're sure?" said Dr. Weber.

"I'll show you." He led them away from his makeshift shelter.

Anaya glanced overhead to check on the vines, still coiling over one another like restless snakes. A few dropped down to nose around her head, then retreated hastily.

"I didn't know how long I'd be here," Dad said, "so I thought I better make the time count. When the vines were dropping down for me, I managed to snap a few of the tendrils and replant them." He came to a stop and pointed. "Here."

In admiration, Anaya looked at the small patch of cleared earth that her father had turned into a test plot. How many people, with their lives at risk, would have the discipline and courage to run a science experiment?

"I planted three tendrils. I even snared a young water lily that hadn't developed its flower head yet. I planted that, too."

Anaya studied the wizened plants. They all sagged, their leaves limp and yellow against the earth.

"Whatever's in this soil, it's a potent toxin to the plants," Dad said.

"Any theories what it is, exactly?" Dr. Weber asked.

"A bacterium. But we won't know what until we isolate it in a lab."

"Why here?" Seth asked. "Why's this soil special?"

"You sometimes get these rare fungal ecosystems in isolated places. Like the South American rain forest. Totally unique bacteria. Same thing here. If we can isolate it, and culture it, we might have a way to kill these rotters on a mass scale."

Rotters. Anaya couldn't help grinning. She felt a strengthening pulse of excitement and hope. A way of killing all the plants. *Possible.*

"How long did it take?" Seth pointed at the withered plants in the plot. "For them to die."

"Within an hour."

Anaya scratched at her neck, and then noticed that Seth was scratching at his hand. She glanced over at Petra, who was rubbing her cheek. Beneath the dirt on her friend's face, Anaya saw a red patch of skin.

"The soil," she breathed.

Petra looked over at her. "What?"

"We're allergic to it, too!"

"Let me see," said Dr. Weber, peering at her neck, then at Petra and Seth. "I think you're right. Is it very itchy?"

Seth shook his head. "Just like a mosquito bite."

"Makes sense," Anaya's father said, "since you guys have some of the same DNA as the plants."

Dr. Weber said, "The reaction looks fairly mild, but we need to keep an eye on it. If it spreads, or you have any shortness of breath, tell me."

"Shouldn't we wash the dirt off?" Petra said worriedly.

"No!" said Anaya. "Or the vines'll take us!"

She'd put up with a little itchiness to keep those things off her.

Petra pointed at the wilted plants. "It killed them! How do we know it won't kill us?"

Anaya felt a squeeze of fear around her throat. She'd gotten used to being the one who was immune to all these new dangers: the acid, the sleeping gas, the searing water. Now it turned out she was vulnerable to dirt from her own planet—just like the cryptogenic plants.

"Remember," Dr. Weber said, "you only share a small amount of the plant's DNA. Those vines can't even *touch* the dirt. You guys have very mild reactions by comparison."

"Still," said Anaya's father, "I don't like it. The sooner they can clean off the better. We need to get out of here. We've only got a couple more hours of light."

"We're not getting that canoe back," said Seth, looking at the boat snarled up in the vines.

Anaya exhaled. Without the boat, they were stranded.

"We could swim," Petra reminded them.

"I don't think Dr. Weber and I would make it," said Anaya's father. "Even if it weren't for the lilies."

"I could rip them out," Petra said.

"Too many of them," Seth said.

"Even if we did make it across," Dr. Weber said, "then what?"

"There's your boat at the dock," Petra said to Anaya's father.

"And a whole forest of vines and pit plants to get through," Anaya said.

"Well, we can't just wait around!" Petra said. "What if they don't send a rescue team? Even if they sent another helicopter, they wouldn't see us through the vines!"

She was right. Anaya stared up into the dense weave of vines.

Already the small hole they'd burned was sealing itself up. Those things were unstoppable. She traced them back to the massive pit plant on the opposite shore.

"How much soil do you think it would take to kill that big pit plant?" she asked Dad, pointing to the shore.

"I don't know. Why?"

She looked over at Petra, who was nodding with her. "That's where all the vines come from. We kill the pit plant, then all the vines die, right? If the vines die, a helicopter can see us."

"And the canoe falls down," Seth added. "Even if there's no rescue, at least we've got a boat. And no vines to capsize us."

Frowning, Dr. Weber looked across to the pit plant on the shore. "How could we even get close to that thing?"

Anaya took a breath. Exhaled. "I let it eat me."

SETH LOOKED AT her in shock, and then at Mr. Riggs, who was about to speak, but Anaya cut him off.

"I load myself up with as much soil as I can carry. I wash the dirt off myself, and let the vines grab me. They'll feed me right into the pit plant."

Despite himself, Seth agreed with her logic. The plant must be hungry; it hadn't eaten Brock. Even with all its vines collecting light and eating small animals, that enormous pit plant would need a ton of food to keep itself going.

"Absolutely not," Mr. Riggs said. "Way too risky. If anyone does it, it's me."

"Dad, it'll kill you!" Anaya said. "The acid doesn't hurt me. I go in, dump the soil, and get right out. I can jump really high now! Didn't you see me?"

"What if it seals you inside?" Mr. Riggs asked.

"I cut my way out. I'll take your knife. And I've got these." She pointed to the claws jabbing through her socked feet.

"And she won't be doing it alone," Seth said. There was no way he was letting Anaya do this by herself. He held out his spiky arms. He'd just sawed through a wall of black grass; he was pretty sure he could slash his way out of a pit plant. "I'm going with her."

Anaya turned to him, and Seth didn't think anyone had ever looked at him with such gratitude.

"Me too," said Petra.

"You guys—" Anaya began to say, but Petra cut her off.

"With three of us, that thing doesn't stand a chance."

Seth knew it was just tough talk, but they needed all the toughness they could muster right now. He looked over at Mr. Riggs. He didn't say okay, but he didn't say no, either. Seth figured he must know this might be their only way off the island.

There was no more debate. They dumped out Mr. Riggs's backpack and filled every compartment to bursting with soil. Seth took off his hoodie and knotted it into a sack, and they loaded that up, too. For good measure, all three of them crammed their pockets with more soil.

"Listen to me," Mr. Riggs said sternly. "If anything starts feeling wrong—*anything*—you cut loose, all right? Even if you don't get to the pit plant, you bail. Understand?"

"Let's wash," said Petra. "I want to get this dirt off me."

"Be careful," Dr. Weber said, and Seth noticed her eyes rested longest on him. It was a tender look. Something he'd seen plenty of times in movies, but hardly at all in real life. He felt like he'd just been given an amazing gift.

Down at the shore, he splashed water on his head.

"Keep it dirty around your neck and nose," Anaya said.

"It's so itchy, though," Petra complained.

"Yeah, but we don't want them choking us—or going up our nostrils."

"Good point," Petra agreed.

Seth kept his arms dirty, too. He needed his arms and feathers completely free so he could slash and cut. He looked at Petra and Anaya, standing beside him on the shore, hair dripping, clothes sodden. They were not the picture of likely heroes. As Anaya shrugged the bulging backpack over both shoulders, he reached for his soil-packed hoodie. Petra got to it first.

"Keep your hands free," she told him. "You're the muscle."

He felt himself blush and couldn't help smiling. The muscle.

Mr. Riggs zipped his knife and a chemical light stick into a small outer pocket of Anaya's backpack and hugged his daughter tight.

"It'll work," Anaya said, but she was trembling, and Seth didn't think it was just the cold water.

Mr. Riggs retreated. And suddenly the vines were whipping everywhere. Anaya got snared around her arms and ankles, and yanked into the air. They took Petra next, the soil-filled hoodie hugged tight to her chest, and then it was Seth's turn. Spiraling around his ankles, the vines gripped so tight he grunted in pain. They flipped him upside down and whipped him skyward. His stomach slewed as he soared up, but for one ecstatic moment it was almost like he was flying. Below, the two grown-ups were already so small! He was lifted right underneath the squirming canopy.

Different vines came and took hold of his legs, others released, and he realized he was being passed along over the lake.

In front of him, the vines were doing the same to Petra and Anaya, deftly shunting them toward the shore. The ground trembled, and then split open in a vast gash. His insides went cold. He hadn't fully appreciated how huge this thing was. From this height, he could see its wet walls, though its bottom was hidden in darkness.

"You okay?" he shouted out to the girls.

"Okay," Petra grunted back.

A few stray vines oozed past his dirty feathered arms, but backed off. One brushed his cheek but darted away when it touched the soil around his nose. He wished they would flip him right side up, but apart from that, everything was going according to plan.

On the shoreline, the pit plant trembled and began to open.

Its fleshy lips made a hissing sound as they pulled wide. The thing was so enormous.

Seth watched as the vines carried Anaya directly over the pit plant—and then dropped her. He cried out in shock. She couldn't survive that fall! But ten feet above the pit plant, Anaya bounced back, tethered by a single remaining vine around her ankle, like a bungee cord. She bounced a few more times, and only when she stopped did the vine release her.

Anaya plunged into the pit plant and disappeared. Seth swallowed. It must be deep. He wasn't looking forward to his turn. He calmed himself by going through the plan. Dump all the soil inside, and get out, cutting his way through the top if it sealed on them. They should be out of there in minutes.

He realized he wasn't moving anymore. Hanging upside down, twirling slowly from side to side, he felt suddenly light-headed and breathless. His heart stuttered. He dangled over the lake like a piece of meat on a hook.

"What's going on?" Petra called back to him.

"I don't know. Can you see anything?"

"No! It's too deep."

"What's happening?" he heard Mr. Riggs shout out from the island.

On the shore, the pit plant's lips started to constrict.

"It's closing!" Seth shouted.

It wasn't supposed to do that. But it didn't stop until the lips had mashed themselves together, sealing Anaya inside, alone.

CHAPTER NINETEEN

THE SMELL HIT ANAYA before the impact: the sickening sleep perfume, and the stench of whatever the pit plant had last eaten. She bounced off the pit plant's rubbery walls and landed beside a puddle of some gooey mess she didn't want to think about.

She scrambled up. It was like a small cave, much bigger than the last plant she'd been in. Much deeper, too. With a tight squeeze of fear, she wondered if she'd be able to jump high enough. Already the walls were glistening, trickling with eager little rivulets of acid. Even though she knew it wouldn't hurt her, there was still a primal fear about being inside the gut of a creature designed to digest her.

Where were the others?

Get to work.

Hurriedly she shrugged off her backpack, and started unzipping. It was suddenly darker, and she glanced up, hoping it was just a cloud. In dismay, she saw the lips of the plant slowly twitching closed. Why was it closing so soon? Didn't it know there was more food coming?

Hands shaking, she dumped out the soil. It looked just like ordinary dirt. For a terrifying second, she couldn't believe there was anything special about it, and what on earth was she doing here?

In the fading light, she watched, waiting for the plant to react. She'd hoped the moment the soil touched, the plant would hiss and burn—just like its acid did to human skin.

Nothing was happening.

She kicked the dirt around the bottom of the plant, and emptied her pockets. It didn't look like very much, spread out like this. She needed Petra's soil, too. What was taking both of them so long?

"Petra!" she called out through the opening. "Seth?"

Underfoot she felt a tremor. On the dirt-scattered bottom of the pit plant, a blister appeared, then burst. Black tarlike fluid oozed out.

Was this a good sign?

Anxiously she looked up to see the plant's mushy lips twitching ever closer together. If she wanted to jump out, she was running out of time.

Another boil swelled up, then a third. A swampy stink overpowered the sickly perfume. Everything about that smell signaled rot and death to Anaya. The soil must be working.

She looked back up. Still no sign of the others. She didn't want to be sealed inside alone, without Seth's razor-sharp arms. Dad had told her to cut loose if things went sideways. She'd promised. She only hoped the soil she'd brought was enough to do the job.

She flexed at the knees, ready to leap. From the slick walls of the plant, and the underside of the constricting top, long black spikes poked out, angled down, like an animal unsheathing all its claws.

"WHY DID IT close?" Petra yelled to Seth as they both dangled over the lake.

She couldn't understand it. The thing was huge; it must want more food!

Being stuck up here was not part of the plan. She winced as a vine slid across her body. It wasn't just revulsion at its touch. Suddenly she realized how easy it would be for these things to tighten like boa constrictors, and squeeze the life out of her. She remembered Jolie hanging from the trees.

This was a terrible idea.

"We need to get her out!" Seth grunted, trying to swing himself upright.

A vine nosed around Petra's soil-filled hoodie, and pushed its way into the opening—then recoiled as if scalded. The vine rustled against several others, making a sound like a snake hissing. Other vines brushed together, and the eerie whisper drifted across the canopy, in the direction of the shore. And the pit plant.

Like they were communicating.

"They know!" she cried out to Seth in alarm.

"What?"

"They know about the soil! They know what we're doing!"

She gave a cry as Seth suddenly dropped.

The vines had let go of his ankles, and he plunged headfirst. Maybe it was instinct that made him stretch his arms like they were wings. The colorful feathers spread, but they didn't slow his fall.

"Seth!" she cried, and then gasped as vines tightened across her stomach, and kept tightening.

SETH DIDN'T JUST fall. He was *flung*. Air whistled over his feathered arms, and he felt it just for a second: that little bit of lift. He had hardly any time to savor this brief hint of flight before the lake struck him.

He was under, tumbling, water smacked up his nose, roaring in his ears. Up he came, gagging. He churned his legs, blinking, trying to orient himself. There was Petra, still hanging in the vines. And there was the shore, and the monster pit plant.

He swam for it. He needed to help Anaya. He'd never been a

strong swimmer, and his feathers made him even clumsier. Something sharp stung his left cheek, then his right. Converging on him from both sides were clusters of water lilies, their black-swan heads arched high.

He ducked his head below the surface, feeling the seeds strike his arms. Even underwater the seeds hit him, coming dangerously close to his eyes. When he came up for air, he was not nearly as close to the shore as he'd hoped.

And blocking his way was a raft of lilies, their raised purple heads glinting with sharp seeds.

ANAYA KNEW IF she jumped, she'd impale herself on the spikes.

The other pit plant hadn't done this. Was this one special? Or maybe this was its last defense when dying? Whichever it was, she was pretty sure those spikes were getting longer. Either that or the plant walls were constricting. With a wheezing wet smack, the lips of the plant mashed together and Anaya was plunged into darkness.

Oh no. No, no, no.

Blind, patting the ground, Anaya found her knife and light stick. She bent the tube till she heard a crack. Faintly it began to glow, filling the inside of the plant with a ghoulish radiance. She almost wished she were back in darkness. From every angle, spikes slowly converged on her, aimed at her legs, her chest, her face.

Dad's knife was in her hand. Beneath her feet, the pit plant trembled and bulged more violently, and she staggered into a spike. She cried out as it jabbed her shoulder. She grabbed it and tried to snap it. It was bendy and surprisingly strong. She didn't stop pushing until she felt the spike snap like a broken branch. That took way too long. On the next spike she used the knife, sawing a cut so she could snap it faster.

Even so, she wouldn't be able to cut them all down. There were too many, all of them inching closer.

If this thing was dying, she needed it to die faster.

She remembered the pit plant back home in her driveway. The main vine sprouting from the bottom. That would be about where she was standing, right now. Under her feet grew the massive vine that split into thousands of smaller ones spreading over the lake.

And she also remembered how, in her driveway, all the vines on the house had started to wither, right after she severed the main one. She might not be able to kill the pit plant, but if she could sever its central vine, maybe she could kill the ones growing over the lake. She could clear the way for the others.

She kicked at the floor with her clawed toes, right foot, left foot, piercing the plant's thick flesh. It felt good to gouge out big wet chunks. Spikes pricked the top of her head, and she fell to her knees, using Dad's knife to cut deeper. She stabbed down until she felt soil against her knuckles. She'd broken through!

Digging around with her hands, she found the hard, gnarled vine, thick as the root of a great tree. With the knife's serrated edge, she started sawing. It was so thick.

She knew it wouldn't be long before the spikes impaled her.

THE THICK CORD of vines squeezed so tightly around Petra's torso she worried her ribs would crack.

She could see Seth down there, swimming crazily toward shore, and all those lilies closing in, and she needed to help him. Her left arm was pinned uselessly to her side, but her right was still free, and with her hand she tried to tear the vines loose. A few ripped off, but were quickly replaced by others. They were so strong.

"Get off!" she growled.

Dangling right over her mouth was a sprig of those dark berries. Before she could check herself, she gobbled them up. Thick juice exploded against her tongue—such a weird, exhilarating taste—and she felt a surge of strength.

She fumbled with the knotted opening of the hoodie and reached inside for the soil. A vine looped around her forearm and yanked her hand out before she got any.

"No, you don't," she grunted.

Swift tendrils slid between her fingers, tightening, but she pulled free. The hoodie shook, and a bit of soil spilled out onto the vines. Petra felt them flinch, and loosen.

"Yeah! That sucks, doesn't it?"

She plunged her hand deep into the soil, then smeared it onto the vines that ensnared her. Swiftly they started to uncoil. She flung another handful onto the vines around her legs. They, too, sprang away.

Suddenly she was free—

And falling. Clutching the hoodie to her chest, she closed her eyes tight. As she plunged, panic surged through her, but then she was underwater, and her fear was washed away by joy. She was back in her element. Eyes wide, her vision sharpened.

In the distance, she saw Seth's churning legs. She knotted the hoodie tight around her waist and propelled herself through the water. Passing a floating sock, she glanced down to see gear from the tipped canoe scattered across the lakebed. An open backpack, a baseball cap. A pair of sunglasses.

She dived down, snatched them up. As she neared Seth, she saw him duck his head below the surface, trying to protect his eyes with his hands. Seeds cut skinny lines through the water.

Petra put the sunglasses on. To the left and right, she snapped and ripped as many lily stems as she could. So many of them. A whole jungle! Seeds stabbed and raked at her own skin. One ricocheted off her sunglasses.

She surfaced right in front of Seth, who reared back in shock.

"Geez!" he shouted.

"Cover your eyes!" she said, and pushed his head back under.

They were almost completely surrounded by lilies now. Seeds pelted her face and pinged off her sunglasses. Treading water, she reached into the sodden hoodie and closed her hand around the mud inside. She flung it over the lilies, one fistful after another.

The plants recoiled, their swan heads drooping. Even as they fell back, though, new ones took their place. Petra threw a last muddy handful into the thick raft blocking their way to shore.

Seth came up to gasp some air, and Petra said, "Stay down and follow me. Shield your eyes."

Underwater, Petra ripped frantically at the plants' stems, trying to clear a path through them. Seeds zipped through the water. She would've been blinded so many times if not for the sunglasses.

The lake bottom was rising to meet them. They'd be able to stand soon. Seth patted her ankle, and she swirled back to him. He pointed up. He needed air—she'd forgotten about air. She felt like she could hold her breath forever. Despite all her ripping, the water's surface was still darkened by water lilies. They'd have to make a run for shore.

She stood, head and shoulders above the water. Immediately a lily turned to open fire. It was pure instinct: Petra's hand shot out and grabbed the plant's vicious head. She twisted it away from her, even as it spat out seeds.

Those seeds pelted a nearby lily, ripping holes in its leaves, and severing its skinny neck. The flowered head plopped life-lessly into the water.

Petra thought, *This could work.*

Her own skin bristled with seeds now, but she didn't care. She grabbed another lily head from behind. She felt it trying to turn on her, but she held tight, and spun around, spraying its seeds at the other plants. Severed heads hit the water.

Beside her, Seth surfaced, gasping, and stared at her in amazement as she machine-gunned more lilies.

She paused to push the soaked hoodie into his hands.

Seth understood. He covered his head with it, protecting his eyes. The last of the muddy soil dripped down over him.

Petra gave him a push in the right direction. "Go! Get Anaya out!"

SETH STAGGERED TOWARD shore, pelted by seeds.

Even before his feet touched land, the vines came for him. He'd smeared the muddy hoodie over as much of his body as he could, before tying it around his waist. His head was pretty dirt-streaked, his arms, too, but he wasn't sure about the rest of him. He could feel his skin starting to itch, but that was the least of his worries.

He flared his feathers and slashed at the vines trying to snag him. The vines were more insistent than ever now, like they were protecting something to the death. A thick vine lashed him across the chest so hard it knocked him down.

Panting, he staggered up, and when the vine whipped back for him, he was ready. He sliced it in two. The severed end flopped around on the ground, trying to trip him up. He couldn't even *see* the pit plant anymore, there were so many vines in front of it. He had to get Anaya out—she'd been in there too long.

Every step took forever.

Vines coiled down, encircling him. Swirling and slashing, he lost all sense of direction.

"Petra!" he shouted with rising panic. "I can't see!"

From his left came a barrage of familiar chirps, and a whole bunch of severed vines fell to the ground. There was Petra in her sunglasses, gripping a water lily she'd dragged up from the water, firing seeds to slice down another swath of vines.

"That way!" she said, nodding him in the right direction.

"Petra, look out!" he cried.

All her soil was washed off now, and the vines snatched her off her feet. Seth rushed to her but she was just out of reach. He saw Petra aim the lily's spitting head and clip through the vines. She fell back down, nearly knocking Seth over.

"Stay beside me," he told her.

Together, they advanced through the vines, him slashing, her firing until her lily ran out of seeds.

"Empty," Petra said, tossing the spent plant to the ground.

Up ahead, the vines thinned. Finally he could see the pit plant. "Almost there!" he shouted. He wasn't sure how much longer his strength would last. He was slicing forward through vines, and trying to protect Petra, too. He tore off his hoodie and passed it to her. That would keep some of the vines off her.

With a final push, he was right on top of the pit plant. He fell to his knees, slashing at the fleshy lips. They parted into a thin, hideous smirk. Acid welled up and burned his jeans. From within wafted the horrific stench of dead things.

"Help me open it up!" he said to Petra.

He sank his fingers into the gash and, with Petra, pulled the lips apart several more inches. More vines slithered down on them, but they seemed weirdly sluggish, and he quickly severed them.

"Anaya!" he shouted.

At the bottom of the pit plant, he saw her crumpled motionless inside a cage of interlocking spikes.

"Oh my God," Petra gasped. "Is she—"

Then Anaya turned her head and squinted up at them.

Seth let out a shout of surprise and relief.

"I cut through it!" Anaya yelled, shaking the knife in her filthy hand. "Are the vines dying?"

"I don't know!" he yelled back. "We need to get you out! I'll cut off the top!"

"No, wait! It'll fall on me! There's spikes in it!"

"Let's open it up more!" Petra said.

Pulling hard at the rim, Seth realized the entire pit plant was trembling. The walls spasmed away from Anaya, and the spikes retracted. Slowly Anaya straightened up.

"Can you make it now?" he called down.

"Think so!"

He watched as Anaya flexed her knees, and jumped. It was an amazing thing, the way her legs powered her, straight up like a rocket. Her torso cleared the top of the plant—and then she started to fall back. Seth lunged forward with Petra and grabbed hold of her. Together they hauled Anaya out over the rim. She was blood-streaked, her clothing shredded, and they all held on to each other longer than they needed to. Seth didn't want to let go.

But he had to, when a vine landed heavily on his back. He flexed his arm to slash it, but it just slid off like something dead. Nearby, other vines dangled listlessly. From overhead in the canopy came an eerie creaking.

The pit plant shook convulsively, and Seth scrambled back with Anaya and Petra as the ground started to tremble. Like a piece of rotten fruit, the top of the plant collapsed in on itself. An unearthly wet gargle welled up from its insides, and then silence.

"It's dying," Anaya breathed.

"Look!" Petra said, pointing up at the canopy.

It was suddenly very still: Seth couldn't see any more vines snaking around each other. Wilted bits of vegetation wafted down, pattering on the ground, the lake, the island.

"You did it!" he said, looking at Anaya and laughing in sheer amazement. "You friggin' did it!"

"*We* did it," Anaya said. She turned to the island and waved both arms high at her father and Dr. Weber. "It worked!"

Petra grabbed Anaya's hand. "Sorry we were so late. The vines stopped moving us, and then the pit plant closed!"

"You guys saved my life!" Anaya said. "I was about to get speared when you cut me out!"

"I wouldn't have got there without you," Seth said to Petra. He felt light-headed with triumph, his words spilling out of him. "She machine-gunned the vines with the water lilies!" he told Anaya. "It was incredible!"

"What?" said Anaya.

"I'll show you later," Petra said, grinning.

"Nice shades, by the way," Anaya told her.

Overhead came a creaking, groaning sound like cracking ice. Seth looked up to see the entire canopy sagging. And then it began to collapse. Thick tangles of vines plummeted. Eating sacs the size of watermelons cannonballed down into the lake.

On the island, Seth saw Dr. Weber and Mr. Riggs take shelter under a big pine. That was good. There was a ton of stuff coming down, and he didn't want them getting hit, or splattered with acid.

Still the vines fell, crushing the water lilies. From the corner of his eye, Seth saw something long and green fall toward the lake. The liberated canoe! It smacked into the water rightside up, bobbing.

"We've got a boat!" he shouted.

Huge holes had opened up in the canopy now, and through them came the early evening light. And there was the sun itself, low in the sky.

And silhouetted in front of it was a helicopter, hovering low, with someone leaning out the doorway, waving down at them.

ONE WEEK LATER

CHAPTER TWENTY

ANAYA WATCHED AS THE helicopter lifted off from the military base on Deadman's Island, carrying her father and Dr. Weber. Through the window, Dad gave her a thumbs-up. From the field, she waved back with a nervous smile. Strapped to the underside of the helicopter was a torpedo-sized tank of herbicide.

"Please let this work," Petra said beside her.

The helicopter nosed out over the harbor. The water was darkly blanketed by lilies. Anaya couldn't believe how quickly they'd flourished in the saltwater, fouling the air with their stink. A week ago, the harbor had been filled with anchored boats escaping the vines and pit plants. Now only a few remained, slouched low in the water, abandoned and riddled with holes by the acid-coated seeds.

"Look at all the news helicopters," Seth said.

Anaya counted more than ten, hovering around Stanley Park, their doors slid back, cameras jutting. Surrounded almost entirely by water, the huge city park had been designated a test site. It was completely overrun with black grass and vines, the fields and forest malignant with pit plants. Dad had said the eastern point was a good place to test their new herbicide for the first time.

And now she, along with the rest of the world, was watching, and hoping.

Barely a week ago, she'd been helping load eight bags of soil onto their rescue helicopter at the eco-reserve. She and Petra and Seth had all managed to keep their true identities secret from the soldiers. She'd swapped her shoes with Petra's slightly bigger ones to hide her claws; and Seth had bundled his feathered arms back inside his hoodie.

The moment they'd touched down on Deadman's Island, they'd been summoned before Colonel Pearson and grilled. They told him what had happened on the eco-reserve—while hiding details like razor-sharp feathers, tails, impossibly high jumps. *Everything* to do with the fact that the three of them were cryptogen hybrids.

"Four soldiers die, three kids survive," Pearson had said, looking at them so severely that Anaya squirmed inside. "All for some dirt."

But when the helicopter rescue crew reported how the canopy of vines had died and collapsed, even the colonel had to admit the soil was very promising.

"You're tough kids," he'd said. "Good job."

Right after that, Dad had been whisked into surgery to have the seed removed from his neck. The very next day, he was up and in the lab, helping Dr. Weber, who refused to let her own injuries slow her down. Taking only short breaks to sleep, they'd worked together, first isolating the bacterium in the soil, and then trying to culture it for a herbicide. Now it would get its first test.

Anaya gazed across the water at the towering groves of black grass on the park's shoreline. Dad's helicopter made several low passes, spraying, then lifted higher to cover the vine-choked tree-tops. The news copters drifted and bobbed, filming everything.

Anaya felt an arm curl around her shoulders and turned to smile at Mom. She wore a pollen mask, like practically everyone else watching on the field. Her eyes were shadowed with fatigue. Her face didn't look as gaunt as it had when she'd arrived four days ago, flying the floatplane the military had secured for her. She'd brought Petra's mom and dad with her, as well as several island patients who needed to be transferred to bigger hospitals.

"How fast will this stuff work?" Mom asked her.

"On Cordova, Dad said the plants started to die within an hour."

She leaned into Mom. Seeing her get out of that floatplane, she'd felt such a complicated tangle of emotions. First, there was love and sheer relief, but it didn't come with the feeling of safety she'd yearned for. She'd been through so much alone, and *knew* too much, to feel like Mom could solve all her problems, and keep her safe. And then there was absolute dread, too, knowing that she would have to tell Mom what she was.

Luckily, it was Dad who'd mostly done that part, and afterward Mom said all the right things, and hugged her really tightly. Anaya knew Mom and Dad could never think of her exactly the *same* way again; she just hoped they still loved her as much, and could *keep* loving her—no matter what came next.

She looked over at Petra, watching the test spray with her own parents. She knew Petra had been worried sick about how to tell her own parents, and Dr. Weber had helped her out. Afterward, when Anaya asked how it went, Petra had laughed it off by saying her mom had always thought she was half alien anyway, so not much had changed, really. She said her father took it harder, but had told her everything was going to be okay.

Anaya's eyes drifted over to Seth. At least she and Petra *had* parents. Seth had no one, except for Carlene Lee, who was still on the base as Seth's de facto guardian—but that didn't count. He had to deal with this all alone.

No, Anaya told herself, that wasn't true. He had *them:* Petra and her—and Dr. Weber. Anaya remembered how, after they'd gotten back to the base and finally had some privacy, Dr. Weber had examined Seth's arms. They were so bruised and cut, and needed stitches in a few places. She'd called him a hero, and then, very tenderly, she'd wrapped his feathers back up with clean gauze. A real mother wouldn't have done it any differently.

Anaya caught Seth's eye now, and smiled. Then she checked his sleeves—it had become a habit over the past few days—to make sure none of his feathers had cut through. But they were safely concealed inside his layers of clothing.

She was terrified of being discovered; she couldn't forget the way Brock, and especially Jolie, had looked at them—and the gun that had been trained on all three of them.

Petra's changes were easier to hide than Seth's. The skin on her legs was still sloughing, but that was simple enough to conceal. Harder was the tail, which had grown enough to make a small bump in her jeans. Probably no one would notice it, but Petra had started wearing a skirt over leggings, just in case.

Anaya glanced down at her own shoes. With some help from Dr. Weber, she'd sawed and filed down her toenails. She wasn't quite ready to call them claws yet. Surprisingly, she'd felt sad cutting them, like part of her was being taken away. But they'd started to grow back the very next day, and she could already feel them pushing against the toe of her shoe.

Not for a second could she forget what she was. Even on the eco-reserve, when her only focus was staying alive, she was aware of how different she was. Every whiff of the sleeping gas, every splash of acid in her face, every time she jumped high or kicked with her claws. These things were all part of her now, at least for the time being. And if she was honest with herself, she kind of liked it. She liked her unblemished face. Even more, she liked her new leg muscles, her speed: the sheer power of herself. She wasn't sure what awaited her, but right now, at this moment, she felt like she could handle it, especially if she didn't have to go through it alone. Petra and Seth would be keeping pace right beside her.

The helicopter dipped out of sight behind the trees, and Anaya knew they were now spraying the fields on the eastern point. Dad had told her the plan. It was crucial the herbicide worked on *all* the cryptogenic plants, including the buried pit plants. Dad wanted to see if the herbicide could penetrate the soil to reach them.

"Nothing's happening," Petra said, staring at the wall of black grass.

"Give it time," Anaya replied, but she felt the same impatience. She wanted to see the grass wilt instantly. She wanted to see the vines writhe, like they had when they touched the soil on her skin. But looking into the treetops, she couldn't see any frantic snaky movement.

"We need this to work," Petra muttered.

"The whole *world* needs it to work," she added.

Every day the news got worse. Crops were ruined, food shortages were becoming more common, and rationing had started in some countries. The death toll mounted and mounted. Despite all the emergency and military forces fighting the plants, tens of thousands of people were killed every day. Strangled, gassed, melted. Nowhere was safe. This new herbicide was the world's best chance right now.

Anaya looked across the field, at all the other hopeful specta-tors. There was a group of Dr. Weber's lab staff. And there was Carlene Lee, with a bunch of soldiers. Anaya had seen her talking quite a bit with one soldier in particular, and it made her ner-vous. She hoped Carlene was keeping her mouth shut.

And farther along the field was Colonel Pearson, binoculars to his face, with a bunch of other important-looking people, some of whom had flown in today just for the test. Pearson lowered his field glasses, and checked his watch. Anaya didn't think he looked pleased, but then again, when did he ever?

The helicopter lifted back into view. Before heading home, it dipped low and strafed a huge raft of water lilies between the park and the base, using up the last of the herbicide. Anaya saw the chemical mist settling over the plants, and the long flowered heads reared back, taking aim. But the helicopter was already out of range and coming in to land.

The moment it settled on the pad, Pearson and his offi-cers were walking toward it. With a clenched stomach, Anaya watched them talk to Dad and Dr. Weber. She couldn't hear a word they said, but she had a good idea that Colonel Pearson was asking why it was taking so long. Which was crazy, because most herbicides took at least twenty-four hours to start working. She knew Dad would be reminding him of this, and Dr. Weber would be backing him up, and telling the officers they needed to be patient, and this was a first try, after all.

But Anaya couldn't help feeling a creeping disappointment and dread as she looked back at the water lilies and the vine-choked trees and the vast, unbowed wall of black grass.

None of it looked one bit different.

THE CURRY THAT Anaya's mom had made was delicious, but Petra didn't have much of an appetite. In the living room of the little apartment, everyone was sitting with plates balanced on their laps, eating and talking.

"It may just be a question of the concentration," Mr. Riggs was saying. "Maybe it's not potent enough for a big spray."

"It could also be the medium we're using to deliver it," Dr. Weber said. "It might be antagonistic to the bacteria. We probably rushed the lab tests. I *know* we rushed them."

Petra could tell everyone was as bummed out as her, even though the grown-ups were all trying to sound positive, and saying it was ridiculous to jump to any conclusions before twenty-four hours had passed. Words like *enzymes* and *titration* and *stabilizing agents* were bouncing around. All she knew was that, eight hours after the spray, the cryptogenic plants looked just as healthy as ever.

"You're not the only ones working on this, though, right?" her father asked.

"No," Mr. Riggs replied. "We sent soil samples and our data to ten other government labs around the world."

"If we don't nail it, someone else will," Dr. Weber added, but Petra wondered if she was really as confident as she sounded.

"We need to get back to Salt Spring," Mom said.

"What?" Petra turned immediately to Seth and Anaya, and was glad they looked as startled as she felt. "But we're safe here! You said things were terrible over there!"

"That's exactly why we need to get back," her father told her. "They need me at the hospital, and the RCMP needs your mother."

Petra felt her cheeks heat in embarrassment. Of course her parents were needed over there, and part of her wanted to go home, too. But she also wanted to stay here, and not just because it was safer. The idea of being separated from Anaya and Seth gave her a terrible pang. And wasn't it better to be closer to Dr. Weber, who knew better than anyone what might happen to their hybrid bodies?

"I think Petra's also concerned she might be noticed," Dr. Weber said, and Petra nodded gratefully.

"Yeah. What if my tail keeps growing," she told her parents, "and my body keeps, you know, changing?"

"If the tail becomes an issue . . . ," Dad began, and Petra wondered if *tail* was a hard word for him to say. "I can get one of the surgeons at the island hospital to take care of it."

"It would be a risk," Dr. Weber said. "People would talk. One news outlet gets hold of it, and we're in a mess. I'd rather bring in one of my own people, and have it removed in secrecy." She looked at Petra. "If that's what you want."

"Of course it's what I want!"

"There might also be other health issues that arise," said Dr. Weber delicately. "And I'd rather she were here so I could take care of her."

"We should stick together," Seth blurted out, "the three of us!" He sounded so sincere, and Petra felt touched. She wished she could tell him she felt the same, but when her eyes flitted to her father, he was giving Seth a strange look.

As for her mother, she regarded Dr. Weber with her cold police gaze. Petra knew she'd had a lot to accept in the past few days, and it was probably hard to like the person who'd told you that cryptogens had abducted you, implanted their DNA inside you—and, oh, that your daughter was only half human. Without any of your husband's DNA. She wondered if Mom could even really believe it all yet.

"I'm not sure I've got a clear picture of what we can expect," Mom said now, looking at Anaya's parents. "In terms of . . . next steps."

"Neither do I," Dr. Weber said frankly. "We didn't finish the MRI scans, and I haven't had time to assess the ones we did, since we've been working all out on the herbicide. The first step would be getting the three of them back in the MRI."

Just thinking about what she might discover gave Petra's pulse a jolt.

"I don't want to change any more," she said. "I want to go back to normal!"

Or as normal as she could ever be, with a water allergy. But before they'd left the eco-reserve, Dr. Weber had taken a sample of the stinking lake water, and promised she'd try to synthesize it. At least that way, Petra would have a supply of usable water her whole life. But first she needed to go back to normal.

"We need to kill the plants first, right?" she said to the doctor. "Then we might stop changing."

Dr. Weber said, "Petra, even with all the plants gone, we don't know what will happen to the three of you."

"Well, that's not very helpful," Dad said.

"I know this must be incredibly hard," the doctor replied. "I promise you, I will do my best for your children. But I do think keeping them here, and their identities secret, is crucial."

"On an army base?" Anaya's mother said skeptically.

"Why are we assuming the army's reaction would be so negative anyway?" Petra's own mother asked. "Our kids are heroes. They did what professional soldiers couldn't. They rescued Mike, saved Dr. Weber's life, and got us the soil. If it works, they've saved the world. Where's the problem?"

Petra looked at Mom, startled. She'd just called her a hero— all of them. She couldn't help smiling.

"But there's already rumors on the base," Anaya said.

"Remember what Jolie said on the island? People are talking about us. And she was terrified when she saw Seth's arms. She pulled a gun on us!"

"I'm afraid that might be most people's reaction," Dr. Weber agreed. "Including Colonel Pearson. You three share DNA with cryptogens that are trying to destroy the world."

"I agree," said Petra's dad. "And frankly, I think our chances of keeping this secret are better on Salt Spring. All it takes is one soldier seeing Seth's feathers, and our kids end up in military lockup."

Petra turned to Seth, who was looking at his bulky sleeves self-consciously.

"You can't keep those hidden much longer, Seth," her father told him. "We could probably take care of that right here."

Seth looked over in confusion. "What do you mean?"

"Well, it would be fairly straightforward for Dr. Weber and me to remove them. With clippers we could—"

"I don't want them clipped," Seth said firmly.

"Seth, come on," said her father, "you can't want to keep—"

"Dad!" Petra said. Seth was the only one here without parents, and he didn't need anyone giving him a hard time. "Drop it!"

But he didn't. "There's no point keeping—"

Seth stood so suddenly that Petra gave a little gasp.

"No one is clipping my feathers." His eyes focused with a rap-tor's intensity, and his arms spread slightly. Petra thought they actually swelled, as if all his feathers were straining against their bandages, ready to razor through. A prickle of unease traveled over her skin; she didn't know what he was about to do.

"It's Seth's choice," Dr. Weber said calmly, "and I promised I'd honor that."

With relief, Petra saw Seth's shoulders relax. Limply his arms fell to his sides and he sat back down. "Sorry," he mumbled. But Petra could tell her father was shaken.

"CSIS is already looking to move us to another facility," Dr. Weber said. "We'll be more secure there."

"Where is it?" asked Anaya's father.

"I don't know that yet."

"We're not being separated from our daughter again," Anaya's mother said.

"I would make sure you could accompany them, wherever we are."

Dr. Weber's phone trilled and she looked at the screen. "Excuse me, I need to take this," she said, standing and walking into one of the bedrooms.

"I don't like this," Petra's mom said to Anaya's parents. "I feel like we're losing control over our own kids."

"I think Dr. Weber's an honorable person," Mr. Riggs replied.

"Maybe, but everyone has someone in charge of them. She works for CSIS. What if she gets orders we don't like? I say we go home."

"Mom," said Petra, "I am not going home and turning into a friggin' crocodile!"

Her father gave a dismissive wave of his hand. "You're going by some dream drawings, right? Look, this herbicide is going to work, sooner or later, and once the plants disappear, life goes back to normal."

She let out a deep breath. How she wanted to believe her father. Go home and have everything magically return to the way it was.

"Well," said Mr. Riggs, "I need to stay here until we get a workable herbicide." He looked at his wife and daughter. "And I want you guys here with me."

"What about this talk of moving everyone to another facility?" said Petra's mother. "I'm not a fan."

"If it's the best way of keeping our kids safe, and healthy, I think it's a good idea," Anaya's mother said, "but I plan to be there."

They stopped talking when Dr. Weber returned to the room, looking solemn.

"What is it?" Petra asked.

"They've found others," she said.

Petra was so startled she couldn't think of what to say.

"Kids like us?" asked Seth. "Immune to the plants?"

Dr. Weber nodded. "Not just that. The boy they found in Halifax has claws on his hands and excessive hair growing on his legs."

Petra looked at Anaya, who seemed barely to be breathing.

"And in Toronto a girl was brought into Emerg, and one of the nurses secretly took some footage on her phone."

"Do you have it?" Seth asked.

Petra crowded around with the others while Dr. Weber cued it on her phone. The footage was shaky, shot through a hospital dividing curtain. Petra saw a girl about their age in a hospital gown, crying softly while two doctors examined her. The doctors kept blocking the view, but through the gaps, she caught a glimpse of an arm bristling with feathers. They were a different color than Seth's, but appeared just as sharp.

Petra looked across at Seth, who watched the girl, mesmerized. She was pretty, and Petra felt an unexpected stab of jealousy.

On screen, the male doctor gave a cry and pulled back, blood dripping from his hand. "Stay still!" another doctor told the girl. And the girl shouted back, "Get away from me!" And then both doctors stepped back as she spread her arms threateningly. "Nurse!" the female doctor shouted over her shoulder. "We need security!" Then the video image went sideways and cut out.

"What happened to her?" Seth asked, frowning with concern. "Is she okay?"

"Apparently they sedated her. My colleagues in the States also just reported several teenagers with exactly the same profiles as you three."

"So the secret's out?" Petra asked urgently.

"So far, we've managed to contain it," Dr. Weber said. "But it won't be long before it leaks. This changes things. We may need to move you all quicker than I thought."

Petra locked eyes with Anaya, then Seth. They weren't alone. Dr. Weber had already told them about her own son, and guessed there must be others out in the world, but it was different now, *knowing*. They weren't solitary freaks. There were kids the same age, with the same feathers and claws and hair and skin and tails. The same ability to jump high, or slash things apart. Or swim underwater.

"You were right," she said to Anaya. "We must be part of some big experiment. We're lab rats."

And yet, she felt strangely reassured. They weren't alone.

"*Failed* lab rats," Anaya said, looking at her parents. "So they sent down the plants, and we started to do better."

Petra suppressed a shiver. "To see if they can come themselves."

"Okay, slow down," said her dad. "There's an awful lot of guesswork here. If you guys were supposed to be specimens, who's been studying you? Where've the cryptogens been all this time?"

"Well, they must've been here at some point," Anaya's mother said, then added with difficulty, "the night the children were conceived."

"So, have they been hiding out on the planet all these years, watching us?" Seth asked.

The idea was almost too creepy for Petra to fathom. Night

faces at her window. Looking over her as she slept. *Examining* her in her sleep?

"Doesn't make sense," Mr. Riggs said. "If the planet was truly hostile to them, they couldn't have survived here for any length of time."

"Maybe they wore suits," Petra said. "Or sent robots. Or they've been watching us from a spaceship, I don't know. They must be able to do all sorts of stuff we can't. Anyway, if we wipe out all their plants, they'll give up on Earth, right?"

This was her grand hope, and she didn't want anyone chipping away at it.

"Maybe so," Mr. Riggs said. "Farmers without a crop don't last long. Let's hope tomorrow we see some damage to those plants."

SETH WOKE FROM a flying dream, heart pounding in his temples.

He'd been soaring so quickly it was almost like being pulled. As if someone was expecting him, and was eager for his arrival. He wasn't high in the sky this time, but skimming low over land, because it was misty on all sides. He looked over his right shoulder at his splendid wing, the feathers glinting almost metallically in the sunlight. And there was Anaya, furred and sleek and bounding alongside him. Over his left wing, keeping pace through the water, was Petra, light glistening off her flanks, fierce but graceful in the water. What joy he felt to be with both of them, and all traveling in the same direction, all headed somewhere momentous. And then his attention was focused forward, straining to see what awaited them.

When he woke, his chest was damp with sweat, and his arms ached as if he'd truly been beating them. Sitting up, he rubbed his temples, and then put on his clothes. He could tell by the curtains the sun hadn't risen yet, but he felt awake and restless.

He slipped out of his room and left the apartment he'd been sharing with Carlene since Petra's and Anaya's parents arrived. He knew his way around the building by now. Down a long, windowless corridor, hang a right, and then he was at the doors. Outside, it was overcast and the air still had a cool bite to it, which would have been refreshing if it weren't for the sulfurous stench given off by all the water lilies in the harbor.

He'd overheard Dr. Weber and Anaya's father mention that the plants were emitting methane, and how that could eventually change the planet's atmosphere, warming it, altering its chemical composition. Making it ready for *them*.

The sky was brightening in the east, but it would be at least half an hour before the sun broke the horizon. He nodded at a masked soldier on patrol near the parking lot, and headed toward the east field.

Petra was standing near the high chain-link fence, looking across the water at the black grass in Stanley Park. He was happy, but somehow not surprised, to see her.

"Any change?" he said quietly, walking up beside her.

"Don't think so," she said, as if they'd already been talking for a while.

The dream made him feel incredibly close to her, like they'd shared an amazing experience. He wanted to enjoy the feeling before telling her about his dream. Or maybe he wouldn't. He should probably just keep his dreams to himself. The last time he'd shared them, she got really angry.

"I thought I heard some vines cracking earlier," Petra said, "but it was just a bird getting eaten."

"Hey," said a voice behind them, and Seth turned to see Anaya walking toward them.

"Hey," Seth said back, and now felt the full strangeness of it: all three of them being in the same place, at the same moment, as if by agreement.

"Couldn't sleep either?" Petra asked.

"Dream woke me up," Anaya said. "It was so vivid."

Seth knew the answer to his question before it even left his lips. "Were you running?"

Startled, she looked at him. He had his answer.

"Not just running," Petra said. "You were taking these huge leaps."

"Yes," Anaya breathed. "And you were swimming. You were so fast!"

Petra turned to him. "And you were between us, flying."

He nodded. His skin prickled in the cool air. He remembered

when he'd first seen both of them in his dreams. Never did he think one day they'd see *him* in theirs.

"How could we all have the same dream?" Anaya said.

"Did I have scales?" Petra asked.

"No," Seth told her.

"Oh, good," breathed Petra. "I didn't see any either."

"I was covered in hair," Anaya said.

Petra touched the back of her head and asked, "Did you guys get the headache?"

Seth nodded.

Anaya said, "And we were going somewhere. Where, though?"

"This is so weird," Petra said, her face pale in the coming dawn.

"Is it?" Seth asked. "We've been having the same kind of dreams all our lives. Only now we're in them together."

"I don't want this," Petra said abruptly, and Seth worried for a moment she was going to freak out. "I just want normal."

Gently he asked, "You sure?"

"Of course I'm sure! What're you talking about?"

"What about the swimming?"

"Shut up, Seth!"

"In the lake," he said quietly. "You *loved* the swimming."

Her face softened and became wistful. "I did love it. It was amazing. I felt like I was in exactly the right place. But it was also like I was a completely different person." She shook her head, as if trying to dislodge a nasty thought. "So, yeah, the swimming was great, but there's all the other stuff. Like getting a tail and my skin sloughing off. Turning into one of *them*."

"I want wings," Seth said. "I want to fly."

Had he ever said it, so simply and bluntly? He felt his feathers taped against his skin, and felt proud of them. Their dazzling color, their sharpness. They let him do all sorts of things.

"You really think you could fly?" Anaya asked him.

"If my feathers keep growing, maybe."

He watched their faces closely, and was relieved there was no revulsion in them.

"That would be . . . amazing," Petra said.

He let out a breath. He'd been so afraid they'd think he was a freak. "So, no, I don't want to go back to normal," he said.

Anaya kicked at the ground. "Normal. For me, that means a snotty, zitty mess. I was enjoying not being feeble."

"You're enjoying being pretty, too," Petra said wryly.

Seth saw Anaya's face redden. "Okay, fair," she said. "But I'm also growing fur and claws, so I can probably say good-bye to that one."

"We'll always be *us*," Petra told her kindly, and Anaya returned the smile.

"Look!" Seth shouted, pointing.

Along the edge of Stanley Park, some of the massive stalks of black grass had yellowed. With a snap, one of the stalks cracked and fell, quickly followed by a second.

"It's working!" said Anaya.

"Yes!" shouted Petra. "Yes, yes, yes!"

Seth had never believed people really jumped for joy, but he did now.

"Call the colonel!" Anaya shouted at a soldier across the field. "Call everyone! It's working!"

Within minutes, people were hurrying out of buildings. Soldiers of all ranks, Colonel Pearson still buttoning his jacket, Dr. Weber pulling a sweater over her tousled head.

Across the water, the wall of black grass was turning the color of curdled milk. Amid the darkness of the mighty firs and cedars, jagged streaks of yellow started to appear. It was the vines, withering and snapping as they fell through the branches.

Seth turned to see Anaya's and Petra's parents rushing toward them. He watched them hug, and felt the old familiar clench of loneliness. The girls had their families, and sooner or later they would go home without him. Even if he got his wings, would it make up for losing his friends?

"Look at that!" Mr. Riggs said as more black grass cracked and fell under its own weight. "It's coming down. Under twenty hours, and it's coming down!"

Cheers went up from the soldiers. From the city, Seth heard shouts carry across the water. On rooftops and balconies and even on the streets, people had been watching and waiting and hoping for this moment. A news helicopter buzzed overhead and started filming. Car horns were honking downtown. From a rooftop, someone sent up a fountain of fireworks. Their lights fluttered down like a dozen shooting stars whose wishes had come true.

"The water lilies, too!" Dr. Weber shouted, coming over to them. "Look!"

The bat-shaped leaves were turning a sickly green, and their seed-spitting heads drooped into the water.

Colonel Pearson marched over and shook hands with Mr. Riggs and Dr. Weber.

"You make this stuff work a bit faster and I can load my soldiers up with it," he said. He turned to Seth and Anaya and Petra. "You're brave kids. You and your families are welcome to stay on the base as long as you like." And he marched off, shouting orders to his deputies.

"We're going to win," Anaya said. "We're going to get rid of this stuff!"

"And maybe go back to normal," Petra added.

Seth saw Carlene Lee out on the field with the soldiers, happily watching the plants die in Stanley Park. Before long, he knew she'd be filling out forms, and trying to match him up with new foster parents.

Maybe Dr. Weber heard him sigh, because she put a hand on his shoulder. "I wanted to talk to you about something. I asked Carlene if I could be your guardian for the time being. She said she'd be happy to do the paperwork."

Seth looked at her, amazed. "You're serious?"

"Absolutely."

"So you'd be my foster mother?"

"If that's all right with you."

He suddenly couldn't speak, so just nodded, then nodded some more, happiness blooming through him.

It started to rain, heavily all at once. Seth pulled up his hood. Beside him, Petra swore and ran for the base. But after a few steps, she stopped and turned back.

"Weird." She held out her bare hands. "No itch! You see any rash?"

Seth looked at her skin and shook his head.

Jubilantly Petra tilted her face to the rain, then her smile melted away.

"No," she muttered, gazing at the dark, pregnant clouds.

And suddenly Seth understood. The last time rain like this had come, it came with seeds. These drops were so big they seemed to bounce. They came down harder. After a second, he realized some of the raindrops weren't soaking into the ground. He frowned. They just rested there like tiny, clear eggs.

Then, as he watched, the rain began to hatch.

ACKNOWLEDGMENTS

There are a lot of very unpleasant plants in this book. I owe a huge debt of thanks to Dr. Stefan Weber, a specialist in botany, who answered my endless questions about plant biology and behavior, and enthusiastically helped me imagine terrifying new types of invasive species—even making wonderful drawings for me. He also came up with the name "cryptogens" for my fictional plants and their creators.

This novel had many early readers: Philippa Sheppard, Nathaniel Oppel, Stefan Weber, Steven Malk, Hannah Mann, Kevin Sylvester, Kevin Sands, Jonathan Auxier—all of whom made very insightful comments that guided me forward through subsequent drafts.

I'd also like to thank my editors, Suzanne Sutherland and Nancy Siscoe, whose expertise helped this novel to germinate and bloom.

THE NEXT STAGE OF THE OVERTHROW
IS ABOUT TO BEGIN....

THE OVERTHROW BOOK 2

HATCH

KENNETH OPPEL

CHAPTER ONE

ANAYA

THIS WASN'T NORMAL RAIN.

It came as a sudden deluge, pockmarking the water and misting Anaya's view of the battered city across the harbor. It lashed down on the field of Deadman's Island, where she stood with Mom and Dad, Petra and her parents, Seth, and Dr. Stephanie Weber. And it wasn't *right*.

Just minutes ago, all her attention had been focused on Stanley Park, where the cryptogenic grass and vines were dying. Yesterday they'd been sprayed with an experimental herbicide, and now they were wilting and cracking. Up till now, nothing had been able to kill these plants. They'd spread worldwide, crowding out crops, sending strangling vines into houses, waiting underground to trap and eat animals and people in their acid-filled sacs. But the herbicide that Dad and Dr. Weber had created—it *worked*. And seconds ago, Anaya had been cheering along with everyone else on the army base who'd rushed out to witness this huge triumph.

But now came the rain. Mostly it was real rain. She could feel it, wet against her face. But among the raindrops were ones that were too big to be normal. They didn't soak into the earth but bounced and settled on the grass like gleaming translucent beads.

"Hail," Mom said.

Her mother was a pilot, and Anaya knew she'd seen all kinds of severe weather. Hail in May was weird but not impossible. And Anaya *wanted* it to be hail. But near her feet, one of the gleaming beads quivered, swelled, then—

Burst.

She stepped back with a gasp as something swift and wet uncoiled from inside. It happened so quickly that she couldn't tell the thing's size or shape—except that it seemed too big to come from such a tiny space. In a second, it had burrowed into the earth and disappeared.

"Did you see that?" she cried.

"Eggs," Dad said, kneeling down as more of them hatched. Their squirming cargo slithered into the grass. He lunged and caught something in his cupped hands, but it squirted between his fingers and was gone.

"Holy crap," said Seth. "What are they?"

"There's hundreds of them!" Petra gasped, stamping with her foot.

Anaya's shoulders jerked at the sound of a gunshot. Across the field, a soldier fired a pistol uselessly at the ground until someone yelled at him to stop.

"They're everywhere!" she heard another soldier shout.

"We need specimens," Dr. Weber was saying with remarkable calm.

Anaya spotted several more trembling eggs nestled among the blades of grass. She snatched the coffee cup from Petra's father and splashed out the contents. Dropping to her knees, she scooped up the eggs and snapped the plastic lid back on.

"Good thinking," said Dad.

"Let's get that to the lab," Dr. Weber said. "Fast."

As quickly as it had come, the rain subsided. Anaya rushed toward the main building. She felt like she was clutching a grenade. Against the waxed paper was a sudden churning.

"I think they're hatching!"

She sped up, bolting through the doors, down the corridor, and into Dr. Weber's laboratory.

"In here," Dr. Weber told her, opening a large glass terrarium that contained some samples of black grass.

Anaya lowered the coffee cup inside. Very quickly she snapped off the lid. Several tiny translucent creatures spilled out. Dr. Weber sealed the terrarium. Wriggling at the bottom, the things looked like they were trying to burrow through the glass.

"They all want to get underground," Seth said.

"They're larvae," Dad remarked, leaning closer. "Trying to find somewhere safe to grow. And they're not all the same." He turned to Dr. Weber. "Stephanie, can you get that magnifying camera working?"

With a joystick, Dr. Weber angled the small camera mounted above the terrarium. She flipped a switch, and on the monitor loomed some kind of blunt-faced worm.

"Looks kind of like a borer worm," Anaya said.

Growing up with a botanist dad, she'd been shown all sorts of things—not simply weird plants but the freaky creatures that ate them. She knew it pleased Dad that she'd never been one of those kids who squealed at the sight of bugs. He'd taught her to look longer and closer.

"Yeah," Dad agreed. "A flat-headed borer larva."

"So these things are from Earth?" Seth asked hopefully.

"They just fell from the freaking sky in raindrops!" Petra told him.

"I just want to know for sure!" Seth retorted.

"These definitely aren't from Earth," Dad said. "Borer larvae aren't segmented like this, and they don't have lateral fins." He pointed at the long ridges that ran the length of the thing's body.

"They might be for digging," Dr. Weber remarked.

When the worm opened its wide mouth, Anaya took a sharp breath.

"Oh my God," said Petra.

Inside were spiraling blades that looked like the turbine of a drilling machine.

On the monitor another creature now plunged into view. This one had an oversized head, which was mostly taken up with a pair of black-dot eyes. Its narrow body was like a chain of armored blocks, each sprouting spiky hairs. Below its head was a big hump, and through the translucent flesh, Anaya made out something dark and bundled.

"What's that?" she asked, pointing.

"I think those might be the beginnings of wings," Dad remarked. "This one might be a flyer. What else have we got in there?"

Dr. Weber panned the camera across the terrarium. There were a couple more of the bulgy-headed creatures, a few more worms, and then a grub-like thing so blobby Anaya couldn't tell which end was which.

"This little dude's a puzzle," Dad remarked as the camera zoomed in. Dad had always had a habit of calling his specimens endearing names. *Rascal. Scoundrel. Smart aleck.* "He's still completely undifferentiated."

"Meaning?" asked Sergeant Diane Sumner. Petra's mother worked for the Royal Canadian Mounted Police and liked to understand things as quickly as possible.

"Meaning it's hard to tell what the heck it is," replied her husband, Cal Sumner, who was a nurse practitioner at the Salt Spring hospital.

As Anaya watched, the grub thing flopped over to a worm that was busily bashing its head against the floor. She still couldn't tell which end was which until the grub thing unhinged its jaws and inhaled the worm whole.

"That just really happened," Petra said, sounding horrified.

Bloated, the grub was motionless for a few seconds, maybe stunned it had eaten something as big as itself. Its body twitched. Then it flumped over to one of the black-eyed bugs and ate that, too. It finished off all the other larvae in the terrarium. Its swollen body bulged as if its prey were still alive and thrashing around inside. Then it became very still.

"Did it die?" Anaya heard Mom ask.

"What's all that goo?" Seth said.

A pale fluid oozed from the thing's flesh, and at first Anaya thought it must be injured, but the fluid quickly hardened into an opaque gray coating.

"A cocoon?" she asked, squinting.

"It's entered the pupal stage," Dad said.

"Looks more like a shell," Dr. Weber commented. "Hard."

"How could it turn itself into an egg?" Petra asked. "It just hatched!"

"Whatever it is," Dad said, "this troublemaker's definitely a work in progress."

"I don't want to see him when he's finished," said Petra.

"Dr. Weber?"

Anaya turned to a lab technician at a nearby workstation pointing at her monitor. On it was a weather broadcast showing a huge white swirl over the Pacific Ocean. Its eastern edge covered the west coast of North America, including Vancouver.

"That's one heck of a system," said Mom.

"It's like that big rain a couple of weeks ago," Seth said.

In a time-lapse visual, the enormous swirl of cloud expanded, swelling across North America, billowing toward Asia, bellying down to swallow up South America.

"Except this time the rain is eggs," said Anaya. "Not seeds."

"Is this it?" asked Petra. "Are they invading?"

They.

Anaya stared at the creatures behind the glass. "These aren't them, are they? The cryptogens?"

That was the name they'd given them. It meant "species of unknown origin." Maybe it was more scientific than the word *aliens,* but it was no less scary.

"Not a chance," said Dr. Weber, nodding at the terrarium. "These things aren't higher-order life-forms. They're oviparous. Egg layers. Insects, by the looks of it. It's definitely a new invasion, but not the big one."

"Just another bit of an alien ecosystem," Dad said. "First they sent down the flora; now we're getting some fauna."

"Step away from your workstations!"

Anaya jolted at the booming voice and spun around.

Colonel Pearson strode into the laboratory, soldiers fanning out behind him.

"What's going on?" Dr. Weber demanded.

He knows, Anaya thought with a clenched heart. *Pearson knows what we are.*

"I want all your records, your hard drives, all external storage units," Pearson told the lab staff.

Anaya saw them glancing nervously at Dr. Weber as they pushed back their chairs and stood. Soldiers immediately took over the computers, tapping keys, unplugging devices.

"Colonel Pearson," Dr. Weber said, "this is completely unacceptable!"

Her voice was filled with indignation, but Anaya had the feeling she would not come out the winner in this battle.

"This lab," she told the colonel, "is under the authority of the Canadian Security Intelligence Service."

"Not anymore," Pearson said. "I want a full briefing on your findings. And I mean *all* your findings, Doctor. The parents will be detained in their apartment for the time being." He nodded to the soldiers nearest him. "Take the children downstairs to the holding cells."

"What's all this about?" Sergeant Sumner said in her steeliest RCMP voice.

"Come with me," a soldier said to Anaya.

Instinctively, she stepped toward her father, but the soldier tugged her smartly away and unclasped handcuffs from his belt.

"You're not serious!" Dad exclaimed. "Handcuffs?"

"Arms behind your back," the soldier snapped at her.

She'd been brought up to be respectful and obedient, but right now she was overwhelmed by confusion—and anger.

"This is crazy! We helped figure out how to kill the plants! And you're arresting us?"

"You've got no cause for this!" Dr. Weber said.

"I have ample cause, as you know," said Colonel Pearson.

Because we're only half human, Anaya thought.

Sergeant Sumner took out her phone and began dialing. "I'm calling my superintendent."

Pearson himself snatched the phone from her hand. Sharply to his soldiers he said, "Cuff them all. Now!"

Anaya felt the loops of steel close coldly around her wrists.

"Ow!" Petra cried out as a soldier snapped her arms behind her back.

"There's no need for this!" Mr. Sumner objected.

"Don't touch them!" Anaya heard Seth shout. And then someone cried out in pain.

When she turned, she saw that Seth had ripped off the bandages on his right arm, revealing his feathers. Their tips bristled, razor-sharp. They were longer than the last time she'd seen them on Cordova Island. Their colors were even more vibrant now, exploding along his arm in a dazzling pattern.

On the floor, a bright line of blood led to the soldier who'd tried to manacle Seth.

"You cut me!" the soldier snarled, cradling his wounded hand.

Immediately, three other soldiers had pistols out, aimed at Seth.

Everyone knows now, Anaya thought numbly. This past week, they'd tried so hard to keep their changing bodies secret: Seth's feathered arms, Petra's growing tail, her own clawed feet.

Seth pulled back his bristling arm, ready to lash out again.

"Seth!" Dr. Weber yelled. "Don't!"

"You crypto freak!" the injured solider spat at Seth, and Anaya saw the hatred in his face—and the fear.

"Lower your arm, boy!" Pearson barked at Seth.

"Don't shoot him!" Petra wailed.

"Seth," croaked Anaya, hardly able to breathe. "Stop!"

Slowly Seth dropped his arm to his side. At once, two soldiers smashed him against the wall and manacled him.

Anaya was given a hard shove toward the exit.

"Hey!" she protested.

"Stop this!" Dad shouted, and grabbed the soldier, but immediately two others pulled him away, twisting his arm behind his back so he winced in pain.

"You can't do this!" Mom shouted at Pearson. "You can't separate us from our kids!"

A scuffle broke out between Petra's parents and the soldier escorting Petra from the lab. Anaya gasped as Sergeant Sumner actually punched a soldier in the face—and was instantly wrenched away and handcuffed, along with Mr. Sumner.

Anaya was pushed through the doorway into the corridor. With a last backward glance she saw Mom's beautiful face compressed in anguish, and Dad looking more furious than she'd ever seen. Then she lost sight of them. She felt like a long, invisible tether had snapped, ripping a hole in her belly.

Beside her, Petra called out, "Mom?"

And this was what started Anaya crying. Because her friend's voice was filled with the childish hope that her mother, even now, could somehow protect her. Anaya knew that Petra had never gotten along with her mom, and yet she was still the person Petra wanted most right now.

"Don't worry!" Anaya heard Sergeant Sumner call out from the lab. "We'll sort this out! The RCMP knows where I am."

"This is a big mistake," Seth shouted as he, too, was marched into the corridor.

The soldiers escorted them through a fire door and down several flights of stairs.

"I'm a freaking hero, okay!" Petra yelled, her voice echoing off the concrete walls. "I got the dirt that's killing the plants. What'd you guys do? Huh? You can't treat us like this!"

Then her voice broke and she was crying again and saying she wanted to go home, couldn't they just let her go home?

Anaya took a breath, tried to stop herself from shaking.

Downstairs now: a dim concrete corridor with windowless doors.

The guard unlocked one of these doors and shoved her inside, alone.

READ THE OVERTHROW'S
STUNNING CONCLUSION IN . . .

THE OVERTHROW   BOOK 3

THRIVE

KENNETH OPPEL